STATE OF QUALMS

VIRGIL JONES MYSTERY THRILLER SERIES
BOOK 17

THOMAS SCOTT

Copyright © 2023 by Thomas Scott. All rights reserved. No part of this book may be reproduced in any form or by any electronic or mechanical means, including photocopying, recording, or by any information storage and retrieval system without written permission from both the publisher and copyright owner of this book.

This book is a work of fiction. No artificial intelligence (commonly referred to as: AI) was used in the conceptualization, creation, or production of this book. Names, characters, places, governmental institutions, venues, and all incidents or events are either the product of the author's imagination or are used fictitiously. Any resemblance to actual persons, living or dead, businesses, companies, events, locales, venues, or government organizations is entirely coincidental.

For information contact: ThomasScottBooks.com

HIGH ROAD PRESS

— Also by Thomas Scott —

The Virgil Jones Series In Order

State of Anger - Book 1
State of Betrayal - Book 2
State of Control - Book 3
State of Deception - Book 4
State of Exile - Book 5
State of Freedom - Book 6
State of Genesis - Book 7
State of Humanity - Book 8
State of Impact - Book 9
State of Justice - Book 10
State of Killers - Book 11
State of Life - Book 12
State of Mind - Book 13
State of Need - Book 14
State of One - Book 15
State of Play - Book 16
State of Qualms - Book 17
State of Remains - Book 18
State of Suspense - Book 19

The Jack Bellows Series In Order

Wayward Strangers - Book 1
Brave Strangers - Book 2

Visit ThomasScottBooks.com for further
information regarding future release dates, and more.

*For Ron D. & Oscar E.
Man, what a ride, huh?*

Qualms:

/kwä(l)ms/

An uneasy feeling of doubt, worry, or fear, especially about one's own conduct.

"We're good, Virgil. I give you my word."
—Murton Wheeler

"Trees resonate at the same frequency as humans. I've always found that fascinating."
—Mason Jones

CHAPTER ONE

A SULLEN MAN WALKED IN THE RECESS OF THE NIGHT, the fallen boy hobbling alongside with a steady but uneven gait, his fingers wrapped tight around a walking stick that had a rubber stopper on the tip of the cane. The stopper was worn and made faint compression noises if he put too much weight on it…dry little poofs that sounded like a hospital blood pressure cuff, or an old woman secretly trying to pass gas during a Sunday church service.

By age, he wasn't really a boy anymore, but the older man couldn't help but think of him that way. Not since the accident. They were brothers, separated by little more than five years, their mother gone for decades now, and their father…well, their father was part of the reason they were out walking a back alley in Paoli, Indiana.

The passageway was filthy with smelly dumpsters pushed against brick walls, old damp cardboard boxes reverted back to pulp, and bits of newsprint stuck to ankle-high window grates like flies on sticky paper. Their car was parked more than two blocks away, out of view from the prying eyes of other night dwellers and, more importantly, the security cameras.

The cameras, it seemed, were everywhere these days.

The man carried a small satchel strapped across his broad shoulders. The bag contained three things: A note for the authorities, their list of targets, and a hammer. The list told them where to go.

The hammer would, as it had before, speak for itself.

When the two men turned the corner out of the alley, they paused for a few seconds as the building came into view less than a block away. The older man subconsciously squeezed his elbow into his side, the shape of the hammer against his ribs a comfort that registered somewhere in the lizard part of his brain like a shot of dopamine. The hammer was there. It was a part of him. It spoke to the sullen man and told him what to do. He looked at his younger brother with a measure of pity and frustration. He kept his voice low and said, "How's the leg?"

"Hurts." The fallen boy wasn't much for talking, especially when his leg was barking at him.

"Almost there." The sullen man didn't talk much either. Not when there was work to do. "Get your hands, now."

They both slipped into their gloves, then started walking again…one with a cane, one with a hammer.

THE BUILDING WAS OLD YET FAMILIAR IN A comfortable sort of way. The hum of florescent lighting, the well-known thump from the compressor when the air conditioning unit kicked on, or how the downspout at the exterior corner of exam room four vibrated against its mounts if the wind blew out of the Southwest. And if someone put their weight on it just so, the click of a loose piece of linoleum flooring right inside the main entrance near the reception area.

It was the click that got the attention of Doctor Paul Campos. The office was closed for the day, the dental hygienists and other staff long gone…home to their families, dinner, kids, and pets. Or maybe out for a night on the town…a movie, or perhaps a few drinks and a little nine ball down at the local tavern. But Campos was working late, alone, and trying to get caught up on the never-ending flow of paperwork. His office manager usually took care of the business affairs...things like insurance forms, billing statements, patient charts, the quarterly tax prep for the accountant, and nearly every other piece of paper a dentist's office generates. Except she was taking a much needed vacation down in the Ozarks and wouldn't be back until Monday morning. So Campos, in addition to his regular duties of what he liked to call drill 'em and fill 'em, was working late and trying to stay ahead of the paperwork curve while his manager was finishing off all that the Missouri Dragon had to offer. Slaying, is what she'd called it before she left. Campos liked it. He'd smiled and told her to have a good time, but now he couldn't wait for her to get back. When he looked at all the paperwork on his desk, he thought he should probably give her a pay raise.

Click.

Campos turned his ear toward the sound, then set his pen aside and pushed his chair back, his hands gripping the edge of his desk, his knuckles white. For a moment, he thought he might have imagined the noise. Campos knew old buildings could sing their own song, a tune that carried an unusual rhythm that was never quite the same from one day to the next. Plus, he'd been putting in so many extra hours over the past week that he felt like his brain might be playing tricks with him.

He gave his head a little side-to-side wiggle and silently laughed at himself. When he checked his watch, he saw it was almost nine o'clock. If he hurried, he could be done in less than a half hour and take in a beer or two himself down at the tavern. Friday nights were good, and as a longtime widower with no children, Campos enjoyed the company whenever he could find it. He was about to let the noise go when he heard the second sound…the sound that always followed the first.

The flooring had bubbled in that one particular spot in front of the reception desk—the result of a leaky roof Campos had to have replaced a few years ago. Insurance covered the roof, but the adjuster told him that the interior water damage would have to be a separate claim. Campos wasn't cheap…far from it, but he didn't want two claims against his policy at the same time. And there really wasn't that much water inside, so he said to hell with it, mopped up the water, and left it at that. The bubble appeared the very next day after the flooring had dried out, but Campos didn't really care; it was more character and charm for the old building. But now, whenever someone stepped on that spot, it clicked as the bubble compressed. When they stepped away, the flooring popped back up and…clacked. That was the second noise he heard.

Clack.

Campos swallowed and stood from the chair, his hands still gripping the desktop, his back stiff, his shoulders rolled forward. "Hello? Is someone there?" He walked over to his office door, then looked back at his phone and wondered if he should call 911. Then the rational part of his brain told him it was probably one of the girls coming back to retrieve a forgotten purse or a cell phone, not a burglar or someone else up to no good deed. Had he locked the front door after everyone had left for the day? He tried to remember but couldn't, then thought it didn't matter if he had or not. He didn't even lock his doors at home. *This is Paoli, Indiana, not Chicago or Los Angeles.*

He stepped out of his office and headed toward the reception area. "Hello?"

———

When the floor clicked, the older man looked at his brother, eyes wide, his mouth a tight line. It was a familiar look the younger man knew well. He drew his shoulders in and let his head shrink into his chest. It made him look like a turtle. The man put a finger to his lips, then pointed at the floor.

The younger man nodded—half apology, half acknowledgment. They waited a few seconds before moving. When the boy lifted his cane, the floor clacked.

From down the hall, they heard someone say, "Hello? Is someone there?"

The two men moved toward an alcove between reception and the patient area, one moving fast, the other limping along as quick as he could, his cane making little old lady farting noises with each step. Once they were around the corner and out of sight, the man reached into the satchel.

"Hello?" Closer now.

Time for the hammer to talk.

CAMPOS CAME DOWN THE HALL, TURNED THE CORNER, then stopped as he took in the reception area. He looked at the front door, the desk, the counter, and then the floor where the bubbled linoleum was. When he stepped on the bubble, it clicked. When he took the weight off of his foot, it clacked.

Someone is inside, he thought. *But why?* Without any forethought, he reached across the reception counter and picked up the phone. It was the last act of a dying man because the hammer had the final say, a single blow that, ironically enough, sounded like the clack that the bubble always made.

Only wetter.

Together, the two men dragged Campos's body back to his office and dumped him on the floor. The older man looked at his brother and said, "I'm gonna take out his teeth." He rooted around in the doctor's pockets and came out with a set of keys. He tossed them to his brother and said, "You better grab our charts from the filing cabinet. Pop's too. One of those keys should get the lock open. This is the one that'll finish us if we don't get out clean. Lock it back up after you've got them."

The sullen man yanked the hammer from the top of Campos's head, then got down on his knees. He was about to go to work on the dentist's teeth when his brother said, "I always kinda liked the old geezer."

The older man stood, then walked over to his brother and got right in his face. "See that asshole on the floor? Pop died because of people like him. You were crippled for life by the same group of idiots."

The younger man looked at Campos, then back at his brother. "He didn't never hurt me none. Gave me free dental care after the fall."

"Fuck him. He helped kill Pop and got you crippled for life. Go get the charts. Now." Once his brother was out of the room, the older man went to work on the dentist's teeth…a sickening, bloody, moisture-laden chore that took nearly a dozen blows with the hammer. When he was finished, he tossed the hammer aside, pulled the note from his satchel, and centered it on Campos's chest.

Two minutes later they were out the door and gone, the sullen man and the fallen boy.

They had more names on their list, and the sullen man wanted them all.

CHAPTER TWO

The landscape, ever-changing, moved forward with a will all its own...a force of nature that blew the winds of chaos into their lives after the death of a single man, one who Virgil Jones, lead detective of the state's Major Crimes Unit, still missed, and always would. They had been brothers of a sort. Yet outside of Virgil's own family, Rick Said, a self-made billionaire, was one of the closest friends that Virgil ever had.

When Said died, his publicly traded holding company, Said, Inc., ended up adrift, its captain gone, its course uncharted, the rocky shores looming ever closer even as the executive officers fought to right the ship. Some thought they couldn't do it...save the company, but then, through an odd and almost unheard-of turnabout, one man stepped forward with an idea that changed everything and steered Said, Inc. back toward safety and the black seas of profit where capitalism was still alive and well.

Hewitt (Mac) McConnell, former governor of Indiana, had resigned from office with less than six months left in his final term. It was a strategic maneuver that allowed him to enter the private sector through a back door deal that would accomplish two things: One, he'd take Rick Said's company from public to private. The other? With the blessing of Patty Stronghill—Said's niece and only living heir—Mac, who had the vitae, would serve as chairman of the board and CEO.

While the move had been both deliberate and tactical, it came with costs, both personal and professional. Tens of millions of dollars were spent on the endeavor, most of the funds coming from the Pope Foundation out of Lucea, Jamaica. The foundation was run by a woman named Nichole Pope, and through her philanthropic contributions and business dealings with the state, she now held a minority position with the company. It didn't hurt that she and Mac were also lovers.

But after a few turbulent months of rough water, the ship was afloat, the crew had manned their stations, and it looked like there would be smooth sailing for everyone.

Well, almost everyone.

Virgil Jones didn't like it.

He had his reasons. Lots of reasons…

Virgil and his adoptive brother, Murton Wheeler, were discussing it on a bright, cloudless Sunday afternoon as they sat down by the pond that separated their two properties. A few years ago, Murton and his wife, Becky, who also worked for the MCU, had asked Virgil if he'd be willing to deed half his land over to them on the far side of his pond so they could build their dream house. Virgil and his wife, Sandy, readily agreed, and now Virgil and Murton were at once brothers, partners, friends, and neighbors.

Murton reeled in his line, examined the empty hook, then set about torturing another worm. With that done, he cast his line back out with a side-arm flick of his wrist, waited for the bobber to settle, then propped his pole against the chair. He cracked open two Red Stripe beers, handed one to his brother, and said, "I think part of the problem is you're only looking at the negative parts."

"You just used the word 'part' twice in the same sentence," Virgil said.

"So shoot me. Either that or stop with the grammar

lessons. Besides, the first usage was singular, and the second was plural. Ergo, your statement is hereby nullified."

Virgil turned his head and let his eyes go flat. *"Ergo?"*

"It's an adverb…a synonym for the word therefore."

"I know what it means, Murt. And nullified? What's with that?"

"I think I picked up some new lingo hanging out with Mac during the transition. But never mind all that. You're avoiding the topic du jour, Jones-man."

"No, I'm not. I simply don't want to talk about it anymore."

Murton let a drizzle of syrup creep into his voice. "It helps if you share your feelings with the ones you love."

"Good idea," Virgil said. "I'll be right back."

"I'll give that crack an F plus. C'mon, Virg, I'm serious. I'm trying to help. You gotta look at the big picture."

"That's exactly what I'm doing, and, as it happens, I don't like the big picture. I don't even like the individual small pictures that constitute the entire montage."

"I'll tell you what you're doing," Murton said. "You're pointing out every single thing you can think of that rubs you the wrong way, then lumping it all together under the subheading of 'change is bad.'"

Virgil valued his brother's opinion, and in truth, he thought Murton was probably right. But the personal and professional changes in his life seemed to be hitting him all at once. The whole thing made him feel like a well-used punching bag in the back corner of a gym. "I'm not sure I would characterize it that way."

"Then how would you?"

Virgil pulled his line in…a diversion to give him time as he formulated his response. His answer came out as a question. "Do you think Mac did the right thing?"

"Which thing are we talking about? His resignation, the fact that he's taking over Said's company, or would it have something to do with your lovely wife's new position as governor of our nation's nineteenth state?"

"Throw a dart," Virgil said with a small measure of disgust. He set his cane pole in the grass and didn't bother to bait another hook.

"I'll do exactly that if it will burst your bubble of doom and gloom."

Virgil turned his chair slightly so he could look directly at Murton. "Didn't it strike you that Mac's move seemed a little opportunistic?"

"In what way?"

"In that the whole plan…resigning as governor, taking over Said's company, having Sandy move up through constitutional succession…every single one of those things served his own agenda."

"What would you have him do, Jonesy? Fall on his own sword? The man has been a politician for almost half his life. His term was nearly up, and an opportunity presented itself. He weighed the pros and cons, then took action. That's how the man operates. I don't think I'd have done it differently if I was in his shoes."

"He could have waited."

"For what?" Murton said.

"For another six months. If Mac had done that, Sandy could have walked away."

"How do you know that's what she would have done?"

"I don't. But I know Sandy takes her job seriously, and when she decides to do something, she goes all in."

"So you're upset that you have to be First Gentleman of our fine state over the next four to eight years?"

Virgil looked away without answering, and Murton let him. After a few minutes of silence, Virgil said, "What do you think it means for the MCU?"

Murton laughed without humor. "Nice try, Virg.

What you're really asking is, what does it mean for you."

Virgil pointed a finger at his brother in frustration. "No, I'm not." Then, a touch softer: "But, so what if I am? How do you think it's going to look that the governor's husband is running around the state chasing criminals of every stripe?"

"Look to whom, exactly?"

"Anyone. Everyone. What difference does it make? I'll tell you what's going to happen, Murt: Sooner or later someone will jump out of the weeds and start making accusations of impropriety, even if no one does anything wrong."

"Give me an example," Murton said.

Virgil stared out across the pond water. "The MCU doesn't exactly have the best conviction record."

"That's not entirely true. Most of the cases we work don't tend to make it to court, I'll grant you that. But when you look at the ones that do, we're batting a thousand."

"You're making my point for me," Virgil said. "We'll be working under a microscope. What happens the next time we find ourselves in a position where someone has to go down? How's that going to look to the media and the public at large? I can already see the headlines. They go something like this: Governor's

Husband Kills Again. Brother-In-Law Sought For Questioning. Vigilante Governor Takes Matters Into Own Hands."

"You're overthinking it, Jonesy. All we have to do is focus on our jobs. If the bad guys make the play, we take care of ourselves, just like we always have."

"Oh yeah? How do we do that? By being terribly British about the whole thing? Start walking a beat and carrying whistles and wooden batons?"

"I thought we were talking about Mac," Murton said.

"We are. And that's another thing. Did you happen to see the financials on the company?"

"Yeah. What about them?"

"Mac's salary, for one thing. He ended up with enough stock options that he became a multi-millionaire overnight."

Murton gave Virgil a slow blink. "First of all, he was already wealthy. And second, I don't think the guy who also became a multi-millionaire overnight—namely, you—should be making any of this about money."

"I'm not making it about money."

"Sounds to me like you are."

"Well, I'm not. I'm simply saying that because of Mac's decisions, you, me, and quite possibly the entire team of people who make up the Major Crimes Unit could be looking for work…sooner rather than later."

"I think you're overreacting."

"I'll tell you something, Murt. Walking away from the MCU might not be such a bad idea. At least we'd get to go out on our own terms."

"Will you give it a rest already?"

"I'm serious. You wouldn't believe the things I've been asked to do so far, and Sandy's only been in the big chair for a month."

"Like what?" Murton said.

Virgil held up his hand and began ticking an itemized list off his fingers. "Well, let's see…I've been told to get a haircut—"

"You could use one."

"Let me finish, will you? I've been told to get a haircut, my wardrobe is no longer good enough—"

"Was it ever?"

Virgil ignored him and kept going. "As I was saying, I'm no longer able to wear my usual jeans and T-shirt, and apparently my truck—which I love, by the way—doesn't reflect the proper image for the husband of the governor. I'm supposed to start driving a black SUV with tinted windows or some goddamned thing. And to top it all off, in its infinite wisdom, the state has decided that since Sandy and I declined to live in the governor's mansion, they want us to install gates down at the intersection and buy our portion of the road."

Virgil's and Murton's houses were located south of the city, just off Highway 37, on a dead-end gravel road nearly three miles long. Murton was suddenly interested.

"They want you to buy our road? How much is that going to cost?"

"I don't know yet, but I've already put you in for half. It's your road too."

"Very funny," Murton said.

"I'm not joking. Welcome to the big leagues."

"I think I'd like to go back to the minors."

Virgil nodded with enthusiasm. "See? That's what I'm talking about."

"I'm sort of serious here, Virg. How much?"

"What's the matter? Didn't Becky's trust fund kick in yet? I thought once Ellie Rae was born, you guys would be fat with cash."

"The trust is complicated," Murton said. "But even if it wasn't, I don't want to spend it on a gravel road."

"Complicated?"

"Most of it is for Ellie Rae's education. The rest of

it doesn't come into play until after Becky's parents are, uh, you know…"

"Dead?"

"Pretty much. Anyway, quit steering the conversation away from my question. How much?"

"Relax. I was just trying to make a point about our situation. The road won't cost a dime. Mac put some sort of provision through the budget before he left office."

"Now he tells me," Murton said. His relief was visible. "What kind of provision?"

Virgil gave his brother a single shrug. "I don't know…some kind of deal where the state picks up the tab, then deeds the road over to us."

"What tab? It's a county road," Murton said.

"I'm not entirely familiar with the finer points of the whole thing. I think the state is negotiating with the county. Once they come up with a figure, the state will give the funds to the county, then we get our very own private road."

"That means we'll have a driveway that's three miles long. Who's going to take care of the maintenance? Fresh gravel, the grading, snow plowing, and all that?"

Virgil let his shoulders sag. "I don't know, Murt. It

feels like no one tells me anything anymore. I feel like…uh, like…"

"A First Lady?"

Virgil couldn't help himself. Despite everything that was happening and how he felt, Murton had nailed it. He barked out a laugh and said, "Yeah, that about says it."

"Hey, look at the bright side, Virg. It can only get better from here."

Virgil didn't get a chance to respond because that's when they heard the familiar beat of rotor blades off in the distance. Both men turned and scanned the sky. "Here comes Cool," Virgil said.

Richard Cool was an ISP Trooper and the state's chief pilot, tasked with flying the governor wherever need be, and assisting the MCU as necessary.

"What's he coming here for?" Murton said.

"Hopefully, he's bringing my lovely wife home."

"Then why is he coming in from the South?"

Good question, Virgil thought.

CHAPTER THREE

VIRGIL AND MURTON WAITED UNTIL THE HELICOPTER touched down, then both men walked over to the landing pad—Virgil had put the pad in not long ago at Mac's suggestion—and waited for Sandy to climb out. They had to wait for nearly five minutes as Sandy spoke with someone on the phone.

While they were waiting, Emily Baker, Sandy's personal security guard, hopped out to stretch her legs, and Cool did as well. Virgil looked at them both and said, "Where'd you guys go?"

Cool gave Virgil a toothless smile. "She didn't tell you…Madam?"

Murton sucked on his cheeks. Baker had her head tipped back, and she suddenly seemed to be taking a great interest in the complex workings of the helicopter's rotor blade hub.

Virgil gave Cool a dry look. "That joke is getting sort of stale…kind of like the smell of your aftershave. And, I'm pretty sure if she had told me, I wouldn't have asked you."

Cool took off his aviator shades and said, "I think the word you were looking for there is aroma. As in, my aftershave has a nice aroma. The word smell is a little off-putting. No one ever says something like, 'The aroma in here is like I stepped in dog poop.'"

"Then I'll definitely stand by my original statement," Virgil said. "And just for the hell of it, how about you answer my question?"

Cool shrugged. "I don't have any details, but we went down to Tell City."

"That's all the way down by the Ohio River," Virgil said.

Cool worked the kinks out of his neck. "I'm aware."

"So, what was in Tell City?"

"Other than the second worst diner I've ever had the displeasure of visiting, I have no idea. I just go where they tell me." He belched, placed his hand on his stomach, and finished with, "I may need a colonoscopy, though. Either that or a good old-fashioned cleanse."

"The hose is up by the house," Virgil said.

Cool looked at Murton. "Still working his way through it, huh?"

"We've made significant progress," Murton said.

Virgil turned to his brother. "Have we, though?"

Baker came to Cool's rescue. "The governor had a meeting with the NFS."

"The NFS?" Virgil said. "What's that? The National Freemason Society, or something?"

Baker gave Virgil one of the quickest fake smiles he'd ever seen. It was so short he thought he might have imagined it. Murton leaned in close and whispered in Virgil's ear. "The NFS is the National Forest Service, Jonesy."

"I knew that."

"Uh-huh."

"Why'd she go there?" Virgil said.

Baker tucked her hair behind an ear and said, "I don't know. I had to wait in the lobby."

"On a Sunday?"

"I don't think the lobby minded what day of the week it is." Then, before Virgil could respond: "Listen, could I use the bathroom? The flight back was a little longer than I expected."

"Headwinds," Cool said. "Fought them all the way here. We should have taken the jet."

Virgil looked at Baker, then tipped his head toward

the house. "You know the way."

"Thanks, Jonesy."

As she was walking away, Virgil said, "No problem. Just don't forget to put the seat down when you're finished."

Baker shot him the bone over her shoulder.

Murton looked at his brother. "Your humor is improving."

"At least something is," Virgil said.

SANDY FINALLY CLIMBED FROM THE HELICOPTER, HER phone still stuck in her ear. "Yes, it won't be long, I'm sure. Will you hold for just a moment?" She gave Murton a wink, and Virgil got a peck on the cheek. "Walk with me?"

Virgil tried to keep his voice light but failed. "Is that a request or an order?"

Murton rubbed his face with his hands. "Jesus, Virgil. Take it easy."

Sandy looked at her brother-in-law and said, "It's okay, Murt. We're all under a lot of stress." Then to her husband: "It's a request, sweetheart. I need to speak with you for just a moment."

"And I need to speak with you for more than just a

moment," Virgil said.

Sandy nodded rapidly, then put the phone back up to her ear. "Half an hour. No more than that." Then she ended the call, put her hand on the crook of Virgil's elbow and steered him toward their house...exactly the way a politician would.

After they were out of earshot, Cool looked at Murton, and with a voice full of mockery, said, "So... how's everything going lately?"

Baker ran into Virgil and Sandy as she stepped out the back door. "Will there be anything else, Ma'am?"

"That should do it for today, Baker," Sandy said. "See you tomorrow at six?"

"I'll be here. Have a good night, Ma'am."

Virgil, who'd managed to get his blood pressure back under control was only trying to be polite. He answered for his wife. "You too, Baker."

Baker laughed like it was the funniest thing she'd ever heard.

Once they were inside, Virgil watched as Sandy went straight to the side of the refrigerator and took a quick look at the scheduling board...something that

Huma Moon, their live-in housekeeper and nanny to their two boys—Jonas and Wyatt—had developed to help all the adults in the house stay on top of everyone's comings and goings. Virgil felt like it was getting harder and harder to keep up with the Joneses, even though he was one of them.

"Huma and Delroy took the kids to the game?" Sandy said.

Delroy Rouche was a Jamaican bartender, one Virgil and his late father, Mason, had hired years ago to help run their downtown bar, a joint now called Jonesy's Rastabarian. After Mason died, his will stipulated that Delroy, and another Jamaican, Robert Whyte, along with Virgil and Murton, would all own a piece of the bar together. It worked out well for everyone. Delroy and Robert ran the bar, while Virgil and Murton ran down criminals for the state.

Delroy and Huma had a child of their own, a beautiful little girl named Aayla, so the Jones household was always in a state of perpetual flux. Three kids, four adults, and a golden retriever named Larry the Dog. Sandy loved it, and though he didn't often say so, Virgil did too.

"Yeah. It's been on the schedule for a week or so."

"I see that," Sandy said. "I guess I forgot."

"You have been busy." Virgil kept his voice neutral.

When he glanced out the window he saw Baker, Murton, and Cool still standing next to the helicopter. "Why hasn't Cool left yet?"

"He's waiting for you."

"Why? I'm not going anywhere."

"I'm afraid you are. Cora is on her way to the MCU as we speak."

During the initial transition, Cora LaRue, Mac's former chief of staff, had moved into the lieutenant governor position as Sandy's replacement.

"What for?" Virgil said.

"Would you mind if she filled you in when you get there? I've scheduled another call, and I can't miss it."

It didn't escape Virgil that his wife, the woman he now answered to both personally and professionally, had just ordered him back to work…on a Sunday, no less. "Want to know what I miss?"

Sandy turned, walked over to her husband, and gave him a lingering kiss. When she pulled away, she said, "That?"

Virgil wrapped her up in a hug. "Yes. That. Exactly. I miss my girl."

"Well, right now you're about to crush your girl's rib cage."

Virgil let her go and said, "Sorry." Then: "Really, what's going on?"

Sandy's phone chirped at her. She checked the screen, then said, "I'm sorry, Virgil. Please, let Cora explain. I don't have the time, and I've got to take this call. Would you mind changing before you go in?"

"Sandy…"

"I love you, Virgil."

"You'd better." Then quickly: "I love you too."

Sandy put the flat of her hand on Virgil's chest. "This whole thing—all of it—the transition, the schedule, the chaos…it *will* get better. I promise."

"When?" Virgil said. The question came out as a challenge.

If Sandy caught the challenge, she let it go. "Very soon…I hope. A few weeks. No more than a month or two at the most."

"That's a pretty wide margin of error."

"I have to go, Virg. You and Murton do too. We'll talk later. I promise."

"You're making a lot of promises," Virgil said.

"You don't know the half of it."

And Virgil thought, *Hard to argue that.*

Cool dropped Virgil and Murton on the recently added helicopter landing pad atop the MCU building, then left with Baker, back to the airport. To his credit, Murton didn't ask any questions on the flight from Virgil's place to the MCU. But when Virgil went to open the rooftop door, Murton put the flat of his hand against the steel barrier and stopped him. "What the heck are we doing here, Jonesy?"

"Cora is downstairs waiting for us."

"Why?"

"Beats me. Sandy wouldn't say."

"Wouldn't, or couldn't?" Murton said.

"You're not helping, Murt."

"Heavy is the head that wears the crown, Jonesman. And for the record, I am trying."

Virgil took a deep breath. "I know you are, and I appreciate it, Murt. I really do. But it feels like I'm drowning here."

Murton took his hand from the door. "All you have to do is breathe, Jonesy. Breathe."

"I just told you it feels like I'm drowning, and your advice is to breathe?"

"Well, it will help put you out of your misery…one way or another."

That got a small smile from Virgil. "Yeah, I guess you're right. C'mon, let's go kiss the other ring, or bend a knee, or whatever we're supposed to do."

"I'll bow," Murton said. "You can curtsy."

When they walked into the conference room, Murton gave Cora a tiny bow and said, "Ma'am."

Virgil, who wasn't really paying attention, turned to his brother and said, "Oh, for Christ's sake, will you give it a rest already? If one more person calls me ma'am, I'm going to—"

Cora snorted—her version of a laugh—then said, "I think he was talking to me, Jones-man."

Virgil stuck his tongue in his cheek. "I knew that."

"Right," Cora said. Then to Murton: "And can it with the ma'am stuff, Wheeler. I was Cora before all this craziness, and I'm still Cora. That means I still outrank you."

"Well, not to split hairs or anything like that, but Jonesy is my actual boss, boss. I report to him, and he reports to you. Without that kind of structure in place, it'd be pure chaos around here."

"Like that's not already an issue," Virgil said.

"Thanks for the verbal flow chart," Cora said. "Can we get to it?"

"Sure," Murton said. "I'm waiting on you."

Cora pointed at a chair and said, "Sit. We've got a problem." Then to Virgil: "I thought you were going to get a haircut and some new clothes…"

CHAPTER FOUR

ONCE THEY WERE SEATED, VIRGIL LOOKED AT CORA and said, "Do you have any idea why Sandy was in Tell City meeting with the National Forest Service?"

Cora bent over the side of her chair and pulled a three-ring binder from her bag. She plopped it on the table, then said, "Jonesy, the legislature is in session, there are about ten billion bills in various committees right now, and as the lieutenant governor, part of my job description is to chair the senate."

Murton leaned close to his brother, nudged him in the ribs with his elbow, and said, "In case you've never noticed, I've always been fairly good at reading between the lines. I'm pretty sure that means she doesn't know."

"You think?"

"Knock it off…both of you," Cora said. "There's something we need you to look into."

Virgil touched an ear to each shoulder. "When you say, we…"

"Given the unique circumstances we all find ourselves in for the foreseeable future, moving forward, the governor thought it best that an extra layer of plausible deniability between her office and the Major Crimes Unit would be…mmm, beneficial."

"Is that right?" Virgil said. The disdain in his voice was thick and deep. He glanced at Murton and said, "See, what'd I tell you?"

Then Virgil witnessed something he didn't often see from Cora, and it surprised him. She let her guard down. "Jonesy, I know this transition has been hard for everyone, particularly you. I'm not without sympathy. I'm really not. The changes that have taken place over the last month or so have happened very fast, and I don't think anyone would argue that you're at the top of the list when it comes to level of difficulty or amount of scrutiny. Your position is all but untenable."

"I'm aware," Virgil said. Then he quickly added: "But thanks. I appreciate you saying so. Murt and I were discussing that very thing when we were asked to come down here."

"Believe it or not, I already gathered that," Cora

said, her sarcastic streak once again on solid ground. Then she looked up at Virgil and Murton and said, "Effective immediately, we are instituting a statewide major crimes reporting program. Every serious offense, from murder, arson, terrorism, criminal possession of a chemical weapon, criminal possession of a controlled substance with intent to distribute, kidnapping—"

"Essentially all your basic class-A or level 1 felonies," Murton said.

"Yes," Cora said. "And if you interrupt me again, I'll add your name to the list. But you're correct. All major felonies committed anywhere in the state will automatically be routed through the MCU. Becky already has the system set up, the counties and local municipalities are all on board, and it goes online at midnight tonight."

Murton said, "Huh. I didn't realize she was that far along in the process."

Virgil looked at his brother. "Is that right? How's it feel to not know what your wife is up to all the damned time?"

Murton turned the corners of his mouth down. "I do know, and even if I didn't, it wouldn't bother me. She's good at her job and does what she's asked to do. If I need to know something, she tells me. If I don't, we leave it alone. Maybe you should give it a try."

Virgil ignored him and looked at Cora. "Will there be a backlog?"

"A small one. Nothing the system can't parse out automatically."

"What's your thinking on this, Cora?" Virgil said.

"I've already explained part of it."

"The deniability?" Murton said.

"Exactly. The rest of it will ultimately make things run a little smoother around here. You'll no longer have to seek permission, nor will you have to be asked by county or local law enforcement to assist in their investigations…though we'll still be looking at individual crimes if a verbal request comes in."

"You're saying we get to cherry-pick our own cases?" Virgil said.

Cora pointed the tip of her pen at him. "Our official position is going to be that state law enforcement—specifically the Major Crimes Unit—will assist other municipalities as we see fit. There are too many things happening in this state that we should be involved in, and we're not."

"What's the unofficial position?"

"You get to cherry-pick your own cases," Cora said. "Make sure you pick carefully."

"Who will I be reporting to?" Virgil said.

"All your reports will be filed with the superintendent of the ISP. That's why I want you to pick carefully. He's agreed to leave you alone if you don't make too much noise. If you do make too much noise, guess who he's going to call? Don't bother answering. I'll tell you: It's me. And my plate is full, Jones-man. Do you understand what I'm saying here?"

"Yeah, I'm pretty sure I do. You've given me a new pseudo-boss, more responsibility, less oversight, and when the fecal matter hits the rotary blades, the fan better be pointed in the opposite direction of the statehouse."

"I couldn't have said it better myself."

"We'll do our best, Cora. You know that. You also said there was a problem?"

"There is. Becky did a test run on the system earlier today. The results were…disturbing."

"In what way?" Virgil said.

"In that there have been two murders in the same number of weeks in different parts of the state, all with the same MO. That's why we've got the new system in place. None of the individual departments are talking to each other, much less us."

"A little specificity would go a long way right about now," Virgil said.

Cora opened the binder again and pulled out a letter-sized piece of paper. "This is a copy from one of the cases. The others are identical in every way." She slid the note over to Virgil and Murton so they could see it. The note read:

We have no qualms regarding our conduct. Restoration is not an option.
Others will die unless your B.S. project stops.

Murton looked at the note and said, "What bullshit project does this refer to?"

"That's what I want you to find out, among other things, obviously." She pushed the binder across the table. "All the details we have—which isn't much, by the way—are in there." Then to Jonesy: "Get your entire team briefed first thing tomorrow morning. Call me if you need me, but really, please don't call."

"We'll brief everyone we can as soon as possible," Virgil said. "But Mayo and Ortiz are on vacation for a few more days."

"Where'd they go?" Cora said.

"Ortiz took Mayo spelunking down near Patoka Lake."

"I thought he was from the Southside of Chicago."

"He is," Virgil said.

"And he talked Mayo into following him around inside a bunch of bat-infested caves?"

"They didn't really give me all the particulars," Virgil said.

Cora waved it off. "Whatever. I don't care. Get them up to speed when they get back. And Jonesy, God bless me, keep the press out of my hair. Any questions?"

"I've got one," Murton said.

Cora had her elbows on the table and let her hands flop down on the surface. "Why am I not surprised? What is it, Wheeler?"

"Well, Cool brought us here, then left. How in the hell are we supposed to get home?"

Cora reached into her bag, pulled out a set of keys, then tossed them to Virgil. "You can call an Uber, stick your thumb out and hitch, or go with Jonesy. His new ride is parked right out front. Keep me, and more importantly, the governor, out of the loop."

After Cora was gone, Murton looked at Virgil and said, "See? Things are looking up already."

"That's your take on all this?"

"Sure. Why wouldn't it be?"

"Well, in case you didn't notice, we just got compartmentalized. The MCU used to have the governor's ear. The way Cora laid everything out, it sounds like we'd be lucky if they let us in the statehouse without undergoing a strip search first."

"As usual, you're looking at the negative side of things. Cora basically said we get to run our own show. As far as the governor's ear goes, at the risk of stating the obvious, you're married to the woman, Jonesy."

"I don't like it."

"I'll be sure and pass that along next time I amble over to your house."

"That's not what I meant," Virgil said.

Murton clapped him on the back. "I know, I'm just messing with you. So, are we going to dive into this case by ourselves on a Sunday afternoon, or wait until tomorrow morning?"

Virgil picked up the note and read it again. Then he quickly looked through the binder Cora had left behind. "According to the autopsy results, it looks like both victims were mutilated in one way or another after they were killed."

"Mutilated how?" Murton said.

"We've got one male, and one female. The first victim had both his ankles smashed. The second—the female—had multiple fractures to her pelvic region."

"Both postmortem?"

"That's what it says."

"What about cause of death?"

Virgil scanned the summary report. "Blunt force trauma to the head in each case."

"I hate these kinds of cases," Murton said. "Half of these idiots never get captured at all, and the others just keep killing until they do get caught."

Virgil closed the binder. "Let's start fresh tomorrow morning. I don't think there's much we can do tonight."

"Good idea. C'mon, let's go check out your new wheels."

"I liked my old wheels…"

When Virgil and Murton stepped out front, they found—as Virgil knew they would—a brand new black SUV with windows tinted so dark they looked like part of the sheet metal. Virgil pressed a button on the fob and popped the driver's side door. Murton took the passenger seat.

"I was expecting a Tahoe," Virgil said.

"Maybe our new governor wanted to brighten your day. Do you know how much these things go for?"

"It's a Range Rover, Murt. I've never priced one. Who cares?"

"Well, it's not too shabby if you ask me. And based

on the model we're sitting in, I'm guessing the price tag is somewhere in the neighborhood of a buck and a half. C'mon, let's roll. Try not to scratch it up on the maiden voyage."

Virgil fired up the Rover and pulled out into traffic.

"Why are you going this way?" Murton said.

"Because I want to get out on 465 and see what this pig can do." Ten minutes later they hit the on-ramp, and Virgil gunned it.

"How's it feel so far?"

"Like I'm driving a bus."

"Well, you were thinking about a career change."

"Not as a bus driver."

"C'mon, Jonesy. Start thinking outside the box, will you? I'm not talking about you driving a bus."

"Then what the hell are you talking about?"

"You're kidding, right? With this baby? You could qualify as an Uber XL driver. Play your cards right, adjust your attitude a little, and you might—and the key word there is *might*—make Diamond status. I hear that's where the real money is."

"Do not make me pull over. I will let you out. Hey, what are you doing?"

"Giving you a one-star review on Yelp. Maybe the bus driver idea was the way to go. I think you're more of a Greyhound type of guy after all."

"You're a riot. Anyone ever told you that?"

"Sure. All the time. Say, what do you think this switch is for?"

"I'm hoping it's the ejection button for the passenger seat. Why not give it a try?"

Like that...all the way back.

Virgil was smiling though by the time they exited 465. "I've driven worse vehicles, I guess."

He slowed to make the turn down their gravel road, then was slightly annoyed when the two state trooper squad cars blocking the intersection refused to move. Virgil honked the horn, then raised his hands in a what-gives gesture.

One of the troopers got out of his vehicle, his hand on his gun. Virgil found the switch for the blue flashers behind the front grill and lit them up. The trooper relaxed, then walked over to the driver's side of the Rover.

Virgil buzzed the window down and said, "How about it on the barricade?"

The trooper's face reddened slightly. "Sorry, Detective. I didn't recognize the vehicle, and the windows are so dark I couldn't tell it was you."

Virgil knew the man was only doing his job, and in truth, he'd have been more upset if they had just waved him through without checking. "No problem. All quiet on the home front?"

"Yep. Got a new ride, huh?"

"So it would seem," Virgil said.

"I'll make sure it gets on the list. Can I take a peek at the registration?"

Virgil squinted an eye at the trooper. "I didn't steal it."

"No sir, I didn't mean to imply that you had. But I need to make sure the information gets passed along to the other troopers who'll be on duty."

"How about you just take down the license plate number and vehicle description?"

The trooper bobbed his head and said, "That'll work. Sit tight." He took a pad and pen from his breast pocket, then moved to the rear of the vehicle. Twenty seconds later he was back. "You're all set, Detective. Let me move my squad car so you can get through."

"Appreciate it."

The trooper started to turn away, then stepped back. "Mind if I ask you a question?"

"What is it?" Virgil said.

"We heard that the state is turning this into a private road."

Virgil nodded. "That's what they tell me."

"Did you think of a name yet? I mean, if you've got your own road, its gotta have a name, right?"

"I haven't put much thought into it," Virgil said. "Why do you ask?"

"Well, this sure is a nice car for a state cop, detective or not."

"I didn't have a lot of say in the matter."

"Lucky you," the trooper said. "Gravy Train Lane comes to mind."

"Keep up the good work, Troop," Virgil said. Then he buzzed the window back up, looked at Murton, and said, "Not one single word, Murt. You hear me? Not a peep."

CHAPTER FIVE

Virgil dropped Murton at his house, then said, "Mind if I come in for a minute?"

"Of course not," Murton said. "What's up?"

"I'd like to have a word with Becky."

They found her in the living room with Ellie Rae. Some sort of ridiculous cartoon program Virgil had never seen before was playing on the TV. Over the background noise, Virgil heard a toilet flush in the guest bathroom. "Do you have company? And what the hell is that on the television?"

Becky ignored Virgil's first question, and answered the second. "It's a TV program for infants and small children called Cocomelon. Nursery rhymes and that sort of thing."

Jonas came into the room, cleared his throat, and

held out his hand. Virgil spun around and said, "What the heck are you doing here?"

"Watching TV with Aunt Becky and Ellie Rae."

Virgil pointed at the television. "Aren't you a little old for this kind of thing?"

"It's sort of addictive," Jonas said. "And besides, you're trying to distract me. I heard what you said. You owe a buck to the swear jar. Fork it over."

"I'm a little short on cash right now," Virgil said.

"Got your phone?" Jonas said.

Virgil was suddenly suspicious. "Yeah. Why?"

"In addition to cash, I accept PayPal, Venmo, or Apple Pay."

"I don't even know what Venmo is," Virgil said. Then he turned to Murton. "Can I borrow a buck?"

Murton gave Jonas a dollar, then looked at Virgil. "You should have gone with Apple Pay."

"Why?"

"Because Jonas charges two points a week on the vig. My rate is five."

"Whatever. I think I can handle five points until tomorrow." Then to Jonas: "Head on home, Son. Tell Mom I'll be there in a few minutes."

Jonas's shoulders visibly slumped, and Virgil caught it. "What is it, pal?"

"Mom's not home. She had another meeting or something."

Virgil glanced at Murton and saw him mouth the word, *breathe.* He looked back at Jonas and said, "Tell you what, buddy. I got a new car today. It's parked in Uncle Murt's driveway. Why don't you go check it out? We can take it for a spin in a little while."

Jonas re-inflated. "Cool. Later, Aunt Becky. See ya, Uncle Murt."

Once Jonas was out the door, Virgil turned to Murton and Becky. "See? This is exactly the kind of thing I'm talking about. Mac told Sandy—and by extension, me—that being governor would be less demanding of her time. So far, that doesn't seem to be working out very well."

Becky handed Ellie Rae off to Murton. "Would you mind changing her clothes?"

"I'm not very good at it," Murton said. "She doesn't have any core strength. It's like trying to dress an earthworm."

"Practice makes perfect," Becky said. Then to Virgil: "It's still early in the transition, Jonesy. Give it a little time. Things will smooth out."

Virgil ran his fingers through his hair. "I guess so. That's what everyone keeps saying. I'm getting a little tired of it, though. Anyway, that's not why I'm here. You got a second, Becks?"

"Sure. What's up? And listen, I know it's not my business, but weren't you supposed to get a haircut?"

"It's on my list of things to do."

"Let's talk in the kitchen," Becky said.

Virgil followed Becky into the other room, and once they were there, Virgil said, "I wanted—"

"Hang on a second," Becky said. She pulled a chair away from the table and into the middle of the room. "Have a seat. I'll be right back."

Virgil sat down, and a minute later, Becky returned with a bath towel and a set of electric clippers.

"Becky?"

"Yes, Virgie?"

"What do you think you're doing?"

"I'm going to give you a haircut while you tell me whatever it is you wanted to talk about."

"Becky, I don't think—"

"Relax, Jonesy. I know what I'm doing. I've been cutting Murt's hair for years."

"Really?" Virgil was surprised. Though he was loath to admit it, Murton did have a nice haircut.

"Yeah. Looks pretty good, doesn't it?"

Virgil tried to play it off. "I guess so…if you like that George Clooney kind of look."

"Well, I hope you do because that's really the only style I'm good at." Then, before Virgil could protest, she clicked the switch on the clippers and got started.

"Hey, not too much, okay? Just a trim."

"Uh-huh. Hold still. So, what's up?"

"I'm sure Murt will give you the finer points later tonight, but it looks like we've got some nut job running around the state killing people. Mutilation after the fact. Your new system kicked them out of the database."

Becky laughed through her nose and said, "Duh. Who do you think told Cora?"

"Yeah, okay. I guess what I'm trying to say is this: I was wondering why I wasn't more involved in the process. In case you've forgotten, I run the MCU."

Becky grabbed Virgil's head and turned it to the side. "Sit still, will you? Let me ask you something: How much do you know about computers and their interconnectivity across various data sets when using multiple programming languages?"

"Excuse me?"

"That's what I thought. You weren't involved because there wasn't anything you could do."

"Being informed comes to mind," Virgil said.

Becky turned his head the other way…maybe a little more forcefully than necessary. "You were informed, Jonesy. You signed off on the program right before Mac stepped down."

"I don't remember doing that."

"There was so much going on at the time, I'm not surprised. I've got the form in my office if you'd like to examine your signature."

"I'll take your word for it," Virgil said, his voice dry.

"Good. Now please hold still. I'm almost finished."

"We're having a meeting first thing tomorrow morning. I'd like you to be there."

"Sure. Whatcha need?"

"I want you to start deep backgrounds on the victims. Go all the way back to their childhoods if you have to. We need to figure out if there are any commonalities, or if this nut job is hitting people at random. If we can establish that, it will save us some time. It might save some lives, too."

"I can do that."

"I'll also want the names of the detectives who did the initial investigations."

"No problem," Becky said. "Anything else?"

"Yeah, one more thing. Starting tomorrow, all our reporting goes to the superintendent of the ISP, not Cora. That means I want to see every single report before it goes out the door."

"That sounds more like a conversation you should have with Sarah."

Sarah Palmer was the operations manager for the MCU, and the girlfriend of Andrew Ross, one of the other detectives with the Major Crimes Unit.

"It is, and I will. I just want to make sure that everyone is on the same page. Cora is still running the show, but she's distancing herself—and by extension, Sandy—from any fallout that might occur given the nature of my relationship with our new governor."

"Gotcha." Becky turned off the clippers, ran her fingers through Virgil's hair until she was satisfied, then handed him a mirror. "What do you think?"

"I'm afraid to look."

Becky punched him in the shoulder and said, "Shut up. Take a look. It's nice."

Virgil grabbed the mirror, already prepared to be mad, but when he saw the way his hair looked, he was impressed. "Jeez, Becks. That's pretty good. Fantastic, actually."

"Told ya." Then she took out her phone and said, "That'll be fifty bucks. I accept PayPal, Venmo, or Apple Pay."

"Becky…I don't have any of those things set up on my phone. Besides, I thought you did it because you love me."

"I do love you, but with what you pay me, a girl's gotta have a side hustle."

"How about I owe you?"

"How about you whip out a credit card?"

Virgil laughed, pulled out his wallet, then handed Becky a credit card. "What are you going to do? Write down the number or something? Then what?"

"What century, exactly, are you living in?" Becky said. Then she pulled a tiny white box out of her pocket, stuck it into a port on her cell phone, and swiped Virgil's card.

"What's that thing?"

"It's called a Square. It allows you to accept credit card payments on the spot." Becky handed Virgil the phone. "Sign with your finger."

Virgil shook his head and took the phone. "Jesus Christ, don't ever let Jonas see this thing."

Becky hollered into the living room. "Hey, Murt?"

"Yeah?"

"We need a new idea for Jonas's birthday present." Then she looked at her phone. "What? No tip?"

Virgil went outside and found Jonas playing with the display unit in the Range Rover. "What are you doing?"

"Setting up your system. Give me your phone, and I'll get the Bluetooth going."

Virgil reluctantly handed over his phone, then said, "Don't mess anything up."

Jonas ignored him and said, "Got your ears lowered, huh?"

"I think you're spending too much time with Uncle Murt."

"We have been talking about a trip out to Vegas over the holidays."

"What?"

Jonas laughed. "Gotcha, Dad."

Virgil waited until Jonas was finished, then he started the Rover and backed out of the drive. "Where are we going?" Jonas said.

"Shopping. I guess I need to buy some new clothes."

"You can say that again."

"Hey…"

Jonas laughed. "It's like shooting fish in a barrel

with you. You're the fish, in case you didn't know." Then: "You better turn around and go back to Uncle Murt's."

"Why?" Virgil said.

"Trust me, Dad."

Virgil turned the Rover around, then pulled into Murton's driveway.

Jonas popped the door. "I gotta run back inside for a second. I'll be right out."

"Jonas?"

"Two seconds, Dad, really."

It wasn't two, but thirty seconds later, Jonas reappeared with Murton in tow. They both climbed into the Rover, and Murton pulled his door closed, then clapped his hands together. His smile was brighter than ever. "I can't begin to tell you how long I've waited for this moment."

Virgil scratched the right side of his cheek with his middle finger. "Me either."

The sullen man, Luke Quinn, and his brother, Caleb, were sitting in their father's house…a modest log cabin buried deep in the woods of Southern Indiana. The house had been willed to them both with the stipulation that Luke would continue to care for his younger brother who could no longer work because of his mangled hip and leg.

The whole ordeal…their father's death, Caleb's disability…it was something they didn't like to dwell on, unless they'd been drinking. Caleb grabbed his cane and limped over to the kitchen counter. He turned back to Luke and said, "Another beer?"

"Yeah, and bring me a couple of fingers of GJ while you're at it." GJ was Gentleman Jack whiskey.

"You've had quite a bit already."

"You're not my keeper."

Aren't I? Caleb thought.

"What was that?"

"I said I could use a little help. I only got one free hand."

"Then make more than one trip."

"Says the guy with two good legs."

Luke sighed, then heaved himself out of his chair.

"You sound like an old man when you get up," Caleb said.

"Thirty-five isn't old. I'm tired, is all. Work all week, take care of you. It's hard sometimes."

"I do my share, Luke. I try to, anyway."

Luke wrapped a sloppy arm around his brother's shoulder. "I know you do. I just thought life would be different for us somehow." He released his grip on Caleb, then poured himself another drink.

"That looks like more than a couple of fingers of GJ, you ask me."

"I'm not asking." He grabbed his drink and beer, then walked back into the other room. Caleb grabbed a beer with his free hand and followed his brother.

"Do you think we're doing the right thing?" Caleb said.

"How many times are you going to ask me that?"

"Probably until I get an answer that makes some sort of sense. Those people we killed? They never did anything to us. Not directly."

"Direct…indirect, makes no difference to me. They got themselves involved in something that killed our father and permanently fucked up your life. You want to let them get away with it?"

"No, I don't. But—"

"But nothing," Luke said. "You told me that you'd follow my lead."

"I am following you, Luke. I'd follow you to hell and back after everything you've done for me. I just think we need to go after the people who are really responsible for everything that happened to our family."

"We are. When you're fighting a war you shoot the guy in front of you on the other side of the line and keep advancing. You don't try to outflank him and sneak into the general's tent."

"So we're in a war now?"

"I was trying to make a point. Is this about that dentist?"

Caleb looked away. "Maybe. I don't know. He was a nice old man. We knew him. He helped me when I was all busted up."

"You're still busted up, and he was also part of the problem. Don't you see that, Caleb? It's people like him who take on a cause without looking at all the facts. Then, like fools, they delude themselves into thinking they're doing something good. But all they're really doing is making themselves feel better."

"And how is that different from what we're doing?"

Luke drained the last of the whiskey from his glass, then threw the tumbler at Caleb. But Luke was drunk, his aim was off, and the glass shattered against the wall.

"Nice, Luke. Real nice. Are you trying to hurt me more than I already am?"

"I wasn't even trying to hit you."

"You're getting pretty hammered, man. Go to bed, huh?"

Luke reached into the satchel and pulled the list of names out of the bag. "I'm hammered all right. And I'm going to keep hammering until we get every last person on this list. Are you with me, or not? Hey, where are you going?"

"To get a broom and dustpan. Gotta clean up the glass."

"I made the mess. I'll clean it up my damn self." But when Luke stood from the couch, the room began to spin. He fell back on the sofa, and less than a minute later he was snoring, his arm hanging off the side of the couch.

Caleb grabbed a blanket, covered his brother, and thought, *You made the mess all right. God help us all if you ever figure that out. And who's taking care of who?*

CHAPTER SIX

When Virgil walked into the MCU the following day, he found Sarah at her horseshoe workstation in the center of the operations area. Sarah glanced up, did a classic double-take, and said, "Excuse me, Sir. Do you have an appointment?"

Virgil loved Sarah like a daughter, and had ever since she came into his life a few years ago on a case that nearly destroyed her own sense of self. Her fiancé at the time had been beaten to death, and she was so distraught—not to mention without a place to stay since her home was a crime scene—that Virgil and Sandy let her stay with them while her emotional wounds healed. It didn't take long before Andrew Ross took notice and swept Sarah off her feet. They now lived with each other, along with Sarah's daughter Olivia, in the house where Virgil and Murton had grown up.

Virgil subconsciously rubbed the back of his head and said, "Sarah, I was really hoping you'd be the one person around here who wouldn't give me any grief about my, uh, new style."

Sarah came out from behind her desk, walked over to Virgil, then held him at arm's length and gave him a head-to-toe appraisal. "I'm not giving you grief, Jonesy. I'm impressed. You look great. New do, sharp outfit, and unless I'm seeing things, you've got a little spring in your step."

Virgil didn't want to admit it, but he knew Sarah was right. Becky's haircut looked good, Murton had helped him pick out some fancy—yet casual—work clothes, and the whole thing had him feeling like a new man. And, while driving into work, he'd discovered that the Range Rover was actually one hell of a nice ride. Virgil suddenly felt like he'd spent the last decade looking like a schlub. "Thanks, Sarah. I gotta admit, I do feel pretty good."

"And you should," Sarah said. Then, right down to business. "Everyone is waiting in the conference room except for Oscar and Rafael. They won't be back for a few more days."

Virgil nodded rapidly. "I know…about Mayo and Ortiz, I mean. Did everybody get copies of the case notes?"

"They did."

"Good enough," Virgil said. "Listen, we can talk about this later, but starting today, all completed case reports will be routed straight to the superintendent of the ISP. I'd like to review them before they go out."

"I'm aware. Murton emailed a memo to that effect last night. It was waiting for me when I arrived this morning."

Virgil's eyebrows went up. "Did he?"

"Yes. I understand we've got an interesting case."

"It looks that way," Virgil said. He started to creep away. As much as he loved Sarah, she could be a little chatty in the morning…the polar opposite of Virgil's ante meridiem brain. "I better get to it."

"Do you want me to contact Mayo and Ortiz and call them back?"

"I don't think so…at least not yet. Let me get a handle on things and we'll take it one step at a time, huh?"

"You're the boss."

Sarah's statement hit Virgil in his sensitive spot. "I'm glad someone thinks so." He moved away and started down the hall, feeling like the spring in his step might have just unwound itself a little.

Sarah noticed and said, "Hey, Jonesy?"

Virgil stopped and forced his face to relax before he turned back around. "Yes?"

"Remember how I felt after Gary died? How nothing seemed right and I wasn't sure I could keep going minute by minute…let alone day to day?"

Virgil walked back toward Sarah. "Yes, of course I do. Why do you ask?"

"Because it was your words that got me through everything and headed down the right path."

Virgil pulled his chin in slightly. "Mine?"

"Well, not only yours…but you were the one who kept telling me over and over that things will get better, and that I just needed to give it time. And as hard as that was to do, I eventually discovered that you were right. My advice? Listen to yourself once in a while, Jonesy."

Virgil gave her a fatherly hug and told her he'd try.

JOYCE PARKER COULDN'T REMEMBER A TIME WHEN she'd felt more relaxed and at peace. She'd spent two weeks down in Missouri at a luxury resort, eating, sunning, and slaying a dragon that was the Lake of the Ozarks. It took her nearly eighteen months to save enough money for the trip, but it had been worth every penny, no matter what her friends thought. A few of them tried to tell her she was wasting good vacation time by going to what they called the Redneck Riviera, but Joyce didn't care. Besides, everyone who was anyone knew that the real Redneck Riviera was the southern part of Alabama along the Gulf Coast, not the Lake of the Ozarks.

During her stay, she'd updated her Facebook and Instagram feeds with pictures of herself wining and dining, showing off her new swimsuit collection, and best of all, the handsome young man she'd spent the last week with. Was she almost twice his age? Yes, but he didn't seem to mind. It was a week-long whirlwind fling, with Joyce and her friend promising each other they'd do it again next year. Of course, Joyce knew it'd never happen, as she suspected her companion did as well. But that was part of the fun. What was the harm? All in all, it had been a wonderful trip, and when Joyce woke bright and early on a fine Monday morning, she found herself not only relaxed, but refreshed and ready to jump back into her work, running the show at the dental clinic.

She was humming a little tune to herself as she

walked up the front steps of the old building. She'd been smiling all morning, and her jaw was beginning to ache. When Joyce went to put her key in the lock, she leaned on the door with her shoulder. The door was every bit as aged as the building itself, and if she didn't put some pressure on it, the lock wouldn't budge. But this time—much to her surprise—the door popped right open. It wasn't even locked.

Joyce thought Doctor Campos must have arrived early for some reason. *Probably trying to get caught up on the paperwork before I get back,* she thought with another smile that made her jaw ache a little more.

She stepped through the entryway, checked her watch as she walked, her short sensible heels clicking away on the old linoleum flooring. The others wouldn't be in for at least another hour, which would give her time to get back into the rhythm of managing the office.

As she approached the reception area, a dark brown —almost black—spot on the floor got her attention. She cocked her head to the side and thought, *now what?* Maybe the roof had started leaking again. She looked up at the ceiling but didn't see any visible signs of water marks. Then she noticed the same dark spots on the reception counter, and the more she looked around, the more spots she discovered. They were on the walls too. It looked like someone had dropped a gravy bowl, and the contents had splashed everywhere.

Joyce called out in confusion. "Doctor Campos? I'm back. What's with the mess out here?"

She stepped on the floor's bubbled spot and heard it go, *click, clack.* It made her jump a little, and the fact that she was startled unnerved her somehow. The bubble had been part of her work life for so long she hardly noticed it anymore.

When she started down the hall toward her boss's office, she followed a trail of small dark spots on the floor, spread about three feet apart. The spots were slightly out of round, and faded from dark to light the further she went. It reminded her of an ink stamper that was about to run dry.

"Doctor Campos? Paul? Are you back here?"

When Parker opened the office door, the first thing she saw was the hammer, which immediately made her think of the faded spots in the hallway. She walked in, bent over, and picked up the hammer. It was crusted over with what looked like the same goop on the floor.

Later, she'd wonder if it had been her relaxed state of mind, or even fatigue from all the traveling. Still, those thoughts were days away because in the here and now, when Joyce turned toward Campos's desk she saw the mangled body of her boss on the floor. The top of his skull was caved in, and his jaw looked like it was no longer attached to his face. Then four things happened almost at once: Joyce screamed, turned, ran hard and fast straight into the office door's edge, and knocked herself out.

When she hit the deck, the hammer was still in her hand.

Virgil walked into the conference room where he found Mimi Phillips and Chip Lawless—the MCU's crime scene technicians—along with Murton, Ross, and Tom Rosencrantz.

Rosencrantz—a senior detective with the MCU—was still dealing with the loss of his girlfriend, Carla Martin, and their unborn child. They'd been gunned down outside the statehouse a few months ago, a devastating hit that still haunted not only Rosencrantz, but the entire Major Crimes Unit.

Virgil looked at him and said, "Rosie."

Rosencrantz lifted his chin at Virgil but didn't say anything. Despite the way they'd left it—Ross and Rosencrantz had flown to Jamaica and killed the man responsible for Martin's death—there was still a bit of tension between Virgil and Rosencrantz about how everything went down. Virgil had been there as well, and once they returned, both men thought they'd smoothed out any wrinkles in their relationship. But the relational iron—unlike each man's attitude—was running low on steam, and the fabric of their lives still looked as though it'd been hung out to dry instead of pressed back into shape. Virgil knew there was still some work to do, but he was also aware that it was up to Rosencrantz to make the next move.

Virgil looked at Murton and said, "You sent out a memo?"

"What? I'm here to help. And, good morning to you too, by the way. You're looking sharp. I should know. I picked everything out."

Virgil turned his palms up. "Well, you know what they say…there's no accounting for taste."

Mimi stood and walked over to Virgil. She ran her fingers over the cut of his jacket and said—with a voice that sounded like movie theater popcorn—"Hey, did you go on one of those makeover shows, or something? You look like a new man."

"More like a kept man," Lawless said. "You know, with that haircut and your new duds, it's getting harder and harder to tell you and Murton apart."

"You've been hanging out with Ross again, haven't you?" Virgil said.

Ross laughed and said, "Someone has to show the kid the ropes." Then to Lawless: "I'll bet he starts wearing a diamond pinkie ring."

Chip shook his head. "Too flashy. My money's on a birthstone…with a matching brooch on his lapel."

Virgil held his arms out to his sides and turned a complete circle. "Okay, go ahead. Take a good look and get it all out of your system. This is your one and only chance."

"I think they just did," Becky said. "Nice spin, though. How's the plié coming along?"

Virgil dropped his arms. "Yeah, yeah. Let's get started, huh? Murt, did you bring everyone up to speed?"

"Yep."

"Good," Virgil said. He looked around the table. "Does anyone have any questions regarding operational procedures?"

"Doesn't sound like much has changed," Ross said. "Other than the fact that our reports go to a different destination."

Virgil opened his mouth to answer, but didn't say anything. He wanted to tell everyone about the changes he'd had to endure over the last month, then realized that Ross was essentially correct. When it came to his squad and their duties, they were mostly unaffected.

"You should either say something or close your mouth," Murton said. "If you don't, you're going to drool all over your new clothes."

Virgil closed his mouth, swallowed, then said, "Becky, did you get in touch with the investigators?"

Becky opened a file folder and said, "I did. Both of them are county detectives. And I don't know if this means anything yet, but I did notice that both of the murders were in the southern part of the state."

"How far south?" Ross said.

"One in Jackson County. The other—the female—was in Brown County."

"Those two counties border each other," Murton said. "Looks like we might be able to rule out a traveler."

"Maybe," Virgil said. "But let's not jump to any conclusions right out of the gate." Then to Becky: "Does Sarah have a copy of your information?"

"Yes, everyone does."

"I don't," Virgil said.

"Uh, yes, you do. I emailed it to you this morning."

"Oh, okay, right. I didn't have time to check before I came in."

"Too busy primping," Murton said.

Virgil ignored him and hit the intercom button. "Sarah, will you get in touch with the investigators from Brown and Jackson Counties? Let them know that we'll be down this morning to speak with them."

"I'm on it, Jonesy."

"Thanks, Sarah." Then Virgil looked at Ross and Rosencrantz. "I want you guys to take the Brown County case." He turned to Becky. "I want every scrap of paper they've generated on both victims, right down to the color of their socks."

"I've already started," Becky said.

"Good. Ross, Rosie, interview the investigator, then reinterview anyone they talked to. The more information you can gather, the easier it'll be for Becky to do a thorough background. Murton and I will take the Jackson County case and do the same. Questions?"

When nobody had any, Virgil finished with: "Okay, let's get started. It's probably going to be a long day."

Everyone stood and was just getting ready to file out of the room when Sarah walked in. "Looks like we've got another one. The system just kicked it out. Same type of murder weapon, and a similar note left with the body."

"Where?" Virgil said. It was half question, half bark. He dropped his head, then held his hand out, palm forward. Then, much softer, "Sorry. Where, exactly?"

"Orange County. The victim was a dentist in Paoli."

Virgil took a deep breath. "Okay, I hoped it wouldn't be necessary, but get in touch with Mayo and Ortiz. We're going to need them."

"I already did," Sarah said. "They're waiting on your call."

CHAPTER SEVEN

Virgil picked up the phone, then noticed that Rosencrantz was hanging back. He set the phone down, then looked at his friend without speaking.

Rosencrantz held his stare for a few seconds, then said, "Got a minute?"

"Sure. How're things?"

Rosencrantz looked away. "About like you'd expect. It comes in waves. One minute I'm fine, and the next I feel like I'm being pulled underwater by some sort of invisible riptide."

In some ways, Virgil could relate to what Rosencrantz was saying. He'd been present when his father, Mason, was killed. And he'd nearly lost Sandy a number of years ago when she was pregnant with Wyatt. But neither of those things were the same, and

Virgil, while sympathetic, found himself feeling both relieved and guilty at the same time over his slight lack of empathy. "It gets better, Tom. I know that's no kind of answer, but it is the truth."

"I'm not sure I want it to get better. When Carla died, a piece of me died with her. When she was buried, a part of me went into the ground as well. I feel… stuck."

Virgil parked his butt against the edge of the table. "From what I understand, that's not uncommon. People often get stuck in various stages of grief. Have you talked to anyone about it?"

"I don't need a shrink, Jonesy."

"I didn't say you did."

"Then what are you saying?"

"You've got one of the best partners a guy could hope for. You and Ross haven't talked about it?"

Rosencrantz drew his lips into a tight line. "We have. Not much since we took care of business down in Jamaica."

"I really wish you'd have handled that differently."

"You've made that abundantly clear," Rosencrantz said. "On multiple occasions."

"Yeah, I guess I have," Virgil said. "For all the good it's done."

"Christ, Jonesy. What the fuck would you have me

do? Turn back the clock? I'll tell you this: Even if I could, I wouldn't do one single thing differently. And you know what else? I think you'd have done the same thing if it had been Sandy instead of Carla."

"Look, Tom…I don't want to rehash all of that again."

"Then why'd you bring it up?"

"I, uh, well, I don't know, to tell you the truth. Maybe it's because of the pressure I'm feeling myself with everything that's been happening lately. How about we chalk it up to lesson learned?"

Rosencrantz shook his head. "Or, how about we admit that the rules aren't the same for some people around here?"

Virgil tried to keep his voice calm. "You're out of line, Rosie."

"Am I? How about you tell it to your reflection?"

"What the hell is that supposed to mean?"

"It means when Ross made your problem with Roje Brenner finally go away—and you've got to admit, it was a pretty big problem—you essentially gave him a pat on the back. I'm surprised he didn't get a medal."

Virgil pointed a finger at Rosencrantz. "That was different, and you know it."

"Get your finger out of my face. The only difference is that it was done for you. Ross and I took care of my problem ourselves."

Virgil lowered his hand and reminded himself that Rosencrantz was a longtime trusted friend and coworker. He waited a few seconds before he responded. Once he had his emotions under control, he said, "When I asked if you've talked to anyone, I wasn't only speaking of Ross."

"Who'd you have in mind?" Rosencrantz said, a little calmer himself.

"Someone who's been through it."

"Like who?"

"Sarah comes to mind. So does Delroy. Have you forgotten what we did for him and Huma?"

"Of course not. But you know what it reminds me of?"

"What?" Virgil said.

"Every example you've given me is a reminder of you rewriting the playbook when it suits your own agenda."

"What the hell are you talking about?"

Rosencrantz let out a sad chuckle. "When the cops got rough with Sarah after Gary was killed, you beat the living hell out of the guy who body slammed her in her own house, then cuffed him to his squad car in the central booking parking lot and walked away. You did it in the heat of the moment with no forethought whatsoever. When Huma and Delroy were in trouble down in Jamaica, you threw the rule book out the window and opened up on anything that moved. How is that different from what I did?"

Virgil looked at his shoes for a few seconds. "Maybe it's not. I guess what I'm trying to express to you is this: The things I've done over the course of my career…the things I might have done differently…they all land on me, and me alone. I can take the heat. I always knew I could suffer the career hit if it ever came to that. I'm just trying to look out for you, man."

When Rosencrantz didn't respond, Virgil looked at his friend and said, "You started this conversation by asking me if I had a minute to talk…" Virgil let the statement hang.

"I wanted to tell you that I'm sorry for putting you in a difficult position, and I'm sorry I've been such a jerk lately. Thanks for listening." Then Rosencrantz turned and walked out the door, closing it softly behind him.

And Virgil thought, *way to go, Jonesy.*

A FEW MINUTES LATER, MURTON STEPPED INTO THE conference room and said, "You ready to roll?"

"Yeah, almost. I've got to call Mayo and Ortiz."

"No, you don't," Murton said. "I just spoke with them while you were tied up with Rosie. Becky emailed them all the intel we have on the other two victims, along with what we know about the Paoli case, which, admittedly, isn't much. They're headed that way now."

"Thanks, Murt."

"You okay?"

"Yeah. Tom's hurting, though, and it seems like every time I try to help, I end up making him feel worse."

"What happened?"

"He came in to apologize for being a jerk—his words, not mine—and as usual, I managed to steer the conversation into an argument."

"He'll be okay, Jones-man. Just give him some time."

"You sound pretty sure of yourself."

"Why wouldn't I be?" Murton said. "Becky ran into him the other night down at the bar. He was sitting on a stool talking to Delroy. They were both laughing like crazy."

"Was he drinking?"

"Just coffee, as far as I could tell. C'mon, you

worry too much. Let's go figure out who's killing these people. That always makes you feel better."

Virgil pushed his butt off the table. "Yeah, I guess so. You got the case notes?"

"Yep. Say, would it be okay if I drove the Range Rover?"

"Sure. How come?"

"It seems nice. I'd like to get a feel for how it handles. Maybe I'll get one."

"On your salary?"

Murton laughed. "You're forgetting about the trust fund."

"I thought you said it was complicated, and that it was for your daughter's education."

Murton nodded with vigor. "It is extremely complicated. But if I buy a new one now, by the time Ellie Rae is ready for college, it'll be a seventeen-year-old beater I can give her for transportation. That makes it an educational expense."

"That's a little weak, Murt."

Murton shrugged it off. "I'll be able to sleep at night. Let's roll, huh?"

Two hours later, Virgil and Murton turned into the parking lot of the Jackson County Law Enforcement Center. Murton parked the Range Rover in a visitor's spot, then had to move because Virgil thought the space was a little tight. "What? I don't want to get it all dinged up the first week."

"You thought it was a pig the first time you drove it," Murton said.

"I was being facetious. I already like it better than the Raptor. In fact, Delroy is dropping the truck off for me at the motor pool today. They're going to strip the lights, siren, and radio out of it. I'm going to sell it if you're in the market for a new vehicle."

"No thanks. First of all, I only buy new. Your truck is used. Not only that, but it's been run hard and put away wet, if you take my meaning. Plus, I'm not a truck person. You get a truck and the next thing you know everyone wants your help when they move."

"Nobody ever asked me to help them move," Virgil said.

"That's because nobody likes you."

"Hey."

"Relax. I'm just kidding. I know a guy who might want it, though."

"Who?"

"Don't worry about it," Murton said. They walked

up the steps of the law enforcement center. Murton grabbed the door and held it open for Virgil. "I'll ask. If he's interested, I'll let you know."

Virgil was mildly suspicious, but he didn't press the issue. They walked over to the counter, their badges hanging from neck chains and resting across their chests. Virgil rapped on the plexiglass partition with his knuckle—a polite little tap, tap, tap—then held up his badge and gave it a wiggle. The deputy behind the desk walked over to the window and said, "Help you?" Then his eyes opened a little wider. "Say, aren't you—"

Virgil cut him off. "Detectives Jones and Wheeler to see Lieutenant, uh…" Virgil had to check his paperwork because he couldn't remember who they were seeing. He opened the file folder, took a quick peek, then said, "Lieutenant Joe Navarro. He should be expecting us."

The deputy nodded, picked up the desk phone, and made a call. A few seconds later, he pushed a button, the interior lobby door buzzed, and Virgil and Murton stepped through. "Down the hall, last door on the left."

"Thanks," Murton said.

"No problem," the deputy said. Then to Virgil: "Give my regards to the governor?"

Virgil stopped. "Sure. Have the two of you met?"

"In a manner of speaking."

Virgil gave him the brow. "What manner would that be?"

"I was at the race the year she waved the green flag."

Virgil chuckled. "Not to split hairs or anything like that, but I don't think being at the race qualifies as actually meeting her."

The deputy chuckled right back. "Well, if we've gone to hair-splitting, I was in the snake pit for that race. Remember the fat fuck who lifted his shirt and tried to get her to lower the zipper on her catsuit?"

Virgil squinted an eye at the deputy. "Yeah. What of it?"

"That was me," the deputy said with delight. "I still have dreams about that day. You're a lucky guy."

"Want to hear something that'll break your heart?" Virgil said.

"Maybe."

"The catsuit is still in the closet. I get to see it whenever I want."

If Virgil thought he was going to burst the man's bubble, he was mistaken because Murton laughed, looked at the deputy, and said, "It looks a lot better on his wife, though."

As they were walking down the hall: "Why do you always have to do that?"

"Do what?" Murton said.

"Make me the butt of your jokes."

"That's a little like asking the dent in your rear bumper why you're always backing into things." Then Murton pointed at an open office door and said, "Here we are." He knocked on the edge of the doorframe and said, "Lieutenant Navarro?"

Navarro stood from his desk chair and said, "That's me. Detectives Jones and Wheeler?"

"That's right," Virgil said. "Mind if we come in?"

"Not at all," Navarro said. "I'm glad you're here. Have a seat."

Virgil and Murton took the two chairs that fronted Navarro's desk, and the three men spent a few minutes doing what all cops do when they meet for the first time. They spread a little manure around the room talking about their jobs, pay rates, the women who'd gotten away, and the criminals who didn't.

When it was time for business, Virgil opened the file folder and said, "We'd like you to tell us everything you can about the victim…John Harwood."

Navarro reached into his center desk drawer and pulled out a file folder of his own. "I'm afraid there isn't much. Mr. Harwood owned a used car dealership.

One of those places where they do their own financing…you know…buy here, pay here, or whatever they call it. I'll tell you something, places like that aren't really selling cars. What they're actually doing is selling you the financing. The car is nothing more than a bandage for your puckered-up ass after all the papers are signed."

"Sounds like maybe the guy didn't have too many friends," Virgil said.

Navarro shook his head. "That's where you'd be wrong, Detective. The fact is, people loved him. He was kind, helped out the community with charitable contributions, and provided a good working environment for his employees. There wasn't one single person we spoke with that had anything negative to say about him, not counting the ex-wife, of course."

"Of course," Murton said. "What did she have to say?"

"She wanted to know if he was killed fast or slow. When we told her he died instantly from blunt force trauma to the head, she seemed both pleased and disappointed at the same time."

"She have an alibi?" Virgil said.

"Yes, she does. And it's a good one. She was in the hospital getting ready to undergo a triple bypass. Big woman, that one. After we spoke with her, the docs actually told us that her blood pressure went down."

"What about Mr. Harwood's employees…or customers, for that matter," Murton said.

"It's like I said a minute ago. Everybody loved the guy. Even his customers, which is a little hard to believe."

"Why?"

"Well, you know how it is with guys like Harwood. He made his money off the backs of the working class in our community. He sells them a used car, writes his own contracts, charges interest rates that'd make a bookie blush, and to top it all off, sets the whole thing up so their loan payments are automatically deducted from their paycheck every week."

Virgil was skeptical. "And out of all those people, none stood out as suspects?"

"No one we could find. We only went back about three months on the customer list, though. Don't have the manpower, let alone the time to track down every person who ever bought a car from the man."

"Tell us about the scene," Murton said. "Where he was found, and all that."

Navarro went back to his file. "Mr. Harwood was discovered early on a Saturday morning…that would have been two weeks ago, shortly after six by his lot attendant. He'd been stuffed into the backseat of one of the vehicles on the lot. Cause of death—which I've already mentioned—was obvious. Our county coroner reports that both Harwood's ankles had been smashed to pieces postmortem. He said the X-rays showed so many breaks and fragments he couldn't identify the individual bones from one another."

Virgil looked at Murton. "Sounds like a nut."

"That's what I'm afraid of," Navarro said.

"It's actually good news," Murton said.

"How do you figure?"

Virgil answered for his brother. "There's obviously some pretty deep anger issues involved. People who exhibit violent tendencies against their victims after they've already killed them tend to unravel after a period of time."

"How long?" Navarro asked.

"That's the million-dollar question," Murton said. "Did the lot attendant come back clean?"

"Like the Pope at Christmas Mass."

"What about your crime scene people?" Virgil said. "They find anything?"

"A ton of prints off the vehicle, as you might expect. We put them all through the system."

"Any hits?"

"Only two, both minor offenders...one was a DUI,

and the other was nothing more than a bench warrant for unpaid parking tickets."

"You talk to them?" Virgil said.

Navarro tipped his chair back and crossed his arms over his chest. "Yep. It wasn't them. The DUI is our town drunk. He was in the tank that weekend."

"What about the bench warrant guy?" Murton said.

"The bench warrant guy, as you called him, is a seventy-three year old woman who thinks parking meters are the scourge of the twenty-first century. I should know. She's my mother."

"Did you throw the book at Mom?" Virgil said with a grin.

"Like I need that kind of grief," Navarro said. "Plus, I'd miss my Sunday dinners. The woman knows how to cook. If she'd have told me about the tickets, I could have taken care of them."

"Why didn't she?"

Navarro laughed. "Told me it was none of my business, if you can believe that."

"What's the status of Mr. Harwood's dealership?" Virgil said.

"Closed since the incident."

"What about security cameras?" Murton said.

"Two on the front of the building, but they were wired into the computers."

"Did you happen to grab them? The computers?"

Navarro nodded. "There were only two. We've got them down in the evidence locker. We haven't gotten beyond the password screen."

"We'll take care of that," Murton said. "We've got the tech to open them up. Maybe we'll get something from the cameras."

"I hope so," Navarro said. "I'm sorry, Detectives. I know I don't have much for you, but the fact is, there wasn't a lot to work with. We've got the murder weapon—your standard claw hammer—the note that was left behind, and the computers."

Virgil puffed his cheeks and said, "Well, you're right. It's not much, but it's a start. Do you have the original note? I've seen a copy, but I'd like our techs to give it the once-over."

Navarro pulled a clear ziplock bag from the file and handed it to Virgil. "Like the hammer, you won't find any prints."

"I'm sure you're right, but it'll give our techs something to do. There are two more cases connected to this one, so with a little luck and some legwork, we might be able to break it open."

Navarro leaned forward. "I thought there was only one other case."

"Another came through this morning down in

Paoli," Virgil said. "Two of our other detectives are headed that way right now."

"Think this guy is working his way south?"

"Could be," Murton said. "But it's too soon to tell. If you'll have someone get those computers and the murder weapon, we'll get out of your hair."

Navarro stood and said, "Follow me. I'll take you down to the evidence locker myself."

As they were walking down the hall, Navarro looked at Virgil and said, "How's the governor these days?"

"Hard to say. She's been so busy I don't get to see her much lately."

"I saw her at the race a few years ago."

Murton grinned. "Snake pit?"

Navarro nodded with enthusiasm. "Yeah. The fat fuck out front? He's my second cousin on Mom's side."

CHAPTER EIGHT

THE BROWN COUNTY INVESTIGATOR, LIEUTENANT KEN Mayhall, gave Ross and Rosencrantz almost the same case synopsis that Virgil and Murton had gotten from Navarro out of Jackson County. The only major differences being the gender of the victim, and where she worked.

They sat in Mayhall's office and went through the finer points of the investigation. "The victim's name was Lori Reddick," Mayhall said. "I didn't really know her personally, but I knew of her. She ran one of those little tourist shops in Nashville. Sold handmade soaps, candles, knickknacks, that sort of thing. She seemed like a nice lady. The wife used to drag me into her shop every once in a while."

"That's where she was found?" Rosencrantz said.

"Yes. Late last Saturday. Not this past Saturday, but a week ago. Her husband said she was working late, trying to get caught up on her invoicing, inventory, purchase orders, and whatnot."

"Who found her?" Ross said.

"Her husband, Frank. Says he got worried when she didn't make it home by ten. He called both her cell and the shop. When he didn't get an answer, Frank went to the shop and found her dead on the floor." Mayhall reached into a box sitting near the edge of his desk and pulled out an evidence bag that contained a bloody hammer. "She took a single blow to her head with this…then apparently multiple blows to her pelvic region."

"Was there any indication of sexual assault?" Rosencrantz said.

Mayhall shook his head. "Coroner says no."

"The husband check out?" Ross said.

"He did. He's a volunteer firefighter and was out on a run most of the evening. We've got some idiot or idiots going around starting barn fires. It's probably teenage kids, but if I ever get my hands on them I'm going to wring their scrawny little necks."

Ross and Rosencrantz were both sympathetic regarding Mayhall's caseload, but the arson didn't interest them. The killing did. "Any chance the husband did it either before or after the fire call?" Ross said.

"I can't come up with a scenario where that fits. We spoke with the station chief, and everyone who was on duty that night. Frank Reddick was at the station before the call came in—I guess it was his turn to cook dinner for the crew—and everyone told us the exact same story. He was there before she was killed, worked the fire when the call came in, then got home right before ten to an empty house."

"That doesn't exactly prove he didn't go there before he went to the station."

"You're right," Mayhall said. "It doesn't. But Reddick ran a one-woman show. When we checked the receipts from her shop, she was still open for business well after dispatch called in the fire. So unless a dead woman was ringing up her customers, that sort of takes the husband out of it."

"Maybe he went to the shop after the fire, but before he went home," Rosencrantz said.

"Nope. When Mr. Reddick returned to the station, he discovered he had a flat tire. Everyone was pretty beat up by then…the barn had been a total loss…so instead of changing the tire, one of the other guys on the crew gave him a lift back to his place."

They sat quietly for a few seconds, then Rosencrantz said, "If he got a ride home, how did he get to the shop later that night…when he found his wife?"

"He walked," Mayhall said. "They live about three blocks from the shop, right off the main drag. Look, I know you guys have to track down every lead, but it wasn't the husband. He's clean, although I almost wish he wasn't."

"Why's that?" Ross said.

"Because it'd make my job, and yours, a heck of a lot easier. Lori Reddick was one of those women everybody loved. She was kind, made her own goods, and sold them at a fair price in a quaint little shop in a quiet little town. Hell, she even did volunteer work on the side. I don't know who killed her, but it wasn't because of who she was."

"It might be, though," Ross said. "You don't usually see this type of violence after the fact. Did she have any defensive wounds?"

"None," Mayhall said. "We initially thought it was a robbery gone bad, but the cash drawer wasn't touched. We checked the receipts against the money, and it matched to the penny."

Ross leaned forward in his chair. "You mentioned she did volunteer work."

"That's right."

"What kind?"

"A little bit of everything. Church bake sales, library reading club for the kids…like that."

"You're not giving us much to work with here, Lou," Rosencrantz said.

Mayhall had his elbows propped on the edge of his desk. He spread his hands apart and said, "It's all I've got. There were no witnesses, we don't have any suspects, and we can't determine a motive."

"What about security footage?" Rosencrantz said. "Anything there?"

Mayhall shook his head again. "The shop had an alarm system…like the kind you'd find in a house, but no cameras. Nashville is a pretty quiet town, even during the peak of tourist season. With the exception of the local pizza and beer joint, they roll the sidewalks up pretty early. Hell, after nine o'clock in the evening you could use Main Street as a bowling alley. That's not an exaggeration." He handed Ross and Rosencrantz another evidence bag. "Here's the note that was found on Reddick's body. I don't know what else to tell you other than good luck, and let me know what you come up with."

Ross and Rosencrantz were almost to the front door when they heard a woman call out from behind. "Excuse me, Detectives?"

Both men stopped and turned. "Yes?" Ross said.

The woman tried on a quick smile, then let it drop, like maybe it didn't suit her personality. She glanced at Rosencrantz, then looked directly at Ross and said, "Would you mind excusing us for a moment?"

Ross had a very direct way about him, and sometimes it caused others to take offense. He looked at the uniformed woman, took note of her name and rank, then said, "Why?"

"Forgive me, please. I'd like to have a word with Detective Rosencrantz. Alone, if you don't mind."

"I might not," Ross said. "Does it concern the Reddick case?"

"No, it does not."

"Then I don't mind." Ross looked at Rosencrantz and said, "I'll be in the squad."

"I'll be right out."

Once Ross was out the door, the woman looked at Rosencrantz and said, "I'm Sheriff Lisa Young."

Rosencrantz shook hands with the woman and said, "How may I help you, Sheriff?"

"Please, call me Lisa."

Rosencrantz tried on a small smile of his own, but

his heart wasn't in it, so he let it fade. "Very well. How may I help you, Lisa?"

Young seemed like she wasn't quite sure how to begin. She took a breath and said, "Do you know how many female sheriffs our state has?"

Rosencrantz looked away briefly and raked his bottom lip with his teeth. "I don't have an exact accounting."

"I'm sorry. I've never been very good at this sort of thing."

"I'm afraid I don't know what you're talking about," Rosencrantz lied. He knew what was coming, and while he appreciated the woman's efforts, he simply didn't want to talk about it.

"I was at Carla's funeral."

"Thank you for that, but I don't remember seeing you there."

"I'd be surprised if you remembered anyone being there at all."

Rosencrantz nodded at nothing. "You're not too far off the mark," he said. "I know there were a lot of people in attendance, but no matter their own sense of loss or good intentions, they were all a blur…a single mass I couldn't seem to separate from one another. It was like looking at the forest from a distance and trying to pick out an individual leaf."

"That's a very good analogy," Young said.

"I remember nearly every single moment of that day. How I felt when I woke in the morning…you know, that two-second respite you have before reality sets in?"

"I do know. How many seconds are you up to now?"

"I'm afraid it's gone the other way," Rosencrantz said. "It feels like I'm aware of it before I ever open my eyes."

Young reached out and touched him gently on the arm. "That's good news, actually. It means you're healing, whether you know it or not."

Rosencrantz's nostrils flared slightly. "I hope you'll forgive me for saying this, but how would you know?"

"I do forgive you, even though it's not necessary. I lost my husband while he was on the job. He was writing a ticket along the side of the highway and was hit by a drunk driver. I have some idea what you're going through right now."

Rosencrantz tried to keep the bite out of his voice but failed. He tipped his head slightly and said, "Do you? Do you really? They didn't bury your unborn child with your husband now, did they?"

Sheriff Young took a small involuntary step back. "I'm sorry. Perhaps I shouldn't have said anything.

When I took this job, I wasn't prepared for the difficulties I would encounter. I reached out to Carla for help. I wouldn't say we became friends or anything like that, but we were friendly with each other. Peers, I guess you could say. She spoke very highly of you. I could tell how much you were loved by the look in her eyes and the tone of her voice."

"Look, Sheriff—"

"It's Lisa…please."

Rosencrantz flapped his arms and let them fall against the sides of his thighs. "Fine, whatever, Lisa. It's not a scab I want to keep picking at. I don't need a support group, a shrink, or perfect strangers walking up and telling me that they know how I feel, okay? I'm sorry for your loss. Have a nice day."

Then Rosencrantz turned and walked out the door.

When he got in the car, he slammed the driver's side door closed, started the engine, and began to pull away. "What was all that about?" Ross said.

"People not minding their own fucking business."

"Care to be a little more specific?"

"No."

"Maybe I should drive."

"I'm fine."

"Are you?"

Rosencrantz slammed on the brakes and threw the shift lever into Park. He punched the center pad of the steering wheel—hard—and the horn of the squad car let out a single, sharp honk. *"Goddamnit."* He opened the door to get out, but Ross grabbed his arm.

"Where are you going?"

Rosencrantz pulled his arm free and said, "I'll be right back."

When he walked into the law enforcement center, he found Sheriff Young still standing in the hall. She was looking at the framed pictures of the department's fallen officers, and she seemed to be studying one in particular. When Rosencrantz spoke, it was to her reflection in the portrait. "Your original question? The one about how many female sheriffs the state has? I'd like to change my answer."

Young turned and faced Rosencrantz, a single tear caught in her lashes. "Why?"

"Because it matters," Rosencrantz said.

"In what way?"

"In that the number is one less than it should be. You were trying to do a kind thing for a stranger, and I acted like an asshole. I'm so very sorry for the way I just spoke to you. It was completely uncalled for."

Young stepped forward, wrapped Rosencrantz in a hug, and held on for a long time. When she finally pulled away, she pointed at her husband's picture on the wall. "His name was Jerry, and sometimes I miss him so much that it's hard to breathe. Want to know what really hurts?"

"Beyond the obvious?" Rosencrantz said.

Young wiped her tears away and said, "It's the days when I'm busy and I realize that I haven't thought about him at all. Then I get home at the end of my shift and it hits me like the whole house is coming down on top of my head. It makes me feel guilty as hell."

"Mind if I ask you something?" Rosencrantz said.

"What is it?"

"How long ago did you lose him?"

"It'll be three years next week," Young said.

"Do you have any family?"

"Parents are gone…both his and mine."

"Siblings?"

Young nodded without enthusiasm. "Yeah, but siblings are hard sometimes. Most times, in fact. We were never very close."

"Did you ever speak with Carla about the loss of your husband?"

Young looked down at the floor before she answered. "No, I never did."

"Why not?"

"Because she was so happy. I didn't want to dump my personal life in her lap."

"I don't think she would have seen it that way," Rosencrantz said. He took one of his cards from his pocket and gave it to Young. "I'm not very happy…if you ever want to talk." That got him a small chuckle. "And believe it or not, I'm actually a pretty nice guy."

Back in the squad car with Ross: "What's with the sheriff?"

"Nothing. She was trying to be nice, and I didn't handle it well. I had to go back in and apologize."

"Did she accept?"

"Yep." Once they were on their way, Rosencrantz glanced at his partner and friend. "Have I been a jerk?"

Ross didn't hesitate. "Yeah."

CHAPTER NINE

When Oscar Mayo and Rafael Ortiz finally arrived at Campos's dental clinic, they were met by a lone Orange County deputy who casually glanced at his watch and said, "I guess the state pays by the hour, huh?"

"We were actually called away from our vacation," Mayo said. He glanced at Ortiz. "Not that I mind. Anyway, we got a little turned around on the way over. Sorry if we held you up. Where is everyone?"

"Got a crime scene tech still inside, but the coroner already has the body, and the county investigator is back at the station doing an interview. I'm Deputy Jim Harding, Orange County Sheriff's Department. I was told to wait for you guys…if your names are Mayo and Ortiz, that is."

"That's us," Mayo said. Both men introduced themselves, then asked if they could take a look inside the building. Harding twirled a set of keys around his index finger and said, "Follow me. Got to clear it with the tech, though."

They walked up to the front door of the old building, and Harding put on a pair of gloves before unlocking the door.

"You locked your crime scene tech inside?" Ortiz said.

Harding snorted. "Nope. Other way around. She locked me out." He put his shoulder on the door, stuck the key into the lock, then gave it a twist. Once he had the door cracked, he stuck his head inside and said, "Yo. State fuzz is here. Can they come in?"

From somewhere in the back of the building, Mayo and Ortiz heard a woman's voice call out. "Yeah, but tell them to put gloves and shoe coverings on, watch their step, and don't touch anything. And you stay outside."

Once they were geared up, Mayo and Ortiz stepped into the building. Both men kept their hands near their sides and stayed clear of the blood spatter on the floor in the reception area. They found the tech in the hallway between the lobby and Campos's office. She was down on her knees, looking at a spot on the floor with a magnifying glass. The sum total of her greeting went like this: "Don't step on any of these spots."

"We won't. I'm Detective Mayo. This is my partner, Detective Ortiz. We're with the state's Major Crimes Unit. What have you got?"

"A clue," the tech said. "Might be a good one too." She stood carefully, then said, "I'm Edna Weeks, lead tech with Orange County. My partner is already gone. He ran some evidence back to the lab."

"Edna, huh?" Mayo said. "That's a name you don't hear much anymore."

"No kidding. Tell it to my mom. It was her mother's name. I got lucky."

"You mentioned evidence," Ortiz said. "What'd you find?"

Weeks gave them a shrug. "The usual…carpet fibers, hair samples, that sort of thing. And teeth. A lot of busted teeth."

"Teeth?" Ortiz said.

"Yeah. Someone knocked all the victim's teeth out with a hammer."

"All of them?"

Weeks nodded. "That's what the coroner said. Listen, we've already photographed and dusted the place, so be careful what you touch, or you'll have powder all over your clothes."

"What's the clue?" Mayo said.

"C'mon, I'll walk you through it." Weeks led them back to the front reception counter. "See the big pool of blood on the floor?"

"It's a little hard to miss," Mayo said.

Weeks gave him a look. "It's called setting the stage. Based on the amount of blood in this area and the spatter pattern, it looks like they killed the victim out here, then dragged him back to his office. There are a few streaks on the hall floor from the victim's heels. That was confirmed before the coroner took the body. Anyway, once they had him in the office, they knocked his teeth out."

"You keep using the word, *they*," Ortiz said. "You're saying there were two killers?"

"No. I'm not attempting to be that definitive. There could have been a dozen killers. A whole biker gang could have come in here and taken the victim apart. What I am saying, though, is this: There were *at least* two killers. I'm all but certain of it."

"What's your thinking?" Mayo said.

"That's the main thing I wanted to show you," Weeks said. She pointed down the hall. "See those individual spots on the floor?"

"Yeah," Mayo said. "What are they?"

"Hang on a second," Weeks said. "Let me get the

pictures. It's easier than crawling around on the floor and using the magnifying glass." She disappeared into Campos's office, then returned with a small stack of photographs in her hand. "Let's go into the waiting room. That area has been completely processed, and it's clean."

Mayo and Ortiz followed the tech to the waiting room where they pulled three chairs into a tight little group next to a coffee table. Weeks got the photos in the proper order, then went through her thought process.

"Okay, this first shot was taken from where we were just standing…near the reception counter, looking down the hall toward the victim's office." She set the photo on the table, then took out another. "Now, there are two things to see here: This is a closer view of the spots on the hallway floor, and as you can see, we used a tape measure to mark the distance between each one. The distance is almost exactly the same—three feet—from spot to spot…plus or minus two inches."

"You said there were two things," Ortiz said. "What's the other?"

"The spots begin to fade from one impression to the next. Look how dark the first one is compared to the last."

Both men looked at the photo, then Mayo said,

"Okay, so how does a bunch of progressively faded, equally spaced blood spots get you to at least two killers?"

"I'm getting to it," Weeks said. "One more picture first." She took another photo and set it down next to the others. "This is an extreme closeup of the third spot. It's the best one because just enough blood has been cleared from the first two, and the others are pretty faint. The fourth one wasn't bad, but this is the best. Tell me what you see."

Mayo and Ortiz each examined the third spot carefully, but neither man knew what the tech was trying to demonstrate. When they said as much, Weeks smiled with a hint of superiority and said, "I should probably be a detective." She took a pen from her pocket and pointed the tip at one side of the spot. "See how it's darker here on this side?"

"Yeah," Ortiz said. "What of it?"

Weeks continued without answering. "And see these little arcs? They're concentrically uneven. In fact, if you look closely, you'll notice that the spots themselves aren't quite perfectly round."

"That's a good catch," Mayo said. "It'd be a great one if I knew what any of it meant."

Weeks looked at Ortiz. "How about you, handsome? Figure it out?"

Ortiz blushed…twice. Once because a pretty young crime scene tech just called him handsome, and again when he finally had to admit to her that he had no idea what it meant.

Weeks gave Ortiz a wink and said, "I saw the victim before the coroner took the body. I'm just guessing, but I'd put his weight somewhere between two twenty, and two fifty. Those marks on the floor? They're from the tip of a cane. The fact that the impressions are out of round indicates that whoever was using it has a severe limp. There's virtually no way a guy with a bad leg, or hip, or whatever, could drag a man of the victim's size and weight by himself while using a cane."

Mayo looked at the pictures again and said, "You know what? I think you're right."

"I know I am," Weeks said. "I assume you've seen the note?"

"Just a copy," Ortiz said. "What about it?"

"The very first word is *We*. Put that together with what I just showed you, and you end up with at least two killers."

Mayo scooped up the photos and said, "Mind if we hang on to these?"

"Feel free," Weeks said. "I've got digitals for my file."

Ortiz looked at Weeks. "The deputy outside, uh, I think he said his name was Harding?"

Weeks made a face and said, "More like Hard-on. The guy's a pig. Why do you think I locked the door?"

"That bad, huh?"

"Nothing I can't handle," Weeks said. "What about him?"

"He told us your investigator is interviewing someone," Mayo said. "Any idea who he's speaking with?"

"From what I heard, it might be one of your killers. Joyce somebody. I guess she's the office manager. Her face was pretty busted up. They're thinking she and the doc got into it, and she, along with someone else beat the hell out of him. One of the dental hygienists found her unconscious, still holding the murder weapon."

Ortiz looked at Mayo and said, "I guess we should have asked that first."

"I'm glad you didn't," Weeks said.

"Why?"

"Because then I wouldn't have gotten to spend any time with you, Rafael."

Ortiz blushed again. Mayo looked at the tech and said, "What about me?"

Weeks gave Mayo a polite little patronizing pat on his knee. "Of course. You too." Then, "I'm sorry, what did you say your name was?"

Mayo and Ortiz left the building and headed over to the Orange County Law Enforcement Center to speak with the investigator and hear what the suspect had to say, if anything.

On the way over, Mayo called Virgil and filled him in.

"I want you guys to work this one hard," Virgil said. "If this Joyce woman did it, I want to know. I also want to know who she's working with. The second you get anything at all, email it to Becky."

"We're on it, Boss," Mayo said.

"How convinced are you that the Orange County tech is right? That we're looking at two killers, not one."

"She made a pretty convincing argument, and when you factor in the wording of the note, it seems likely. I'll email the photos to Becky once we arrive at the law enforcement center."

"Good enough," Virgil said. "Keep Sarah in the loop as well. She'll get updates to everyone."

"You guys making any progress?"

"Nothing worth talking about…at least not yet. Stay on it. I gotta go."

They were on speaker in the squad car, and before

the call ended, Ortiz said, "We did get one more vital piece of information."

"What's that?" Virgil said, the tone of his voice both hopeful and excited.

"We found out from the crime scene tech that I'm the handsome one."

Virgil hung up.

When they walked inside the Orange County Law Enforcement Center, Mayo and Ortiz asked the deputy at the front desk who was handling the Campos investigation.

"You guys with the state?"

Mayo and Ortiz held out their badges, and the deputy gave them a bored nod. "You're looking for a guy named Buckley. First name Jason. He's got your suspect in interview three. That's down the hall to the end, then left, and it'll be the second door on the right." He pushed a button and the interior door buzzed.

Mayo pulled it open and they headed that way. They found Buckley in the hall, introduced themselves, then Ortiz said, "Tell us what you've got."

Buckley was a big man, balding on top, and wore civilian clothes instead of a uniform. His gut hung over his belt line, and he wore a short sleeve shirt with a tie that didn't seem to match anything on the planet. He reminded Ortiz of Detective Sipowicz from the television show, NYPD Blue.

"Got a lot of nothing is what we've got," Buckley said. "The suspect, Joyce Parker, is the office manager for Doctor Paul Campos's dental clinic. One of the other staff members found her unconscious, still holding the murder weapon. She's pretty beat up herself, but the medics put a splint on her nose and taped up her eye. They said she's okay for now." He opened a door next to the interview room and said, "C'mon, you can take a look at her behind the glass."

They walked into the observation room—a small area not much bigger than a storage closet, and stood next to the two-way mirror. "What's her story?" Mayo said.

Buckley stuck a toothpick in the corner of his mouth. "She didn't do it."

"Is that your statement, or her's?" Ortiz said.

Buckley rolled the toothpick to the other side of his mouth. "You asked what her story was, not mine. She says she didn't do it."

"Just trying to be clear," Ortiz said. "What's your take?"

Buckley jerked a thumb at the mirror and said, "I

don't have one. She's either telling the truth, or this is some kind of weird work-related domestic dispute…if there is such a thing."

"How'd she get banged up?" Mayo said.

"Says she ran into a door."

Mayo and Ortiz used to work the night shift as patrol cops, and they'd seen their share of domestic violence. "Never heard that one before," Ortiz said with sarcasm. "What else did she say?"

"She said she came into work early, found a mess on the floor, didn't know what it was, went back to look for the doc, and saw the hammer. She picked it up, then saw Campos's body. According to her statement, she freaked out, turned to run, and hit the door head-on."

"Anything to add?"

Buckley shook his head. "It could have happened that way, but when I tried to press her, she asked for a lawyer. That's why you found me in the hall instead of the interview room."

"Does she have one?" Mayo said. "A lawyer?"

"Public defender is on his way over from the courthouse. He should be here any time."

"Mind if we have a word with her?" Ortiz said.

"You can't. She's requested a lawyer. That means you can't ask her any questions."

"Doesn't mean we can't have a friendly conversation, though," Mayo said.

Buckley swept his arm toward the observation room door. "Be my guest. And good luck. You're going to need it."

CHAPTER TEN

MAYO AND ORTIZ WALKED INTO THE INTERVIEW ROOM, and both men sat next to each other on the opposite side of the table from Joyce Parker. Mayo let a little light shine into his voice and said, "Miss Parker? It's Joyce, right? May I call you Joyce?"

"You're not my lawyer, are you?"

"No ma'am," Ortiz said. "We're detectives with the state. Is there anything we can get you? Maybe a couple of aspirin, or something? You look a little beat up."

"I know my rights. I've already asked for a lawyer, and that means you can't ask me any questions, and you've already asked me two."

"We're just trying to be friendly, Joyce," Mayo said. "The questions weren't germane to the investigation, so they don't count. Really…would you like some Advil, or something to drink? Coffee or water?"

Parker crossed her arms over her chest and said, "I know what you're trying to do. You'll play good cop, bad cop, and try to trick me into saying something so I'll incriminate myself."

Mayo and Ortiz stayed relaxed and quiet. No one spoke for nearly three minutes. Finally, Parker leaned forward and said, "This is insane. I didn't do anything wrong or illegal."

"I'd like to tell you a couple of things, Miss Parker," Mayo said. "The first is this: I give you my word that I will not ask you one single question without your permission. This is just a friendly chat. Detective Buckley already told us everything you said to him, so this is nothing new."

"Yeah, well, whatever. I guess that makes you the good cop. Detective Buckley treated me like some kind of common criminal. The only friendly chat I'm going to have is with my lawyer."

"You and Doctor Campos were close," Mayo said. A statement, not a question.

"What makes you say that?" Parker said.

"Forgive me. I meant in a work sense. I understand you've worked with him for a long time."

"Yes. I ran the office and managed the business side of things, and he handled all the patient care."

Mayo let his arms rest casually on the table. "According to what you told Detective Buckley, I understand you saw the hammer on the floor and picked it up out of curiosity."

Parker uncrossed her arms and leaned forward slightly. "That's right. That's exactly what happened. I had no idea that Paul had been beaten to death. I didn't even see him until I turned around. That's when I panicked and tried to run from the office. But I was so upset I wasn't watching where I was going. I hit the edge of the door and knocked myself out."

"I understand," Mayo said. "It must have been quite a shock."

"That's about the biggest understatement I've ever heard. It was absolutely horrific. One minute I'm reliving my wonderful vacation, and the next thing I know I find my boss with his head caved in and his teeth knocked out. Why are you smiling at me?"

"Sorry," Mayo said. "You mentioned vacation, and my partner and I were on ours when the call came in about Doctor Campos. We had to leave to come here and speak with you. I don't mind, though."

"Why's that?" Parker said.

"Because we were crawling around inside a bunch of dank caves over by Patoka Lake. I'd have rather been out on the water with a fishing pole in my hand, and a cooler full of beer."

Parker made a funny noise with her lips. "Patoka Lake is a smaller version of where I went down in Missouri."

Mayo tipped his head back. "Ah, you must be speaking of the Ozarks. I've never been, but I hear it's fantastic."

"It really is," Parker said. "I just got back last night."

"I'd love to see some pictures sometime."

"I'd show them to you right now, except Deputy Dog out there has my purse...and my phone."

Ortiz stood and left the room. "Where's he going?" Parker said.

"It's sort of spooky, when you think about it," Mayo said. "Detective Ortiz and I have worked together for so long we can sort of read each other's minds."

"That doesn't really answer my question."

"He's going to get your phone. I imagine you stayed someplace nice. There are a lot of great Airbnbs down that way."

Parker shook her head. "Nope. I stayed at the main resort." A little calmer now.

Mayo chuckled. "That sounds pricey. In fact, let me correct myself, there. I know it's expensive. It's one of the main reasons I've never been. I can't really afford it on my salary."

"Me either. I had to save for nearly eighteen months."

Ortiz walked back in with Parker's purse. When he handed it to her, Parker said, "Why are you giving me this? Am I free to go?"

"Not just yet," Mayo said. "I was hoping you'd show me some of those pictures you spoke of."

Parker dug around in her purse and pulled out her phone. She showed Mayo and Ortiz a bunch of photos of her vacation, then said, "I put most of them up on Facebook and Instagram. I know it's silly, but I was trying to make my friends jealous."

"It's always nice to keep your friends updated," Mayo said. "And the jealousy angle can be fun, too. It looks like you covered the entire length of your stay."

"I did," Parker said. "Or I tried to anyway. It'll be at least another year before I get to go back."

Mayo and Ortiz both stood. "We'll be right back, ma'am." They moved toward the door, then Mayo stopped and turned around. "At the beginning of our conversation I made you a promise, Miss Parker. Do you remember what it was?"

"Of course. You said you wouldn't ask me any questions without my permission. So far, you've managed to keep your word."

"I'd like your permission now. Just two or three questions if you don't mind. And don't forget, you are not obligated to answer, but if you do, it could really help your situation here."

Parker thought about it for a few seconds. The detective had been kind to her, and he'd kept his promise. What was the harm? "Okay, let's hear them."

"Do you know anyone who uses a cane?"

The question was so out of left field that it caught Parker off guard. Mayo watched as she closed her eyes in thought. Finally she opened them and said, "Gee, I really can't think of anyone. A few of our elderly patients use them, but I don't personally know anyone who does. I'm sure of it."

"Did Doctor Campos use one?"

"Oh heavens, no. He was getting up there, age-wise, but he was fit as a fiddle."

"Okay, last question then," Mayo said. He took out his notebook and a pen, then set them in front of Parker.

"What's this for?"

"In a moment, please. When you uploaded your pictures to your social media account, did you do that as you took them, or did you wait until you got home?"

"I uploaded as I went. Why?"

"Because if you'll write down your usernames and passwords for your social media accounts, I'm pretty sure I can get you out of here and on your way in no time at all."

"I don't know if I'm comfortable doing that."

Mayo gave Parker a warm smile. "I understand your concern. But don't worry, you can change your passwords after we're finished, and I give you my word we will not monkey around with your accounts."

Parker suddenly got it. "The location tags on the pictures, right?"

"That's right, ma'am," Ortiz said. "All those selfies you showed us? They're your alibi."

Parker scribbled the information down and gave it to Mayo. "Here you go. Try to hurry, will you? I need to get to the hospital and have my nose properly attended to. That's what the medic said, anyway."

"Give me twenty minutes. Think about that cane question a little more while you wait."

ONCE MAYO WAS OUT IN THE HALL, BUCKLEY WALKED over and said, "I caught the whole interview from the observation room. You got her to open up without asking any questions. That's some really great work, Detective."

"Thanks," Mayo said. "Just out of curiosity, how long have you been a detective?"

"Apparently, not long enough," Buckley said. "So, now what?"

Mayo leaned against the wall and instead of answering, he asked a question of his own. "Got a time of death on the victim?"

"Not an exact one, but the coroner says it was either late Friday, or very soon after midnight on Saturday."

"To answer your question, my partner is giving our computer expert the information from Parker's social media accounts. If the geotags and time stamps show what I think they will, you're about to lose your suspect."

"We'll still be able to charge her with evidence tampering," Buckley said.

Mayo's phone buzzed at him before he could respond. He glanced at the screen, then held it out so Buckley could see it. The message from Becky read: *All clear*. Mayo put his phone back into his pocket, then said, "You could charge her with evidence tampering, Detective, but why would you?"

"Because we can, and she did," Buckley said.

"That's not good enough. She didn't do it with intent, and just because you can do something doesn't mean you should."

"That's not your call."

Mayo shrugged. "Maybe it is, and maybe it isn't. But I'm going to walk back into that room before Miss Parker leaves and let her know two things. One is obvious. She's not a suspect in Doctor Campos's death. The other is this: Given the trauma she has had to endure, not to mention everything you and your department put her through, a sitting jury in a civil suit against Orange County would probably find in favor for the plaintiff."

"Hey…"

Mayo got right inside Buckley's personal space. "Hey nothing. This is no longer a county matter, Detective Buckley. It's a state case. Now strap on a sack, go into that room, and apologize to Joyce Parker. Do that, and I'll keep the legal advice to myself."

"Okay, okay. Relax, will you? Christ, you state guys are wound a little tight."

"You would be too if you'd spent the last week crawling around inside a bunch of bat-infested caves."

Just then a harried looking man came around the corner carrying two large briefcases, with a file folder pinched tight between his arm and ribcage. "I'm looking for, uh…" He set the briefcases down, opened the folder, and finished with, "A Joyce Parker. I'm the public defender."

Buckley shook his head. "We don't need you, Matt. It looks like we're probably going to kick her."

"You can take the word probably out of that last statement," Mayo said.

Matt, the public defender, seemed relieved. "Fine by me. I'm up to my neck in it, anyway." He turned to leave, and Buckley moved toward the interview room to go apologize to Parker.

"After you express your remorse, tell her to sit tight," Mayo said. "I've got a few more things to ask her."

"Yeah, yeah."

Ortiz walked over and said, "You get Becky's text?"

"Yes, I did. Social media saves the day."

"You don't hear that very often."

"That's because it's true."

"That was some pretty slick work, partner," Ortiz said.

"We'll see in a minute."

"What do you mean?"

Mayo puffed his cheeks, then let out a breath. "Because now we have to ask her the hard questions."

Ortiz didn't get it, and said so. "What kind of questions?"

Mayo tipped his head at the interview room door. "Follow me and I'll show you."

CHAPTER ELEVEN

Luke Quinn, a career logger like his father before him, had given his life to the forest. He enjoyed the work...the selective culling of deadwood, and harvesting healthy trees for their profit, all while preserving the beauty of what nature had to offer. But that was all gone now, and Luke was lost inside himself, his moral and rational thought processes buried deep within an area of his brain he could no longer access.

Midway Timber—the company he worked for—employed hundreds of people, from loggers like Luke, to truckers, sawmill operators, surveyors, and office staff. When the Department of Natural Resources awarded Midway Timber a contract to thin the Yellowwood State Forest, Luke got promoted to foreman, and that was the beginning of the end for Luke Quinn and his family.

The fanatics…the tree huggers…had shown up in droves, waving their signs and shouting at Luke and his crew like they were about to burn down the forest instead of help save it for future generations to come. The protesters themselves were bad enough, but when Luke and his crew began finding trees with large metal spikes driven deep into their trunks, everything changed. It was one thing to take a stand and make your point about something you believed in. It was something else entirely to put someone's life at risk to save a bunch of trees that were all but dead anyway. Felling trees was dangerous enough to begin with, and Luke's crew didn't need the added stress of kickbacks from metal rods bucking their chainsaws.

On the day of the accident—the day that Luke's father was killed and Caleb became crippled for life—Luke had missed a spike. The tree was showing rot at the base, and its trunk was a tangled mass of knotted oak that would require special care when making the cut. He was so caught up in the physics which would allow him to bring the tree down safely, he simply forgot to check to see if the giant tree had been sabotaged.

Luke turned to his father and said, "Any thoughts on this beast?"

Luke's father, Carl Quinn, looked at the base of the tree, then ran his hand over the knotted trunk. "There's still some fine wood inside this one. But that base is going to give you trouble if you're not careful. Want me to handle the cut?"

"No, I've got it, Dad. Midway made me the foreman, so it's my job to get it done."

Carl put an arm around Luke's shoulder and said, "You're the boss." When his father spoke, Luke could see the pride on his dad's face.

"I don't mean to step on your toes," Carl said, "but maybe we should call the office and have them send out a feller buncher." A feller buncher was a large machine similar to an excavator, except instead of a bucket, the articulating arm held a hydraulic clamp and a disc blade. The clamp grabbed the tree, and the blade would buzz through the trunk in a matter of seconds. Once the tree was cut, the operator could lay the tree on the ground, where the other loggers could buck the limbs before it was loaded on the truck for transport.

"I already called and spoke with the dispatch coordinator," Luke said. "He told me all they have available right now are the wheeled units. You and I both know that the terrain is too steep on this side of the hill for that. We'd need one with tracks, and they've got all of those down in Kentucky."

"So you're going to fell it by hand?"

"I don't think we've got a choice. The contract with the state doesn't leave us much more time."

Carl looked at the surrounding area and said, "Which way are you planning on dropping it?"

Luke pointed over his father's shoulder. "Right down there if everything goes according to plan. If I notch it just right, it should drop right between those two giant pines. We can buck it in place, then pull the pieces out with the dozer."

"You gonna use the 881 for the cut?"

Luke nodded. "Yeah, Caleb is bringing it out. He should be here any minute." Then: "Here he is now."

Caleb hopped out of the pickup truck, then reached into the bed and pulled out a massive chainsaw with a forty-one inch guide bar. He made sure the chain's tension was set, checked the tanks that held the gas and bar oil, then walked the saw over to his brother. "Here you go, Luke. The biggest, baddest chainsaw ever made. She's ready to run."

Luke got his safety gear on, then took the saw and said, "You guys better stand back. Either that, or be ready to run yourselves."

"Want me to wedge it once you've made the initial cut?" Caleb said.

Luke shook his head. "Nope. I don't want anyone near this thing. I'll make the cut, then handle the wedges myself."

"You're the boss," Caleb said.

Carl laughed. "That's the same thing I told him. Let's hope it doesn't go to his head."

"The only thing going through my head right now is a couple of guys yakking away like they don't have anything better to do. How about you two hop in the truck and get out of my way?"

Carl moved toward the truck and pulled his youngest son with him. "C'mon, Caleb. Luke's right. Let's let him work. He needs to keep his mind on what he's about to do."

"You got it, Dad. Race you to the truck?"

Carl laughed. "Like my knees could take that kind of grief."

Luke already had the saw started, and when he saw his father and younger brother move away, he pulled the throttle wide open and began to make his initial wedge cut. Seven minutes later he had the trunk notched out. With that done, he moved to the other side of the tree and started to make a smaller cut where he'd hammer in the wedges to help the tree fall where he wanted. He was doing everything exactly right…just as he'd been trained.

Then it all went bad in a hurry.

THE BASE ROT WAS WORSE THAN LUKE REALIZED, which made the tree unstable. But he was almost done with the second cut, so he pushed on. And that's when his saw blade hit the spike. The saw bucked in his hands, then kicked back hard, knocking Luke on his butt. When he fell, he heard the tree begin to break loose, and he knew in his heart he didn't have time to get out of the way. He wasn't yet to his knees when the tree twisted, then began to fall in the exact opposite direction of where Luke had intended. He rolled away, covered his head with both arms, then waited for the crushing blow that would end his life.

And when the blow came, it took the life right out of Luke…just not in the way he thought it would.

The tree missed Luke but clipped Caleb's pickup, flattening the entire passenger side of the truck where his father was sitting. Caleb had left his door open, and when the tree started to fall, he yelled for his father to get out, but Carl was slower than his son and fumbled the door handle. His death was instantaneous.

Caleb dove for cover, but even at his young age, he wasn't quite quick enough to clear the truck before the tree came crashing down. It clipped his leg, shattered his hip, and crushed his knee and ankle.

When Luke saw what had happened, he screamed in horror, then ran to his brother's side. Caleb was unconscious and bleeding badly. When Luke looked at the truck, the damage was so severe he couldn't even see his father's body. There was nothing but blood, gore, and clothing buried under the trunk of the tree.

He'd just killed his father and maimed his brother for life.

Weeks later, after his father's funeral, while sitting at his brother's side in the hospital, a lawyer who represented Midway Timber walked into the room and told Luke that his employment with the company had been terminated for not following proper safety protocols.

And since Luke was already mentally standing on a rocky precipice, the lawyer's words drove him right over the edge of his cerebral cliff.

MAYO AND ORTIZ WALKED BACK INTO THE INTERVIEW room and once again sat down across from Joyce

Parker. "How much longer is this going to take?" Parker said. "My face is killing me."

"We're almost done," Mayo said. "Just a few more questions and you'll be on your way."

"What kind of questions? You said I wasn't a suspect."

"And you're not. But we still have a murder to solve, and quite honestly, we need your help."

Parker put a hand against the base of her throat. "My help? I'm not a police officer."

Mayo gave her a sympathetic nod. "We'd like you to tell us about Doctor Campos."

"What about him?"

"Let's start with his family life. Was he married? Have children? That sort of thing."

"His wife died a number of years ago in a traffic accident. They never had any children."

"Did you and he ever, mm, socialize?"

"Are you asking if we dated?"

"In a manner of speaking."

"We did not," Parker said. "He was quite a bit older than me, and quite frankly, I don't think he would have been interested anyway."

"Why's that?" Ortiz said.

"He never really got over the loss of his wife. He just wasn't interested in other women. But every once in a while he'd show up at the local tavern and have a beer or two with some of the staff."

"But nothing romantic?" Ortiz said.

"No, absolutely not. Why are you asking?"

"We're trying to rule out jealousy," Mayo said. "A jilted lover…that sort of thing."

"I'm fairly certain you can mark that off your list."

"Did he have a partner? Another dentist who worked at the clinic?"

"No, it was just Paul," Parker said.

Mayo looked away for a moment, then said, "As the office manager, I imagine that you have your finger on the pulse of the clinic, so to speak."

"I guess you could say that," Parker said.

"Can you think of any patients or other employees who might have held a grudge?"

This time it was Parker who looked away…not out of deceit, but in thought. But even as she was thinking, her head was slowly moving back and forth. "There isn't one single person I can think of who would ever want to hurt Paul. He was polite, kind, gentle, and treated everyone with respect."

"What about drugs?" Ortiz said.

"What about them?"

"I think what my partner meant to ask was, did Doctor Campos keep any narcotics in the office?"

Joyce let out a sad chuckle. "No, absolutely not. Other than your basic numbing agents—which do not fall under the five controlled classes of drugs—he didn't keep anything in the building."

"But he could prescribe painkillers if need be, is that right?" Mayo said.

"It is, but he was hesitant to do so. The standard course of pain control after basic dental procedures is a combination of Advil and Tylenol...both of which I could use right about now. Are we almost done here?"

"Yes," Mayo said. "Just two more questions. If Doctor Campos didn't have a partner, as you say, who will take over the clinic?"

Parker turned her head to the side. "That's a good question. Honestly, I'm not sure. The business was his alone, so I don't know how anyone could actually buy it, or whatever. But I'm not a lawyer, either, so maybe it's possible. I think the most likely scenario is that the clinic will close."

"Are your patient records on paper, or computerized?"

"Both," Parker said. "The paper copies are locked in the filing cabinets, and the electronic ones are stored on the office server." Then, with a bit of suspicion: "Why do you ask?"

"Because we're going to need to see them," Mayo said.

"I'm afraid that's out of the question. As a doctor of dental surgery, Paul had a professional, legal and contractual responsibility to protect his patients' confidentiality. He took that obligation very seriously."

Ortiz leaned forward slightly and said, "Forgive me for being blunt, but Doctor Campos is dead. I don't think he'd mind."

Parker leaned forward herself. "That's a cruel thing to say, and as a point of fact, you're wrong. He would mind. Confidentiality is fundamental to a doctor's relationship with their patients. And that confidentiality applies to the entire clinical staff, not just the doctor. If I give you access to the patient records, I could be fined or sued. Probably both."

"I don't want to argue your point, but how much confidentiality is necessary when it comes to dental care?" Mayo said. "I wouldn't mind if someone saw my records. What are they going to discover…that I have a few fillings? What's the big deal?"

"I don't make the rules, Detective. But I am compelled to follow them."

Mayo knew she was right, but thought it was worth a shot. "I understand. Just so you know, we'll be getting a warrant to examine the records. I'll make sure you get a copy."

"I'll need more than a copy, Detective. I'll want to be there when you go through the records."

Mayo and Ortiz both stood. "I'll see what I can arrange," Mayo said. "Until then, the clinic is a crime scene. That means you and any other staff have to stay out of the building. Sit tight for just another minute. I'll see if Detective Buckley is finished with your release paperwork."

"If I'm not a suspect, there shouldn't be any paperwork," Parker said.

Ortiz turned his palms up. "Bureaucracy. It's a nightmare for everyone…even us."

When Mayo told Buckley what he wanted him to do, the detective wasn't very enthusiastic about it. "What is it with you guys? First you tell me to kick her, and now you want me to hold her?"

"Just for an hour or so. Tell her there's been a mixup with the paperwork or something."

"There is no paperwork," Buckley said. "Why not let her go?"

Given what he and Ortiz were about to do, Mayo

didn't want to answer that question. "Okay, how about this: Have one of your deputies drive her to the hospital ER so she can get her nose set properly. I'm sure they'll want X-rays and all that. It'll probably take a while."

"What are you two up to?" Buckley said.

Mayo gave him a pat on the back. "Just doing our jobs, Detective. Have a nice day."

Once they were in their squad car, Ortiz turned, looked at Mayo, and said, "Are we going to do what I think we're going to do?"

"Got any better ideas?" Mayo said. He tried to hide his grin, but didn't really pull it off.

CHAPTER TWELVE

VIRGIL AND MURTON WALKED INTO THE MCU facility, each of them carrying a computer, along with the rest of the evidence they'd received from Jackson County Detective Joe Navarro. They set the boxes on top of the counter that surrounded Sarah's workstation, then Murton asked if Ross and Rosencrantz had returned.

"Not yet," Sarah said.

Virgil asked Sarah if she'd take the hammer and note to the crime scene lab so Chip and Mimi could do an examination. "They've been run for prints, but I'd like them to double-check that the county didn't miss anything."

"Sure," Sarah said. "Are those the computers from the used car dealership in Jackson County?"

"Yep," Murton said. "We don't know which one has the security footage, so we brought them both. Either way, the dealership customer records should be on one of these machines as well, so it doesn't hurt to take a look at both of them."

"Where's Becky?" Virgil said.

"She's at the office over the bar. When she heard you guys were bringing the computers in, she went over there." Then, with a hint of friendly sarcasm: "That's where we keep the tech to open them up. Someone told me that once, but I can't seem to recall who it might have been."

Virgil lowered his chin and gave her the brow, but he knew she was right. He looked at Murton and said, "We should have just gone straight there."

"Actually, I'm glad you didn't," Sarah said.

"Why's that?"

"There's an APO waiting to see you upstairs. When you called and told me you were headed back, I thought it would be all right for him to wait in your office. I hope that's okay."

Virgil squinted an eye at Sarah. "That's fine, but, uh, I have no idea what an APO is."

Sarah's face reddened, then she leaned forward, lowered her voice, and said, "APO is an acronym I made up for an officer with the Department of Natural Resources."

"I don't get it," Virgil said. "Why not just say the DNR is here?"

"Have a chat with the man," Sarah said. "It'll come to you."

Virgil and Murton walked upstairs and found the DNR officer roaming the halls. "I got bored sitting in an office. It's not my style." He made a show of looking at his watch, then said, "Which one of you guys runs the show around here?"

"That'd be me," Virgil said, already mildly irritated by the superior tone of voice the DNR officer was using. Virgil jerked his thumb at his brother and said, "My partner, Detective Murton Wheeler. I'm Detective Jones. What can we do for you?"

"Well, for starters, you could teach that hot little tart down at the desk how to tell time. She said you'd be here any minute, but I've been waiting for nearly an hour."

"What's your name, and why are you here?" Murton said.

"Hold on a second, Murt," Virgil said. "The woman

you're referring to is our operations manager. What did you just call her? Hot little tart, was it?"

"Yeah, and it's a good thing that's what she is because her attitude could use a little work. Broads like that need to learn their place."

"You should have met the woman who had the job before her," Murton said. He had a smile on his face as he stepped forward and whispered into the officer's ear.

Virgil watched as the DNR officer's face turned white. When Murton stepped back, Virgil said, "Answer my questions. Who are you, and why are you here?"

"My name is Roy Landry." He reached into his pocket, pulled out two pieces of paper, then handed them to Virgil. "Those are citations for two of your guys…Detectives Ortiz and Mayo."

"You're giving them tickets?" Virgil said.

"Are you hard of hearing? What'd I just say?"

"What are the citations for?"

"How about you read them and see for yourself?"

"How about you drop the fucking attitude and just tell me," Virgil said. He looked at the tickets, though.

"Destruction of property, creating a public nuisance, littering, endangering the safety and well-being of others, and abandonment of campsite."

"They didn't abandon anything," Virgil said. "They

work for me and were on vacation when I ordered them to a murder scene over in Paoli."

"Whatever, dude. They left their gear, their tent was looted, and the animals got into their food supply. The place is a mess, and it's their fault. It also means it's their responsibility. They've got thirty days to pay the fine, or bench warrants will be issued for their arrest."

"If I'm not mistaken," Murton said, "and I rarely am, the director of the Indiana DNR is appointed by, and serves at the pleasure of the governor."

"What of it?" Landry said.

"Think the director likes his job?"

Landry lifted his chin slightly. "I wouldn't know. I've never met the man."

"Better clear your calendar, then," Murton said. "You'll probably have a meeting with him in the next day or two…unless you decide to rip up those tickets."

Virgil held out the tickets with a smile on his face.

"Not a chance," Landry said to Murton. "And what's with your buddy's dopey expression?"

"I've never really been able to figure that one out," Murton said. "But I do know this: His wife is the governor."

Landry deflated like someone had just opened an air valve in his shoulders. "Look, guys, I'm new at this, okay? They tell me to bring the tickets, I bring the tickets."

Virgil still had his hand extended. He shoved the papers—hard—in Landry's chest and held them there. "Did they tell you to bring the attitude as well?"

Landry stuck his tongue in his cheek. "No. Force of habit. I used to work as a guard with the Bureau of Prisons." He yanked the tickets away from Virgil, then tore them up and dropped them on the floor. "Tell your guys they fucked up."

"Somebody sure did," Murton said. "Have a great day."

After Landry had gone, Murton looked at Virgil and said, "I think I figured it out."

"Figured what out?" Virgil said.

"What Sarah meant. C'mon, let's go see if I'm right."

"How about you just tell me?"

"Well, it stands to reason that when Sara said APO, the O must be for officer, right?"

"Yeah, probably. What's the AP part for?"

"You'll see," Murton said.

Both men headed downstairs, and once they were

back at Sarah's desk, Murton looked at her and said, "Aquatic penis officer?"

Sarah grinned. "Yep."

"Why didn't you just say fish dick? Everyone else does."

"I didn't want to use that sort of language. It doesn't seem very professional."

Virgil smiled. "You're the best, Sarah. APO. I love it."

ROSS AND ROSENCRANTZ SHOWED UP BEFORE VIRGIL and Murton had a chance to leave and drop the computers off at the bar for Becky.

"Anything?" Virgil said.

Ross wrinkled his nose. "What's that smell? And to answer your question, not much."

"The smell," Murton said, "is the lingering odor of what Sarah has coined as an APO."

"Fish dick, huh?" Ross said. Then: "What? She's my girl. You think we don't talk about things?"

"Let's go into the conference room," Virgil said. "I want to hear your verbal report."

As they were all walking down the hall, Rosencrantz slid up next to Virgil and said, "Get a quick word before we go in?"

"Sure," Virgil said. Then to Murton and Ross: "You guys go ahead. We'll be right there."

Rosencrantz waited until they were alone, then reached out and put his hand on Virgil's shoulder. "Look, I know I haven't exactly been a prince lately."

Virgil couldn't help it. He barked out a laugh and said, "Well, in keeping with your British theme, I'm fairly certain you haven't even risen to the level of commoner."

And Rosencrantz thought, *no argument there.* "I wanted to apologize…again. And this time I mean it. I mean, not that I didn't before, but Ross, among others, have let it be known that I've been something of a jerk over the last few weeks. I witnessed it today myself. My behavior with the Brown County sheriff was pathetic."

"How bad?"

"Bad enough," Rosencrantz said. "Anyway, I hope you and I are all right."

Virgil knew his friend and fellow coworker was making an effort, no matter how difficult. "Rosie, I wish there was something I could do for you…I really mean that. If you'll tell me what you need, I promise I'll be there for you."

"You've never not been there for me, Jonesy. That's what I'm trying to tell you. I've been through something I wouldn't want my worst enemy to endure. And through it all, I've behaved like an ass." He dropped his hand from Virgil's shoulder. "I'm hoping I can make some sort of amends."

"Amends are a form of penance," Virgil said. "It's not required, nor is it acceptable in this situation. You're a great detective, Tom, and you've suffered the type of loss most of us won't let ourselves even think of. Friendship is a given. So is forgiveness, by the way."

Rosencrantz moved over toward the side of the hall, rested his back against the surface, then slid down on his butt. He ended up sitting on the floor with his knees drawn up, his arms wrapped around his legs. Virgil sat down next to him.

When Rosencrantz spoke, he looked straight ahead, avoiding eye contact with Virgil. "I met someone today."

Virgil—somewhat selfishly—wanted to keep the conversation light. "Was she a looker?"

Despite his feelings, Rosencrantz laughed. "As a matter of fact, she was…is. Whatever. But as it turns out, she lost her husband a while back and seemed to understand what I've been going through. Of course, me being me in the moment, I treated her poorly, then had to apologize. It seems I've been doing a lot of that lately."

"Did she take it well?" Virgil said.

Rosencrantz tried on a small smile. "Yeah, as a matter of fact, she did." Then, "My God, you wouldn't believe the things I said to this woman, Jonesy. She told me her story and I all but told her she was being a whiny little bitch."

"This would be the Brown County sheriff you mentioned?"

"That's the one."

"But she accepted your apology, right? That's what really matters, Tom."

"She did. In fact, I gave her my card and told her if she ever wanted to talk about the vacuum in her life, I'd be there for her."

Virgil, one of the top law enforcement officers in the state, liked to keep his finger on the pulse of what was happening across the different Indiana counties. He'd sent Ross and Rosencrantz down to Brown County for more than one reason. He wanted Rosencrantz to meet and speak with someone who'd suffered a tragedy close to his friend's own. "How is Sheriff Young these days?"

There is more than one way to call someone a

derogatory name, and both Virgil and Rosencrantz knew it.

"You motherfucker," Rosencrantz said with a grin. "You sent Ross and me to Brown County so I'd meet with Lisa."

"I thought it might be of some benefit."

Rosencrantz shook his head. "It's too soon, Jonesy. I can't start seeing someone else."

"That wasn't my intent, Tom. All things being equal, I'd have sent you if the sheriff's name was Larry, not Lisa. Shared grief is exactly what its name implies. I also know the sharing is not halved, or anything like that, but it is divided in some sense of the word. Anyway, the sharing can help. May I offer you some practical advice?"

"Sure," Rosencrantz said.

"If she calls, don't blow her off. If she doesn't, make the call yourself."

"Why?"

"Because the best way to help yourself cope is to help someone else with their own grief."

"It's that easy, huh?"

Virgil ran his hands through his hair and suddenly remembered how short it was. "No, not really. In fact it's a bitch…with a capital B. But you've gotta do it, man. What other choice do you have?" He stood, then held out his arm to Rosencrantz and helped him up.

Once they were on their feet, Rosencrantz said, "We didn't get much out of Brown County."

"Based on everything you just told me, that's not exactly a factual statement. Let's join Ross and Murton in the conference room. We'll talk about it. Something will break."

Virgil didn't know it at the time, but something would break…something he never saw coming.

CHAPTER THIRTEEN

VIRGIL AND ROSENCRANTZ WALKED INTO THE conference room and took their seats. Murton had just told Ross something, and both men were smiling. Virgil looked at his brother and said, "I meant to ask you a minute ago but I didn't get to it. What did you say to that Landry guy when you whispered in his ear?"

"That's what I just finished telling Ross. I may have mentioned that you never hear the shot that kills you. I also let him know that the woman he'd gotten lippy with was the love interest of our resident sniper. I might not have expressed my thoughts in that particular order, though."

Ross took a pen and a small notebook from his breast pocket, flipped through a few pages, then looked at Virgil and said, "What'd you say this Landry guy's first name was?"

"I didn't. What's with the notebook?"

"The name, Boss?"

Virgil knew it was easier to answer than to argue. "Roy. Roy Landry."

Ross wrote down the name, then put the notebook away. When he noticed Virgil staring at him, he said, "What?"

"You didn't answer me," Virgil said. "What's with the notebook?"

"Hit list," Ross said, his expression blank.

"I noticed you had to flip through quite a few pages," Murton said. "Who else do you have in there?"

"That's personal and confidential information."

Virgil couldn't tell if Ross was joking or not. Either way, he got everyone back on track. "Let's make this quick. Rosie, Ross, tell us what you know."

"Not much more than you do," Rosencrantz said. "We spoke with Detective Ken Mayhall, who informed us that the victim—Lori Reddick—was loved by everyone. She had one of those little shops in Nashville…made her own soaps and candles…that sort of thing. Husband named Frank, who is a fireman and was on duty and working an active scene at the time of her death. His alibi checks out. The place wasn't robbed, the victim wasn't sexually assaulted, the murder weapon was a hammer, and the note is identical to the others. Chip and Mimi have the evidence. We dropped it off with them before we came up."

"That's not much, Tom," Virgil said.

Rosencrantz gave him a single shoulder shrug. "Is what it is."

"What about security cameras?" Murton said.

"None," Ross said. "She had a basic alarm system, but no cams."

"Anything out of the ordinary going on in her personal life?" Virgil said. "Did you talk to the husband?"

"He wasn't home," Rosencrantz said. "We went by his place before we came back. We'll do the follow-up tomorrow. The only thing we really know about her personal life is what Mayhall told us. He said she did some volunteer work on the side…bake sales for churches and that sort of thing."

"I doubt church bake sales are going to factor into it," Murton said. Then he finished with, "It sounds like you guys did about as well as we did."

Virgil brought Ross and Rosencrantz up to speed on what they had, then said, "We grabbed the computers from the dealership where our victim was killed. We're going to take them over to Becky at the bar. Hopefully that will get us going in the right direction."

Rosencrantz checked his watch. "It's getting sort of late in the afternoon. I could eat."

"Me too," Ross said.

"So take the computers and head over to the bar," Virgil said. "Not much we can do here. We'll grab a bite and see if Becky can get the computers unlocked."

"Sounds good to me," Rosencrantz said. "See you there."

Once Ross and Rosencrantz were out of the room, Virgil looked at Murton and said, "You don't think Ross actually keeps a hit list, do you?"

Murton looked at his brother and said, "What is it Becky is always telling you? Something about don't ask questions you don't want the answers to?"

When Mayo and Ortiz arrived back at Campos's dental clinic, they discovered the CSI technician had left. Deputy Harding was in the process of locking the front door and sealing it with crime scene tape.

"Skip the tape," Mayo said. "And we'll take the keys to the building."

"I was told to secure the entrances and take the keys with me."

Ortiz held out his palm. "And now you're being told differently. Hand them over."

Harding didn't want to give up. "Look guys, no disrespect, okay? But I've got a job to do…one that comes with orders to follow. How about I seal the joint up, take the keys back to the station, and you can go from there?"

"We just came from the station, Deputy," Mayo said. "I don't want to waste time driving back and forth simply because you were told to do something prior to our arrival."

"What if I call Detective Buckley and get the okay from him?"

"Make it quick," Mayo said.

The deputy stepped away, then pulled out his cell phone. After a few minutes of back and forth, he ended the call, tossed the keys to Mayo, and said, "I'm supposed to stay and observe."

"Observe what?"

"Whatever it is you guys are doing."

"We're going to conduct a basic search of the premises now that your crime scene technicians are finished."

"What are you looking for?"

Mayo tried not to roll his eyes, but failed. "Evidence. You can wait outside."

"Kind of hard to observe what you're doing from out here."

"This is a state case, Deputy," Ortiz said. "That means you have no jurisdictional authority here at the moment. You can either wait outside…like you have been, or you can be charged with interfering in an ongoing state investigation. Your choice."

The deputy didn't like it, but he waited outside. Mayo and Ortiz slipped into their gloves, ripped the tape down, then went inside and locked the door behind them.

Before they left for the bar, Virgil and Murton walked down to the forensics lab and checked in with Chip and Mimi. "I know this is a long shot," Virgil said, "but do you think you'll get any prints from the hammers or the notes?"

"I'm almost positive we won't," Chip said. "I've gone over them with the scope and haven't seen a thing. It looks like both Jackson and Brown counties did everything they could."

"He's right," Mimi said. "I spoke with both lead

techs from each department. They did find trace amounts of talc on the letters, so whoever did this was being very careful. The talc indicates they wore gloves the entire time."

"Okay, well, let us know if you come up with anything at all," Virgil said.

"We have some thoughts on the notes if you're interested," Chip said.

"I am," Murton said. "Let's hear it."

"Some of it is fact, but most of it is speculation. The facts are Mimi's. The speculation is mine."

"We'll take anything at this point," Virgil said.

Mimi grabbed a copy of the note, then said, "Okay, here are the facts: The notes we have were printed on standard weight, letter-sized, generic copy paper. The font is 12 point Helvetica printed from a Windows-based operating system using MS Word, and a smear test demonstrates they came from a laser printer…not an inkjet."

"You can tell what operating system and program were used based on the font?" Murton said.

Mimi rubbed the tip of her nose with an index finger. "Yes. There's no question. The operating systems and the programs all have very minor deviations in their fonts, and since we know what those are, we can match them up pretty easily under a scope."

"Well, that's good, I guess," Virgil said. "But what you're really saying is that the paper, the computer, and the printer are all so generic it won't help us at all. Do I have that right?"

"Pretty much. But those are just the facts. You should hear Chip's speculation. It's worth considering."

"Which is?"

"The note itself is something of a conundrum," Chip said.

"In what way?" Murton said.

"Let me back up a second," Chip said. "There's one more fact. Or maybe fact isn't quite the right word, but it's a definite possibility. You're looking at more than one killer."

"We've already figured that out," Virgil said. "The wording makes it pretty clear. 'We' and 'our' indicates more than one person."

"That's not what I'm talking about. When you read this note, it almost seems like two different people sat down and wrote it together."

Virgil looked at the note again but didn't make the connection with what Chip was telling him. When he looked at his brother, Murton simply shook his head. "Explain it to us."

"Well, for starters, qualms is an interesting word choice, don't you think? Why not use the words worry, or fear? By the way, the archaic usage of the word qualms, by definition, is a faint or sick feeling, and archaic is a way of communicating something old-fashioned. That might be something to consider."

Virgil was intrigued. "Go on."

"The last three words of the first line are almost as interesting. *Regarding our conduct* is an odd way to express something, especially given the nature of the crimes. So, just looking at the first line: We have no qualms regarding our conduct…why not instead say something like: We are not worried about killing."

"Keep talking," Murton said.

"I'm going to skip the next line for a second and come back to it. The third line is nearly—but not quite—as interesting as the first."

"In what way?" Virgil said.

"Three ways, actually. One, it's almost repetitive. We know others will die because they already have, so why bother to put it in every note? And secondly, the only thing of obvious value being communicated is some sort of project must stop or the killing will continue."

"What about the bullshit part?" Murton said.

"That's the third thing," Chip said. "I don't think—though I'll be the first to admit I could be wrong—that the *B.S.* in the note is referring to cow dung. Nor is it nonsensical."

"Why?" Virgil said.

"Because *bullshit* is one word, not two…unless, of course, you're saying, 'the bull shit over by the fence,' or something along those lines."

They all sat quietly with that for a few seconds, then Virgil said, "You were going to come back to the second line…the one that says, 'Restoration is no longer an option.'"

"I did."

"So what have you got?"

"Nothing. I can't make it fit. I have no idea why it's even in the note. Are the killers talking about the people they've murdered? If so, it's useless information because you can't restore a dead body. If they're speaking of something else…an actual restoration of some kind, like a statue or a theater, or whatever, there doesn't seem to be any way to figure out what it is."

Virgil's head was starting to swim. "A few minutes ago you said it seemed like two different people wrote the note together. What makes you say that?"

"Beyond everything I just told you? I'd say the other side of the coin."

"I'm not sure I follow," Virgil said.

Chip scratched at the back of his head. "I could be

completely wrong about the B.S. part. If I am, then as I said, the note really is a conundrum. It has archaic and formal wording in some parts, but on the other hand, it's repetitive and possibly uses incorrect punctuation. You've either got a couple of dumb guys trying to sound smart, or a smart guy and a not so smart guy working together, or two smart guys trying to make you look dumb."

"My money's on the third option," Murton said dryly.

"Write it all up, Chip," Virgil said. "Every single thing you just told us and get it to me in your report."

Chip told Virgil he would. As they were walking out of the building Murton looked at Virgil and said, "What do you make of all that?"

"I'm not sure. It's something to think about, though."

When they arrived at the bar, Virgil and Murton said a quick hello to Delroy and Robert, then found Ross and Rosencrantz upstairs with Becky. Everyone was eating a large chicken and shrimp pizza with Robert's special sauce. "I didn't know we did pizza," Virgil said.

"That's because you don't come in here often enough," Becky said.

"Did you get the computers opened up?"

Becky wiped her mouth with a napkin and said, "The program is running now. It'll probably be a couple of hours."

Virgil took a slice of pizza, then flopped down on the sofa. When he took a bite, his eyes got wide. "Geez, this is delicious."

"Don't talk with your mouth full," Becky said. "It's gross."

Virgil used his hand to wipe a bit of sauce from his chin, then said, "Hand me one of those napkins, will you?"

Becky tossed a roll of paper towels to him. "What took you guys so long to get here?"

"Had a little chat with Chip about the note," Murton said. "He had some pretty interesting observations."

"Like what?"

Before Murton could answer, Virgil's cell phone rang. He dug it out of his pocket, saw that it was Mayo, and said, "What have you got?"

"A question. Ortiz and I are standing inside Campos's dental clinic."

"That's great information, Mayo, but it's not a question."

"I know. I'm just giving you the lay of the land," Mayo said. "I need to know if we should break the rules, or bend them."

"Give me the story. Start at the beginning."

Mayo brought Virgil up to speed on everything the crime scene tech had shown them, along with their conversation with Joyce Parker, and her refusal to give them access to the patient records. "Think we could get a warrant?"

"That's a tough one, Oscar. Judges don't like to violate privileged information without cause."

"The man is dead, Jonesy, and he had all his teeth smashed out. How much more cause do we need?"

"Do you have any demonstrable proof that one of his patients did it?"

"Well…no. Not yet."

"Then you won't get your warrant. I've seen it time and time again."

"Okay, that brings me back to my question. Should we break the rules, or bend them?"

"Think maybe you could be a little more specific?"

"Parker told us the patient records are on paper and locked up tight in the filing cabinets. And let me tell you, she wasn't kidding, either. The cabinets are secured with some sort of fancy guide bar running through the handles. We don't have the keys, so if we bust them open, she'll eventually find out about it. But she also told us that the records are on the computer as well. Ortiz found the clinic's server. So, do we break the rules and walk out with the computer, or do we bend the rules and let Becky work her magic from afar?"

"Bend, Mayo. Always bend when you can. Hang on." Virgil handed his phone to Becky.

"What's going on?" Becky said to Virgil.

Virgil grabbed another slice of pizza, took a bite, then, with a mouthful of food, said, "Mayo needs you to bend a rule."

CHAPTER FOURTEEN

BECKY SPENT A FEW MINUTES LISTENING TO MAYO TELL her everything he'd just told Virgil. Once he'd laid it all out for her, Becky said, "Let me call you right back."

"Okay, but we're kind of short on time here. The crime scene techs have finished, and the office manager is going to come over as soon as she's done getting her nose set at the hospital. I don't know how long that is going to take, but once she arrives we really don't have a legitimate reason to keep her out."

"That's why you should stop talking and let me call you back," Becky said. Then she hung up.

Virgil popped the last bite of pizza into his mouth and said, "What's the problem?"

"You tell me," Becky said. She swept her arm around the office. "All my equipment is tied up and running at full capacity. I've got a sequence looking into the victim's backgrounds for commonalities like you requested, and another one running the program to open the computers that you had Ross and Rosencrantz bring over…the ones from the car lot."

Virgil nodded like a dope. "So turn one off for a few seconds, get Mayo what he needs, then start it back up again."

Becky let out a sigh. "It doesn't work that way, Jonesy. If I shut either of the sequences down, I'll have to start all over. Do you want that kind of delay?"

Virgil wiped his hands on a paper towel. "No, I don't. What about using the equipment at the shop?"

"I could do that, but if I do, there'll be a direct link of the activity that'll lead right back to the Major Crimes Unit. I'm sure Sandy would love to explain that to the legislative oversight committee."

"I'll bet she wouldn't," Murton said.

"I'm willing to entertain suggestions," Virgil said.

"Boy, we don't hear that from you very often," Ross said.

"Maybe his estrogen levels are low," Rosencrantz said.

Virgil shot Rosencrantz a look, then quickly let it turn to a grin. If he was making jokes—even at Virgil's own expense—it was a good sign. He thought about it…the problem, then looked at Becky and said, "The Campos murder is the latest one of three. That means we have an opportunity to gather what could be some significant intelligence." He pointed at the two computers from the car lot that were currently hard-wired into Becky's system. "On the other hand, we may have great video footage of the actual murderers from one of those machines."

"So what do you want me to do?" Becky said.

Virgil crossed his arms and bit into the tip of his thumb. "Let me ask you something: Do Mayo and Ortiz actually have to be present for you to make a remote connection to that server?"

Becky shook her head. "No, not necessarily. But I'll need some information from the router…serial number, model number, IP and MAC address, that sort of thing."

"So if they gave you all that information, you could connect whenever you wanted. Do I have that right?"

"Yes," Becky said. "Unless someone physically unhooks the server from the router."

"How long would it take you to do a data dump once you're in?" Murton said.

"The dump will take a matter of seconds," Becky said. "But getting in could take anywhere from twelve to twenty-four hours."

"Why so long?" Virgil said. "That time we did it at the post office only took a few minutes."

Becky was trying to be patient because she knew Virgil didn't know much about how computers worked. "That's because their system was already up and running. I assume that's not the case here."

"Never assume," Virgil said. "Hand me my phone."

Becky tossed Virgil his phone and said, "What are you doing?"

"Not assuming." He called Mayo, put the phone on speaker, and said, "It's Jonesy. Are any of the computers in the building turned on?"

"Nope. The server box has one little yellow light that's blinking, but all the individual computers are turned off. There are only three, by the way. Two at reception, and one in Campos's office. What are we doing here, Boss?"

"Call you back," Virgil said, and hung up. Then to Becky: "What if Ortiz or Mayo turned on one of the computers?"

"It's a professional office environment, Jonesy. I'm sure they're password protected. Wouldn't do any good."

"I've got an idea if anyone is interested," Rosencrantz said.

"What?" Becky said.

"This woman, uh, Parker...is that right?"

"Yeah, that's her," Murton said.

"Why not let her in when she shows up?"

"To what end?" Virgil said.

"Have Mayo and Ortiz tell her that they want to look at the doc's personal correspondences. He was the victim and since he's dead, privileged information doesn't apply. That means we're allowed to look at his email."

Becky pointed at Rosencrantz. "He's right. Once we've got his email, I can send a packet, and the data dump will happen almost immediately."

"Do it," Virgil said.

WHILE MAYO WAS GETTING BECKY THE ROUTER information, Ortiz went outside and spoke with the deputy. "Do me a favor?"

"After the way you guys treated me? You got some major balls to ask me for anything right now."

"Well, I grew up on the Southside of Chicago, so you're probably right about the major balls. But here's the thing: We've got a boss we answer to, no different than you."

"What's your point?" The deputy said.

"We could have handled it better," Ortiz said. He stuck out his hand to shake. "How about a little interagency cooperation?"

Deputy Harding ran his tongue across the inside of his bottom lip, then somewhat reluctantly shook Ortiz's hand. "Okay, so let's say I'm willing to help you out. What do you need?"

"Nothing too difficult," Ortiz said. "We were wondering if you'd run over to the hospital and bring Joyce Parker here. She's the office manager of the clinic. We need to speak with her."

"I know who Joyce is. She's at the hospital?"

Ortiz nodded. "Yep. Getting her nose set. She ran into a door."

"How do I know you guys aren't just trying to get rid of me?"

"Why would we?"

"You didn't want me inside earlier."

"That was earlier. This is now. Look, all I'm asking is that you run over to the hospital, pick the woman up, then bring her back here. It could be vital to our investigation. What do you say?"

"I don't think so," Harding said.

Ortiz was getting upset. "Why the hell not?"

Harding let out a little chuckle, then pointed over Ortiz's shoulder. "Because unless I'm mistaken, she's pulling up now. She doesn't look too happy, either."

Ortiz turned around and saw Parker getting out of her car, a huge metal nose splint taped across her face. He looked at Harding and said, "Don't let her inside until I come back out."

Harding shook his head. "Man, you state guys need to get your act together. First it's stay, then it's go, then it's bring the woman back, and now it's don't let her in…I'm having trouble keeping up."

Ortiz wasn't listening. He was hurrying back toward the front door of the clinic.

Mayo was on the phone with Becky. He'd already given her the router information she needed and was digging around trying to find Campos's email address. He finally found it listed on one of the doctor's business cards tucked inside the center desk drawer. "Got it," he said to Becky. He read her the email address, then said, "Now what?"

"Turn the computer on, then get the Parker woman to enter the password. Once she does that, go to his email account. I'm going to send a blank email from a fake address. All you have to do is open it."

"What will happen?" Mayo said.

"Once you open it, the email will delete itself and I'll have control over the server."

"Will Parker be able to tell?"

"I'm starting to feel insulted here, Mayo," Becky said. Then she hung up.

Ortiz ran into the office and said, "She's here."

Mayo turned the computer on, then said, "Let her in and bring her back here. Tell her I need to ask her something."

Ortiz was back thirty seconds later with Parker. Most of her face was the color of an overly ripe avocado. She put her hands on her hips, then said, "What do you think you're doing?"

"My job," Mayo said. "I'm hoping you can help me."

"We've already talked about this, Detective. There is no way I'm going to allow you to access any of our patient records without a warrant. I've spoken with Doctor Campos's attorney, and he assures me that you won't be able to get one unless you have sufficient probable cause or direct evidence that indicates a specific patient of the clinic is responsible for the crime. Do you have either of those?"

"No, I don't," Mayo said. He kept his voice friendly and light. "Actually, that's not what I wanted your help with. Please, have a seat." He pointed at one of the chairs in front of Campos's desk.

Parker gave him a frown, but took a seat as requested. "What sort of help are you looking for?"

"I'll get to that in a moment. But first I'd like to explain something, and I hope you'll forgive me for being blunt. When you see the type of violence that befell Doctor Campos, it's usually indicative of a larger and often secret issue. Now, I know you told me earlier that Paul wasn't interested in other women after his wife died..."

"That's right, and I stand by my statement."

"I don't doubt you, Joyce. Is it still okay if I call you Joyce?"

"Yes, I suppose so."

"Great. And listen, you can call me Oscar, okay? So, Joyce, what I'm getting at is this: Even though you and Doctor Campos worked together and had the occasional drink or two with other office staff, you'd have to agree that you didn't know absolutely everything there was to know about the man. Is that a fair statement?"

Parker looked away when she answered. "Yes, I'd say that's probably true. But I don't see how that's of any help."

"What we need to solve this crime is more information...specifically about Doctor Campos himself. This wasn't a random act of violence, Joyce. By your own admission there are no drugs on the premises, and according to the responding officers' report, Paul still had his wallet on his person. That means it wasn't a robbery gone bad. This was a brutal, horrific act by someone who wanted Doctor Campos to pay the ultimate price for something he was involved in."

"Like what?"

Mayo gave her a defeated shrug. "I don't know. That's why I want your help. I'd like to look through his personal emails and see if they might point us at someone. Even if they don't, we may be able to interview other people he knew and corresponded with outside of work."

"I'm not sure I should allow that," Parker said.

Mayo leaned forward, but kept his tone casual. "I'm afraid you don't have a choice in the matter. Doctor Campos is dead. This is a murder investigation. His personal emails are no longer privileged information. Refusal to cooperate in this instance could get you charged with obstruction. I don't want that to happen, Joyce, but I have people I answer to, and some of them aren't nearly as nice as I am."

Parker was conflicted. She wanted to protect Doctor Campos's privacy, even in death. But the detective sitting across the desk had gotten her out of county lockup. Still, she didn't quite trust him. "How do I know you won't try to access the patient records once I let you in the system?"

"Because you're going to be sitting right next to me, watching every single thing I do."

Parker thought about it for a minute, and Mayo let her. Finally, she said, "Okay. I'm going to trust you, Oscar. I hope I don't regret it."

"You won't," Mayo said. "I may need to print some emails out if we find anything. Where is the printer?"

"Out front at the reception desk."

Mayo stood. "Tell you what…as a show of good faith, I'll go turn the printer on while you enter the password to the computer. That way I won't even be able to see what it is. Just don't hit the Enter button until I come back. Deal?"

Parker actually smiled. "Deal."

Mayo stood, then held the chair for Parker as she sat down. "I'll be right back."

Once he was out at the reception desk, he told Ortiz to call Becky. "Have her text me the second she gets the data. Make sure it's a text and not a call. Got it?"

"Yep. No problem. Is this going to work?"

"I sure hope so," Mayo said. "I'm ready to get the hell out of here."

Once he was back in the office, he pulled another

chair behind the desk, switched seats with Parker, then said, "Okay, here we go." He hit the Enter button, and the password screen went away, replaced by little desktop icons. Mayo clicked on the email icon to open the program and said, "Well, we might as well start from the top." He clicked the first email, and as soon as he did, it disappeared.

"What the heck was that?" Parker said.

"I have no idea. Must have been a glitch, or something. Boy, Doctor Campos didn't really use his email very much, did he?"

"No, not really," Parker said. "And you can skip the next five because they are all from his patients. There might be private information in those."

"That only leaves three others," Mayo said. "And unless he had a beef with Pottery Barn, BestBuy, or Amazon, I think I've wasted your time."

"Maybe not," Parker said.

"What do you mean?" Mayo's phone beeped at him before Parker could respond. "Just a second. Let me check this text." He pulled out his phone, checked the screen, and saw a message from Becky that simply read: *Got it.* He slipped the phone back in his pocket and said, "Listen, that was headquarters. I've got to run. But what did you mean about not wasting time?"

"Ah, nothing," Parker said. "I was just about to say who doesn't have some sort of beef with Amazon?"

Mayo gave Joyce a polite little laugh, handed her his card, then moved toward the door. "I'll be in touch if we find anything. Think about all this, will you? If anything comes to mind…anything that might help us catch Doctor Campos's killer, please call me."

Parker said she would, and then Mayo was gone.

CHAPTER FIFTEEN

Virgil was leaning over Becky's shoulder looking at her computer monitor. "Did the data from the clinic come through okay?"

"It looks like it, but I won't know for sure until I unpack it and take a look."

Virgil stood up straight and arched his back. "So do that."

Becky let her chin fall to her chest. "I think all that pizza must have had an adverse effect on your hearing. I already told you I can't do anything else until the sequence on the dealership computers is finished." Becky checked the status bar on her screen, then said, "And before you ask—because I know you're going to—we're about eighty percent through the process."

Virgil crossed his arms. "I wasn't going to ask."

"Right," Becky said. "Give me an hour or so and I'll have your video, Jonesy, but hovering over me like a drone isn't going to make it go any faster. Why don't you guys grab a table in the bar, wash down your pizza with a pitcher of Red Stripe, and I'll call when I'm ready for you."

"She's always ready for me," Murton said.

"What about the commonality program you're running on the victims?"

Becky simply pointed at the door.

Virgil shook his head, walked out of the room, and went downstairs.

THE FOUR MEN TOOK A TABLE AT THE BACK CORNER OF the bar, and Robert came over with a pitcher of Red Stripe beer and a tray of frosted mugs. He set everything down, filled their glasses, then said, "How da governor's main mon, mon?"

Murton looked up, smiled, and said, "I'm good, Robert. How are you?"

"Very funny," Virgil said. "I'm pretty sure he was talking to me."

"Well, if you're only pretty sure, that leaves room

for the possibility that I might be correct." Then: "What? It's better than First Lady jokes."

Virgil ignored his brother, looked at Robert and said, "I'm well." He verbally italicized the word 'well.' "How's everything going around here?"

"We got da place running like clockwork, us. Delroy say you working a tough one."

Virgil nodded. "That's true enough. We've got some nut—or nuts, I guess I should say—running around and killing people."

"You catch him, Virgil Jones. You always do."

"We're actually a little worried about this one," Murton said. "So far, we don't have a lot of useful intel."

"Dat why Becky upstairs working so hard, no?"

Murton took a sip of his beer and said, "She does try to earn her keep."

Virgil was taking a drink of his beer as well, and did a minor spit-take when he heard Murton's comment. He set his drink on the table, wiped his mouth, and said, "You're kidding, right?"

Murton gave his brother a serious look. "No, I'm not."

"Well, in case you've forgotten, she charged me fifty bucks for my haircut."

"It worth every penny, you ask me, mon. It look good."

"Thank you, Robert," Virgil said. Then he tipped his head to the side, squinted slightly, and said, "You look like you got a haircut recently yourself."

"Yeah, mon. I go to da same place you did."

"Is that right?" Virgil said. "How much did she charge you?"

Robert's smile disappeared, and he frowned at Virgil. "She no charge, Robert. We friends."

"What?" Virgil said.

"No charge for family and friends, mon. Dat what she told me, anyway."

"Me too," Rosencrantz said.

"Ditto," Ross said.

Virgil slowly turned his head and looked at Murton.

"What? I'm married to the woman. You didn't think she'd charge me, did you?"

Virgil huffed like a teenage girl. "Well, she dinged me for fifty bucks."

"I've only been once," Rosencrantz said. "But Becky told me I could get one whenever I wanted. No charge."

"Me too," Ross said.

Virgil looked up at Robert and raised his eyebrows. "What about you?"

"Every tree weeks, like clockwork, mon." Then he let out a big Jamaican laugh.

Virgil gave up. He downed the rest of his beer, then said, "Why are you waiting tables, Robert?"

"Monday, mon. It always slow. Delroy went home, and I'm all caught up in da kitchen, me. Besides, I'm not waiting tables. I just come out to say hello."

"I'd take a couple of those pizzas to go," Virgil said. "Ready in an hour or so?"

"Yeah, mon. Robert make sure day ready."

"Thanks. I'll be right back. I gotta hit the bathroom."

Once Virgil was out of earshot, Murton looked at Robert and said, "I don't recall Becky ever cutting your hair."

"Dat because she hasn't."

"Me either," Rosencrantz said.

"Same here," Ross said.

Murton smiled. "I love you guys."

When Virgil got back to the table, he sat down, then said, "Why is everyone looking at me like that?"

"Like what?" Ross said.

"Like once again, I'm the butt of some sort of joke."

Before any of them could give Virgil any more grief, Becky stuck her head out of the office, whistled, and said, "Got them open."

Everyone stood at once, then Virgil said, "Ross, Rosie, one of you guys can get the check."

"We thought you were buying," Ross said.

"Why would you think that?" Virgil said.

"Well, you own the joint," Rosencrantz said. "And since it was Becky's idea for us to come down here, and since she's married to Murt—who is also an owner—there was an implied offer of free beer."

Virgil started to walk away. "Yeah, yeah. Fuckin cops. Biggest bunch of tight-asses I've ever seen."

Ross laughed. "Says the guy with his own private road."

Becky had the large monitor on the wall lit up, and once everyone was seated in the office, she said, "Both of the computers from the dealership have duplicate customer lists. I'll parse those out tomorrow, but the video is ready to go."

"You look at it yet?" Virgil said.

"Nope," Becky said. "As usual, I'm waiting—"

"Becky?"

Becky blinked rapidly at Virgil and said, "Yes, Virgie?"

"Please don't. Just run the tape, will you?"

Becky grabbed the remote, pointed it at the monitor, then hit the Play button. "Here we go. I'm guessing it won't be pretty."

Becky was right. It wasn't.

They watched it three times before Virgil finally said, "Turn it off."

Becky shut the monitor down. "Well, that was a waste."

"Why was the quality so bad?" Virgil said.

"The guy was a used car dealer, Jonesy," Becky said. "He probably had the cheapest system he could get. Most places that use exterior cams only have them to get a break on their insurance rates."

"We couldn't even see their faces," Rosencrantz said. "If it wasn't for the fact that one of them was using a cane, and the other pulled out a hammer and started bashing Harwood's brains to mush, we wouldn't even be able to tell who's who."

Virgil stood and made a lap around the office. He gave Rosencrantz a dry look and said, "Well, as someone recently told me, it is what it is."

"What now, Boss-man?" Ross said.

Virgil glanced at the clock on the wall, then looked at Ross and Rosencrantz. "I don't know. You guys can take off. We'll go through the dealership customer list tomorrow. We might find something there."

"Good enough," Ross said. "See you then."

After Ross and Rosencrantz left, Virgil sat down on the sofa, looked at Becky, and said, "Will you be able to get the dental clinic patient names now?"

"Yep."

"Okay, get started on that, then see if any of the customers from the dealership match with the patient records."

"That's no problem," Becky said. "I can automate that process and let it run overnight. It'll be ready by morning."

"Talk about your long shots," Murton said. "A dental patient from Paoli drives nearly halfway up the state to buy a used car?"

"It's what we've got…for now, anyway," Virgil said. Just then his phone buzzed at him. He pulled it out, checked the screen, and hit the Answer button. "What's up, Mayo?"

"Wanted to let you know we're going back to our

campsite to pack up, and then we'll be headed home. Catch you in the morning?"

"That's fine," Virgil said. "But skip the campsite."

"Why?"

"Because we had an APO come in today and try to read us the riot act."

"What does a fish dick and his riot act have to do with us?"

"Hang on a second, Mayo, will you?"

"Sure."

Virgil looked at Murton and Becky and said, "Why is it that I'm always the last to know about things around here? Mayo knew what APO meant."

"Maybe because you don't spend enough time with the little people anymore," Becky said. "You know… ever since you became First—"

Virgil pointed his finger at her and said, "Don't."

Becky tucked her chin. "I was going to say First Gentleman. But now I have my doubts."

Virgil didn't quite believe her, but he let it go and went back to Mayo. "You still there?"

"Yup."

"Some DNR goon came into the MCU today and tried to issue citations to you and Ortiz."

"When you say citations, I take it you're not talking about the good kind."

"You take it correctly. He said you abandoned your campsite, and in doing so endangered other campers, your gear was destroyed, and blah, blah, blah. Anyway, I pulled rank on him and made it all go away."

"Well, uh, thanks, I guess," Mayo said.

"Try to contain your appreciation. With all the excitement you're expressing I wouldn't want you to lose control of your vehicle."

"What about our gear? Can we put that in our expense report?"

"No," Virgil said. He drew the word out into about four syllables. "You were on vacation."

"Yeah…a vacation that you called us away from."

"Right. But I didn't expect you to abandon your gear. Snooze you lose."

"C'mon, Jonesy, that was some quality stuff."

"Mayo, I saw your gear. The tent had the quality of a generic brand garbage bag."

"It's more of a matter of principle."

Virgil sighed, then said, "Okay, whatever." He didn't want to debate it any longer. "See you tomorrow."

After he ended the call, Becky looked at him and said, "I think he's right. The MCU should pay for their gear."

"I just said we would, Becks."

"Yeah, but you made him work for it."

"All in good fun," Virgil said. "I think he's one of the few people around here who actually understands my dry sense of humor."

"If it was any drier you'd be in danger of spontaneous combustion," Murton said.

Becky's desk phone rang. She answered, listened for a few seconds, then said, "Thanks, I'll let him know." Then to Virgil: "Your pizzas are ready."

Virgil rubbed his palms together. "Great. The boys are going to love it. Listen, I'll see you guys in the morning, huh?"

"Don't eat in your new car," Murton said.

Virgil waved him off. "Yeah, yeah." He moved toward the door, then stopped, turned back to Becky, and said, "By the way, you owe me fifty bucks."

Becky made a rude noise with her lips. "Says you."

Virgil crossed his arms. "Well, what's this business about free haircuts for family and friends?"

Murton winked at Becky, who caught the wink like a pro. "Oh, you're talking about—"

Virgil didn't let her finish. "That's right. You're busted, young lady. Ross and Rosencrantz told me all about it. Robert too. There might be a sucker born every minute, but I'm not one of them."

Becky laughed, stood, and gave Virgil a hug. Then

she grabbed her purse, pulled out the Square, and tossed it to Virgil.

"What am I supposed to do with this?"

"Pry it open," Becky said.

It took Virgil a few seconds, but he finally got a thumbnail wedged into a side seam and pulled the little white box apart. "I don't get it. It's empty."

"It was a joke, Jonesy. I didn't charge you a dime."

Virgil turned about three different shades of red, then laughed. "Huh. Well, okay then…another joke on me. I've got to admit, it was a good one, though. See you guys tomorrow."

After Virgil was gone, Murton turned to his wife and said, "You really didn't charge him?"

"Of course not. I love the guy, but you gotta admit, he's an easy target."

CHAPTER SIXTEEN

The two troopers on guard duty at the end of Virgil's road saw him coming and backed their squad cars out of the way so he could get through. Virgil stopped, lowered his window, and waved one of the troopers over.

"All quiet on the homestead?" Virgil asked.

"Yes, Sir," the trooper said. His nostrils flared, and he glanced at the pizza boxes sitting on the passenger seat. "Are those Robert's specialty pizzas?"

Virgil grinned at the trooper. "Yep, and while you have my everlasting gratitude for being on overnight guard duty, I'm afraid my family would have me drawn and quartered if I gave them up. Sorry Troop."

The trooper waved it off. "We'll survive. We're

brown-bagging it, although I do wish your bar would start a delivery service."

"Too much hassle," Virgil said. "Besides, you'd lose the ambiance of the entire experience."

The trooper laughed. "Says the guy with two takeout pizzas."

"I guess you've got me there," Virgil said. "The governor home?"

"No, Sir. Not yet."

Well, that sounds about right, Virgil thought. "I appreciate you, Troop. Have a good night."

"You too, Sir."

When Virgil walked in the door, he could hear laughter coming from the kitchen. He carried the pizzas with him, and right when he stepped into the room, he stopped so abruptly he almost dropped the boxes. Huma and the boys were sitting at the table with Delroy, their plates nearly empty. Larry the Dog was under the table, licking the floor.

"I, uh, brought dinner home."

"Hi, Dad," Wyatt said. "We already ate."

Virgil set the boxes on the counter. "I can see that."

He gave both his sons a hug, patted Delroy on the shoulder, and Huma got the brow.

Huma fought the brow with a smile and a shrug. "The boys were starving, Delroy said he could eat, I missed lunch, so…"

"You miss a good meal, you," Delroy said. "Jamaican meatloaf. It don't get better dan dat, mon."

"What's the difference between regular and Jamaican meatloaf?"

"I don't think there's any difference," Jonas said. "Other than the fact that a Jamaican man helped make it. We had Jamaican Cheerios for breakfast."

Huma stood and began taking dishes to the sink. "Can I get you a plate, Jonesy?"

Virgil chuckled. "Thanks, Huma, but no. I've already eaten myself. The pizza was so good I thought you guys might want some."

"Well, put them in the fridge. They'll keep overnight and the boys can have some for lunch."

Virgil slid one of the pizzas onto the top shelf in the refrigerator, then grabbed the other box. "I'll be right back."

"Where you going, you?"

"I'm going to run this one back out to the keepers of the gate."

"You a good man, Virgil Jones," Delroy said.

"Thanks, Delroy." Virgil headed for the back door, a little spring in his step. Jamaicans—Virgil had discovered long ago—were good for the soul.

As he was turning out of his drive, Virgil reached down and switched his Motorola police radio to the private channel the troopers were monitoring. Then he keyed the mic and said, "Hold in position." When he got to the end of the road, he hopped out and carried the pizza over to the troopers.

"What's this?"

"When I said I appreciate you, I meant it," Virgil said.

The trooper took the box and said, "Thank you, Sir. This will really hit the spot." Then, with just a whiff of sarcasm: "Everybody else already ate, huh?"

"Something like that. Geez, if I'd been thinking I would have brought you some water or coffee."

"No worries, Sir. We've got plenty." The trooper cracked the lid on the pizza box, took a sniff and said, "Man oh man, this smells fantastic. Can we put in an order for tomorrow night too?"

Virgil laughed through his nose and said, "Sure. Call ahead at the bar, put your order in, then swing by and pick it up before you go on duty out here."

"We might just have to do that," the trooper said. "Have a good night, Sir. And thanks again."

Virgil got the feeling he was being dismissed, but he couldn't blame the man. It wasn't fair to wave a fresh pizza at someone, then stand around and not let them eat it. "My pleasure."

He got back in the Range Rover, turned around, then made the trek back to his house. As he turned into the drive, his headlights swept across the backyard, and he saw a man standing down by the pond.

AFTER VIRGIL'S DAD, MASON JONES, WAS KILLED, Sandy, Murton, and Delroy brought his bloodied shirt and a young willow tree out to his house. They put the shirt in a hole they'd dug next to the pond and planted the tree over it. A small tornado later destroyed the tree so Virgil cut what was left of its trunk into a small cross as a memorial to his father.

When Virgil got down to the pond, he saw a bottle of Red Stripe beer and a bottle opener sitting atop the cross.

"Howdy, Virg," Mason said.

Howdy? Virgil thought.

"It's an informal type of greeting."

"What, you can read my mind, now?" Virgil said.

"No, but I can read your face. How's it going,

Son?" Mason moved toward the cross, shirtless as always, the scars of the gunshot wound in his chest still visible and pink and fresh.

Virgil picked up one of the chairs and turned it toward the cross, then sat down and leaned forward, his forearms resting on his thighs. "Everything's going fine, Dad."

"Are we lying to each other, now?"

"Who says I'm lying?" When Mason didn't answer, Virgil tipped his chin at the cross and said, "What's with the beer? Have you taken up drinking in the afterlife?"

Mason laughed, and it made Virgil's heart ache. "No, can't say that I have. Consumption isn't part of the gig over here."

"Then where'd the beer come from?"

"Huma brought it out a few minutes ago. She's pretty special, that one." Mason picked up the beer and the opener. He cracked the cap, then handed the bottle to Virgil.

Virgil leaned forward, took the beer, and said, "Thanks." Then he heard the back screen door open, and when he looked toward the house, he saw Huma putting a bag of garbage into the bin. She closed the lid, then looked down toward the pond and waved at him. Virgil waved back.

So did Mason.

"How did Huma know I'd come down here? And more importantly, how did she know that you'd be here?"

Mason leaned against the side of the cross and said, "I don't know. Maybe you should ask her."

"I'm asking you, Dad."

"She has a very keen sense of intuition. There's no doubt about that."

"Does she ever talk to you?" Virgil said.

"Yes, she does. All the time, as a matter of fact."

"What does she say?"

"She mostly asks me…and your grandpa Jack, by the way, to watch over you."

Virgil thought, *Huh.* "And do you ever talk to her?"

"It'd be rude not to answer someone, don't you think?" Mason said.

Virgil took a swig of beer. "I guess so. But what I'm really wondering is if she can hear you."

"She hears in her own way, Virg. Everyone does." Mason ran his hand over the top of the cross. "Did you know that trees resonate at the same frequency as humans? I've always found that fascinating. Anyway, I see that your misdirection skills are coming along nicely."

"What's that supposed to mean?" Virgil said.

"It means I asked you how you're doing, and you gave me the easy answer…one that doesn't seem to be the entire story."

Virgil looked out across the pond for a moment, and when he did, he saw the lights flick on at Murton's house. "Looks like Murt and Becky are home."

"Maybe Huma should have brought out a pry bar instead of the bottle opener."

Virgil turned back toward his father. "I don't know what to tell you, Dad. Things have been…tense lately."

"Things are what you make them, Son."

"Meaning?"

"Sandy got a new job," Mason said. "So what?"

Virgil was starting to get upset. "I'll tell you so what. In the last month we haven't seen much of each other. She's off running around taking care of state business all the damn time."

"I think you might be overstating things, Son."

"Am I?"

"I wouldn't have said so if I didn't think it was true. And for the record, are we talking about Sandy's job, or yours, because it sounded like you just described what you do for a living."

"That's different," Virgil said, his defenses up.

"In what way? Sandy's home every night. Granted,

a little later than normal, but she is here. Can you say the same thing?"

Virgil knew his father was right, and it angered him for some reason. "Can we drop it, Dad? I don't want to talk about any of that right now."

"Look at the bright side, Virg. You've got a new look...one that suits you, by the way, a nice new ride, and what is probably the longest, most private driveway in the state. To be honest, I wouldn't have any qualms about the whole thing."

Virgil snapped his head up. "What did you just say?"

"I think you heard me," Mason said. "I'll tell you something, Son: It's time to stop being so selfish and start thinking about this case you're working."

"We've only been on it for two days, Dad. We're doing everything we can. And for the record, I don't think I'm being selfish. I'm simply trying to answer your original question."

"Fair enough," Mason said.

"Why did you use that word?"

"Qualms?"

"Yeah."

"I think you know the answer to that."

"Pretend I don't," Virgil said dryly.

"Things aren't as clear for me over here as you

might think, Virg. Like Huma, I have my own sense of enlightenment, but it's an ongoing journey, not a destination. The road that leads to enlightenment, as the Buddhists would say. Now there's an interesting group of guys to hang out with."

Despite his frustration, Virgil had to laugh. "Great. Have one of them pop in and give me the keys to solve some murders, will you?"

"You've got the keys, Son. You just don't know it yet."

"Then how about you tell me where they are."

Mason waved Virgil's statement away like a bothersome fly. "Ever heard of a guy named Jonathan Lindley?"

"No. Who the hell is he?"

"You should find him. He holds one of the keys you're looking for."

Virgil heard the sound of rotor blades, and when he turned in his chair, he saw the state helicopter off in the distance as it approached the landing pad in the backyard. "Dad, I have no idea what you're talking about."

When Mason didn't answer, Virgil turned back to the cross, but his father was gone.

Virgil helped Sandy from the helicopter, nodded to Baker, then gave Cool the thumbs-up sign before closing the door. Once Virgil and Sandy were well clear of the pad, Cool took off. They watched him go for a few seconds, then Sandy took Virgil's hand, pulled him close, and said, "I owe you an apology."

Virgil laughed.

"What's so funny?" Sandy said.

"I was about to tell you the same thing."

"Virgil, you don't owe me an apology. I've put you in an awkward position, and I'm sorry. I was thinking about it today, and if the situation were reversed, I don't think I'd be handling it nearly as well as you have."

Virgil gave his wife a hug and a kiss, then said, "Someone told me that I've been acting selfish lately."

"Who?"

Virgil tipped his head at the cross.

"Well, I don't think anyone could blame you," Sandy said. "I certainly don't."

"How was your day?"

"Hectic, as usual. I hope I haven't bitten off more than I can chew. And speaking of chewing, I haven't had anything to eat all day."

"Then I've got just the thing. C'mon, let's go inside. I'll get you fixed up."

They headed toward the house, then Sandy suddenly stopped. "You are talking about food, right?"

Virgil tugged her along. "Of course. I brought one of Robert's pizzas home. Actually it was two, but I gave one to the troopers."

"Got anything for dessert?"

"That depends," Virgil said. He opened the back door and held it for his wife.

"On what?" Sandy said as she stepped inside.

"I'll tell you in about sixty seconds. Sit. I'll get the pizza." Virgil popped a couple of slices in the microwave, and a minute later brought them to the table.

Sandy took a bite, then said, "Oh my God, this might be the best pizza I've ever tasted."

"I had the same reaction," Virgil said.

"What were you going to tell me about dessert?"

"Well, it involves the catsuit, if that gives you any ideas."

Sandy swallowed another bite, wiped her mouth, then leaned close to Virgil's ear and whispered, "Meow."

CHAPTER SEVENTEEN

THE NEXT MORNING, VIRGIL AND SANDY WERE UP early together. As they were getting dressed, Virgil looked at his wife and said, "What's on your schedule today?"

"Believe it or not, I've got a pretty quiet day. I've been working as hard as possible to get everything squared away, and after a month, I'm almost there. Things are about to calm down around here, Virgil, just like I promised they would."

Virgil strapped on his shoulder rig, slipped into one of his new jackets, then sat on the edge of the bed and watched Sandy as she finished dressing. "That's great news. Mind if I ask you a few things?"

"Of course not," Sandy said. "What's up?"

"Was the Range Rover your idea?"

Sandy turned and smiled. "Do you love it?"

Virgil shook his head. "No…I love you. I am, however, quite fond of the Rover. It's a hell of a lot nicer than the truck."

"I thought you'd like it. Actually I was praying that you'd like it."

"So it *was* your idea," Virgil said.

"Of course it was. Cora wanted to put you in a Tahoe, if you can believe that."

"I do believe it. Speaking of Cora, she mentioned that it was your idea that all MCU reporting be routed through to the superintendent of the Indiana State Police."

"It was," Sandy said. "We've got to maintain an extra level of separation between your department and my office."

"Permanently?"

"I really don't know, Virgil. Maybe once the public settles in with the idea, we might be able to go back to the way things were. But let me ask you something: Does it really matter? Your reports went there anyway after Cora screened them."

"I guess it doesn't matter. It's just that Cora has been my boss for so long now that I'm having a little trouble making the adjustment."

"Technically she still is your boss. I think she's

simply trying to clear her plate a little. Don't worry about where the reports go, Virgil. Cora is actually doing us both a favor. She's taken the threat of impropriety out of the picture." Then: "Here, zip me up, will you?"

Virgil stood, grabbed the zipper on the back of Sandy's dress and gave it a tug. When he put his hands on her shoulders, he could feel her collarbone sticking out. "Are you feeling okay?"

"Well, I'm about as exhausted as I've ever been, but other than that I feel fine. Why?"

"You're losing weight. Last evening I noticed the catsuit wasn't exactly painted on like it used to be."

Sandy looked over her shoulder and said, "That's a good thing. I thought I was starting to get a little hippy."

Virgil chuckled. "Hardly. But listen, I'm serious. The dress you're wearing right now? It looks about a half size too big."

Sandy turned around and looked at herself in their full-length admiration mirror. She gave her hips a little wiggle and said, "I think I look fantastic."

"You always look fantastic, but you are losing weight. Maybe you should make an appointment with Bell." Doc Bell was their longtime friend and family physician. "Let him give you the once over."

"The only person who is going to give me the once over is you, Virgil Jones. I'm fine, sweetheart. Really. I've been eating less and running at full speed for over a month. The stress has taken its toll as well. To be honest, I'd be worried if I wasn't losing weight."

"But you feel okay?"

"Sure, other than being tired. Tell you what…bring me home a tub of Ben and Jerry's Cherry Garcia ice cream tonight, and I'll eat the whole thing. *Then* you'll be telling me to lose weight."

"I'll split it with you," Virgil said with a smile.

Sandy slipped into her heels and said, "You mentioned there were a few things you wanted to ask…?"

"You never told me what the meeting with the National Forest Service was about down in Tell City."

Sandy puffed her cheeks. "That's a tough one."

"In what way?"

"In that I don't agree with something Mac did while he was in office. I want to change it, but he's insisting that it remain in place."

Virgil and Sandy had always been close to Mac, both personally and professionally, so Virgil didn't feel like he had to hide his feelings, especially from his wife. "You don't answer to him anymore, Sandy. I don't either. I love the guy…you know I do, but if he's still trying to keep some sort of control inside the statehouse, I'd tell him blow it out his butt."

Sandy chuckled. "I'm sure that's exactly what you'd do, but it's also something I can't."

"Care to explain that?"

"Politics is mostly about diplomacy, Virgil. You know that. Mac's not only a friend, but his influence in certain matters didn't automatically go away once he left office. If anything, that influence I just mentioned is probably stronger now that he's in the private sector."

"But he's pressuring you?"

"I don't think I'd use that word. But he is strongly advising me on certain matters."

"Look, you and I both know that Mac is a great guy. But you're the governor now. If you want something done your way, I say go ahead and do it."

"It's not that simple, Virgil."

"Why not?"

Sandy checked her watch. "Okay…Tell City. Remember all the fuss when the state hired contractors to thin the Yellowwood Forest in Brown County?"

Virgil puffed his cheeks. "Yeah, it's pretty hard to forget. Hell, half the demonstrators were acting like they were going to go in there with flamethrowers and burn it to the ground."

"The Indiana DNR—with Mac's blessing—hired a

company called Midway Timber to do the work. They went in, selectively thinned the forest, and essentially, that was that. Now the NFS wants to do the same thing with the Hoosier National Forest. The contract was already in place before Mac left office, and now it's a problem."

"Why?"

"Do you know who owns the Midway Timber company?"

"I have no idea," Virgil said.

"Actually, I don't either, but it's part of a portfolio of companies that used to be run by a guy named Rick Said."

Virgil let that sink in for a minute, and Sandy let him. "You're telling me that Mac is now in control of the company that holds the contract with the NFS to thin the Hoosier National Forest?"

"That's right. But there are larger issues at play."

"Like what?"

Sandy checked her watch again. "Baker is picking me up in about two minutes, and I still have to say good morning to the boys. Can we finish this tonight?"

Virgil was disappointed. He didn't want the conversation to end…not because of the topic, but because he enjoyed spending time with his wife. "I guess so. What time will you be home?"

"In time for dinner. I promise."

"What is it with politicians always making promises?"

"I'm not sure, but at least I keep mine. Make sure you keep yours."

"What are you talking about?"

Sandy gave him a kiss. "Cherry Garcia, Baby. See you tonight."

VIRGIL SET A REMINDER ON HIS PHONE FOR THE ICE cream—he knew he'd forget if he didn't—then drove to work. When he arrived at the MCU facility, he found Ross leaning over Sarah's desk, giving her a kiss. Virgil cleared his throat and said, "Good morning…and get a room."

"Good idea, Boss-man," Ross said. "Can we use your office?"

Virgil laughed and said, "No, but I'm sure Murt wouldn't mind if you used his."

"Someone is in a better mood this morning," Sarah said.

"That's because I finally got to spend some time with my wife last night." Then right down to business.

"Is Becky in yet? I want to take a look at the reports she's generating."

"Not yet," Sarah said. "She called from the bar and said she'd be here as soon as everything was finished."

"Huh. I thought it was going to be finished by now. What about Murt? Is he in?"

"I hope not," Ross said. "You just told us we could use his office."

"I was joking," Virgil said.

"You sounded serious," Ross said. "Anyway, he's with Becky. They're coming in together."

"Okay, thanks." Then to Sarah: "I'll be in my office. Let me know when they get here, will you?"

"Sure. Anything else?"

"Actually, yes. Becky might need to do this, but you can probably get the ball rolling for me. I need to find a guy by the name of Jonathan Lindley. See if you can get his phone number and address. If you can't locate him, have Becky start digging around."

Ross laughed.

"What's so funny?" Virgil said.

"A couple of things…your choice of words, for one. Digging is exactly what you'll be doing if you want to locate Jonathan Lindley. He doesn't have a phone, either, although I'm sure there's an address on record somewhere."

Virgil gave Ross the brow. "You know who Lindley is?"

Ross was something of a history buff and was known for his knowledge of Indiana history in particular. "No, but I do know who he *was*."

"He's dead?"

"Either that, or he's in the record books for being the oldest man ever."

"Ross…"

Ross let a small grin tug at the corner of his mouth. "Jonathan Lindley was born in the mid-1700s and died somewhere around 1830, although I might be misremembering that part. So, yeah, he's dead. Why in the world do you want to know about him?"

Virgil didn't answer. Instead, he looked at Sarah and said, "Check Wikipedia, and get me everything you can find on the guy. Ross, you're with me. My office, right now."

ONCE THEY WERE IN VIRGIL'S OFFICE, ROSS SAT DOWN and said, "Why the sudden interest in Lindley?"

"That's a little hard to explain. But I'd like to know everything you can tell me about him."

"You should crack a book every once in a while."

"Ross..."

"Okay, okay...just making an observation. Here are the basics: Jonathan Lindley was an eighteenth-century member of the North Carolina legislature, land speculator, and one of the original settlers of Orange County, Indiana."

"Paoli is in Orange County," Virgil said.

Ross let his eyelids droop. "I'm aware."

"And that's where Campos was murdered."

"At the risk of repeating myself—"

Virgil waved him off. "Yeah, yeah. So what does an eighteenth-century dead guy have to do with our case?"

"I have no idea," Ross said. "You're the one asking about him."

"What else do you know about the guy?"

Rosencrantz walked into Virgil's office and sat down next to his partner. "Good morning. Who are we talking about?"

Virgil looked at Rosencrantz and said, "Ross is giving me a history lesson on a guy named Jonathan Lindley."

Rosencrantz turned to Ross and said, "The Quaker guy who originally settled Orange County, Indiana?"

Ross nodded. "Yep."

Virgil gave Rosencrantz a skeptical look. "You know who Lindley was?"

"Yeah…I graduated from high school. What's he got to do with anything?"

"That's what I'm trying to figure out," Virgil said. Then to Ross: "Keep going."

Ross tipped his head back in thought. "Lindley was born in Orange County, North Carolina, and made his mark in lumbering and land speculation in the same area. He was also a politician who served in the North Carolina General Assembly and participated in the ratification of the U.S. Constitution. He insisted on amendments to the original Federal Constitution, which ultimately led to the Bill of Rights.

"He was a fierce proponent of anti-slavery, and eventually helped set up the Underground Railroad, and was among the many leaders who called for an end to slave importation from Africa, which was one of the first steps that brought about abolition."

"How'd he end up in Indiana?" Virgil said.

"He was prospecting for land," Ross said. "Apparently he was mesmerized by the old-growth forests in the southern parts of our state. Lindley and his family purchased land at Lick Creek in what would later become known as Orange County, Indiana, named after Lindley's North Carolina birthplace. That's about all I've got. I'm sure Sarah can dig up more on the guy."

Rosencrantz stood, arched his back, then looked at Virgil and said, "Anything else?"

"I don't know yet," Virgil said. "Why?"

Rosencrantz jerked his thumb at Ross and said, "Because me and Rain-man have to go back down to Brown County and speak with Frank Reddick, the husband of the murder victim. He's expecting us later this morning."

Virgil nodded. "Okay, you'd better take off, then. Let me know if you get anything useful from the husband. Doesn't sound like he's a suspect."

"We will," Rosencrantz said.

Once they were out of Virgil's office, Ross looked at his partner and said, "I'm a little surprised you knew about Lindley."

Rosencrantz laughed. "I've never heard of the guy. But I did stop by Sarah's desk before I came upstairs. I said good morning and all that, then asked what she was working on. She told me."

"Good one," Ross said. "Although, I really wish you'd stop calling me Rain-Man."

Rosencrantz gave him a fake grin. "I say it with love."

CHAPTER EIGHTEEN

Shortly after Ross and Rosencrantz left to drive down and speak with Frank Reddick, Becky and Murton showed up with the computer intelligence that had been gathered from the previous night.

Virgil was leaning against the edge of Sarah's desk, waiting on the printout of everything she'd found on Lindley. He said good morning to his brother and Becky, then Sarah handed him a thin stack of papers. "Thanks, Sarah."

"My pleasure, Jonesy."

Murton glanced at the papers and said, "What's that?"

"Something I'd like to talk to you about. My office?"

"Sure," Murton said. "Let me get a cup of Blue, and I'll be right up." He gave Becky a quick kiss and said, "Let us know when you've got something."

As Murton was walking away, Virgil turned to Becky and said, "You brought the data from the dental clinic here?"

"Yeah. The car lot customers as well."

"Is that a good idea?"

"Why wouldn't it be?" Becky said.

"Well, last night you said you didn't want anything tied back to the MCU."

"I was speaking from an operational standpoint, Jonesy." Becky dug into her purse and pulled out a USB thumb drive. "I've got everything on here, and before you have some sort of conniption or something, you've got nothing to worry about. It's just raw data that contains patient names, Social Security numbers, and home addresses. Same for the car lot customers. I'm going to work it all from an air-gapped computer."

Virgil gave her a dull look. "I wasn't going to have a conniption, as you say. And I'm not worried. I was, uh, just checking to make sure you're following proper procedure. It is part of my job, you know."

"Right," Becky said with a dull look of her own. "Just like it's my job to make sure your gun is loaded at all times." Then she pointed up at the railing along the second-floor hallway. "Speaking of guns, it looks like your brother-in-arms is starting to get impatient."

Virgil turned and saw Murton looking down at him, a bored expression on his face. "I said I'd be right up, Murt."

"Wake me when you arrive," Murton said. Then he disappeared into Virgil's office.

When Virgil turned back to the front desk, he saw Becky already walking away. "Hey, Becks?"

Becky waved over her shoulder and kept walking. "I'll let you know, Jonesy."

VIRGIL STEPPED INTO HIS OFFICE, THEN TOOK A SEAT behind his desk. Murton was reclining on the sofa along the side wall, pretending to be asleep. Virgil let him pretend and started looking at the information Sarah had given him regarding Jonathan Lindley.

After a few minutes, Murton sat up straight and said, "If you don't at least act upset that I'm sleeping in your office, it takes all the joy out of my morning routine." Then before Virgil could respond: "What'd you want to see me about?"

Virgil set the papers down and said, "I had an interesting conversation last night."

Murton tipped his head slightly. "It's been my experience that every time you use the word, 'interesting,' as an introductory term preceding the word, 'conversation,' you're talking about Mason."

"Really?"

"Yep."

"Huh. I've never noticed that."

"Well, it's true," Murton said. "So spill it. What'd he have to say?" There were a handful of people who knew that Virgil had occasional conversations with his dead father, but other than Sandy, Virgil's brother was at the top of the list. Murton had—on one rare occasion—even experienced it himself.

"Well, you know how the interactions are usually sort of confusing, or enigmatic?"

"Yeah."

"This one wasn't exactly like that."

"In what way?" Murton said.

"The whole thing was pretty direct. He told me I was being selfish when it came to Sandy's new career and all the changes we've been through."

"So far it sounds like he's right on the money."

"Do you want to hear about it or not?" Virgil said.

"Of course. I'm simply interjecting my thoughts as you go."

"Anyway, he asked me how everything was, and when I told him things were fine, he essentially accused me of lying."

"That's probably because you were, Jonesy. There are a lot of different words you could have used to describe your situation of late…but I don't think fine would be one of them."

"You might be right, Murt, but things are getting better."

"You do seem to have a more positive mood lately. This morning in particular."

"That's because I had a good night…and early morning with Sandy."

"Catsuit?"

Virgil tried to hide his grin but failed. "We're getting off topic, Murt."

"Sorry. Go on."

"Last night I took one of the pizzas out to the troopers at the end of the road, and when I got back, Dad was waiting for me. There was a beer sitting on the cross. He told me Huma brought it out."

"I'll tell you something, Jones-man…I love that woman. If I didn't, Becky and I wouldn't let her take care of Ellie Rae while we're working. But sometimes —and I mean this in the nicest possible way—she's sort of spooky. She has this weird kind of intuition."

"That's essentially what Dad said, although he didn't use the word 'weird.'"

"What word did he use?"

"Keen," Virgil said.

"That fits."

"So, right out of the blue, he asked me if I was aware that trees resonate at the same frequency as humans."

"Do they?" Murton said.

"I don't know. I guess they must. Then he gave me a little grief and told me I needed to look at the bright side of things."

"You do have a tendency to downplay the positive aspects of any given situation."

"I do not," Virgil said, somewhat defensively. "Anyway, he finished with two things that got my attention."

"Such as?"

"For one, he used the word, qualms."

That got Murton a little more interested. "Did he?"

"Yep. Then he asked if I've ever heard of a guy named Jonathan Lindley."

"Who's he?"

Virgil gathered up the papers Sarah had printed out and handed them to his brother.

After a few minutes of reading, Murton looked up and said, "What would a dead guy from the eighteen hundreds have to do with anything?"

"I don't know. But he said that Lindley holds one of the keys we're looking for."

"And that's where Paoli is," Murton said, "along with one of our murder victims."

"That's right. It's also where Lindley is buried. Take a look at the last page of what Sarah pulled up and you'll see that his house is now designated as a historical landmark."

"Do you think it's worth a trip down there?" Murton said.

Virgil tipped his chair back, put his hands behind his head, then said, "Hell, I don't know. It seems like it'd be a waste of time."

"Then why would Mason mention it?"

"How should I know?" Virgil said. "Half the time his messages are so obtuse I can't decipher them until after the fact."

"That doesn't necessarily render them useless."

"Okay, so say we go down there. What are we going to do, go walk around an old cemetery?"

"I don't know, Virgil, but he wouldn't have said anything if it didn't matter."

Virgil knew he was boxed in. "Okay. I guess you're right. I'll get Cool on the line and see if he can fly us down. Do me a favor?"

"Sure," Murton said. "What is it?"

"Get with Mayo and Ortiz and have them help Becky in any way they can. I still believe the link that's going to pull all this together is buried in those contact names. If we can find any commonalities with the victims, we'll be off and running."

Murton said he would, and stepped out of the office.

Joyce Parker was confused about something. It occurred to her as she was cleaning Paul Campos's office. The place was a disaster. The Orange County Sheriff's Department had sent a cleaning crew to help with what they called the 'bio-hazard' mess—a euphemism for Paul's blood—and once they'd finished, they told her the rest wasn't their responsibility.

When she looked around the reception area, she noticed that the fingerprint powder was everywhere, and when she began to clean it up, she discovered the task wasn't quite as easy as she thought it might be.

The damned stuff stuck to everything and didn't seem to want to go away. She used a number of different cleansers and assorted rags, but the more she tried, the worse the mess became. Finally she threw the rags on the floor and said—out loud—*fuck it*. Then, as a faithful Catholic, she crossed herself, said she was sorry to whoever might be listening, and went into Campos's office, sat down in his chair, and cried for a long time.

After Joyce was all cried out, that's when she realized she was confused about something. She picked up the phone and called Detective Mayo.

Virgil got Cool on the line. "What's up, Motherfucker?"

"Well, I'm up to my elbows in gear oil, and since you called, now my phone is a mess as well."

"Would the elbow grease have anything to do with the helicopter?" Virgil said.

"I didn't say elbow grease, Jonesy. I said gear oil."

Virgil laughed. "What's that expression Wu always uses? Potato, tomato?"

"Something like that. Anyway, if you were hoping to fly today, I'm afraid I'm going to have to be the destroyer of yet another aviation enthusiast's hopes and dreams."

"No chance, huh?" Virgil said.

"Nope. I've got half the tail rotor assembly sitting on the hangar floor. It's time for what us aviation professionals like to call required maintenance. Tomorrow at the earliest. Safety comes first."

Can't argue that, Virgil thought. "Okay, I gave it a shot. Thanks, Rich."

Murton walked back into the office and said, "I've got Mayo and Ortiz set up to assist Becky. They seem excited about the prospect."

"And Becky?" Virgil said.

"Let's not dive too deep into the particulars. What'd Cool say?"

"He says we're driving," Virgil said. "I looked it up. If you drive we'll be there sometime tomorrow. If I do, it'll be a little less than two hours."

"I liked you better when you were miserable," Murton said.

BECKY WAS IN THE MIDDLE OF INSTRUCTING MAYO AND Ortiz on what they could do to help her with the data when Mayo's phone rang. He pulled it out of his pocket, stepped out into the hall and hit the Answer button without checking the screen. "Detective Mayo, Major Crimes Unit. How may I help you?"

"Detective? This is Joyce Parker."

"Hello, Joyce. Is everything okay? You sound a little upset."

"No, everything is not okay. I'm sitting in Doctor Campos's office. I was trying to clean up around here, but I found out in a hurry that fingerprint powder doesn't like to cooperate."

"Yeah, that stuff can be a beast. But surely that's not what has you so upset."

"No, I guess it's not. I think the whole thing... Paul's murder and mutilation, the impending closure of the clinic, the fact that I'll be out of a job...it all hit me at once."

"That's understandable, Joyce, and I'm really sorry you have to go through all of that, but I'm not quite sure how I can help you."

Parker sniffed into the phone, then said, "Actually, that's not why I'm calling."

"Oh?"

"Well, when you were interviewing me, you asked if I knew anyone who uses a cane..."

"Do you?" Mayo said, suddenly a little more interested in the conversation.

"No, I don't. I stand by my original answer. Like I said, we have a couple of elderly patients who use them, but they are really old, and they certainly wouldn't want to hurt Paul. In fact, they're so old, they couldn't if they wanted to."

Mayo's disappointment was evident. "You'll have to forgive me, Joyce, but we're sort of in the middle of something here. If you don't know anyone who uses a cane, why are you asking me about it?"

"Because you asked me…during the interview. In fact, you asked me twice. I was wondering why."

"I really shouldn't discuss the matter with you, Joyce. It's part of an ongoing investigation."

"Well, if you say so. I just thought it was an odd question. I mean, if I had said yes, then you would have asked who, right?"

"Yes," Mayo said.

"Which means that you're probably looking for someone who uses a cane, and that particular someone is a suspect in Paul's murder. Do I have that right?"

Mayo was hesitant to answer, but couldn't really see the harm, so he said, "Essentially, yes. We have direct evidence that someone with a cane was in the office either during Doctor Campos's death, or just after. We don't know which. They may or may not be a suspect."

It wasn't a complete lie, but it wasn't exactly the full story, either.

"Okay, well, thank you. That puts my mind at ease. I don't want to have to walk down the street and be afraid of anyone who is using a cane."

Mayo gave her a polite little laugh. "I don't think you've got anything to worry about." Then, before the call was over: "What are you going to do now?"

"I'm not sure I understand the question," Parker said.

"I mean...you know, for a job."

"I'm not really sure. Get my resume together, I guess. I've got to get the patient records in order here first. That will take some time, then we'll see."

"Remember what I said, Joyce. If you think of anything that could help us catch Doctor Campos's killer, you'll not only find closure for yourself and Paul, but you may help save other lives as well."

"I'll get in touch right away if anything comes up," Parker said, then ended the call.

When Mayo walked back into the room, Ortiz looked at him and said, "Why the long face?"

"Ah, it was that Parker woman. She wanted to know about the cane angle, she's upset about the doc, and just now coming to the realization that she's essentially out of work. I feel kind of sorry for her."

Becky slid her chair back and said, "You're going to feel sorry for yourself if you don't get started on those reports."

"Don't I outrank you, or something?" Mayo said.

Becky laughed. "Oh, Mayo, I hate to be the bearer of bad news, but even Murton doesn't outrank me." Then the smile went away. "Now get to it."

CHAPTER NINETEEN

ONCE VIRGIL AND MURTON WERE ON THEIR WAY, Murton turned to his brother and said, "So, things are smoothing out a little for Small, huh?"

"That's what she told me," Virgil said. "Sandy's been going at it pretty hard, but says she's getting everything under control."

"Why do you suddenly sound like you don't believe your own statement?"

Virgil laughed through his nose. "Ah, I do. There's just something bugging me about the transition."

"If you've got it narrowed down to one thing, I'd say that's significant progress."

"You know what? I have narrowed it down to one thing. Sandy said everything would get better and it has."

"So what's the problem?"

"I guess Mac is leaning on her pretty hard over something they can't agree on."

"Big deal," Murton said. "Small's the governor now, not Mac. I love the guy, but she should tell him to mind his own business."

Virgil bobbed his head. "That's essentially what I told her. The problem—in a weird sort of way—is that's exactly what he is doing. He's minding his own business, and now there's a conflict."

"What's the conflict?" Murton said.

"I don't have the full story yet," Virgil said. He recapped the conversation he'd had with Sandy earlier about her meeting down in Tell City.

Murton listened quietly until Virgil was finished, then said, "So the National Forest Service wants to selectively harvest old-growth trees from the Hoosier National Forest? Man, it'll be like the Yellowwood all over again…only worse. If Small is against it, why not cancel the contract?"

"I don't know, Murt. I don't think it's that simple. The DNR is involved, along with the NFS, and Sandy's office. Mac had the contract put in place before he stepped down."

"That sounds like our guy," Murton said. "He wrote

a contract with a company he'd eventually end up controlling."

"Exactly. But that's not the entire story. According to Sandy there are larger issues at play."

"Like what?"

"I don't know. That's as far as we got with the conversation before she had to leave. I guess we're going to talk more about it tonight."

"You probably could have had the entire conversation if you didn't spend all your time with the catsuit."

"That's another thing," Virgil said. "Have you noticed that Sandy has lost weight recently?"

Murton sucked his cheeks in. "She has thinned out a little, I'll give you that. But she looks great." Then he turned and looked out the passenger window. A few minutes later when he spoke, it was at his own reflection. "I'm sure it's stress-related, Virgil. I wouldn't worry about it."

Virgil caught the delayed response, along with the use of his proper name, but let it go.

JOYCE PARKER DID THE BEST SHE COULD WITH THE fingerprint powder mess, and even though the building wasn't much cleaner than it had been, it was better. *Good enough to work in, anyway,* Parker thought. And there *was* work to do. Suppliers had to be notified, as did the patient's insurance carriers, the bank, there were taxes to attend to...the list seemed to trail away inside Parker's head like a wisp of smoke caught in the wind.

The first thing she did was check the bank balances and the outstanding invoices. She didn't want anyone trying to wiggle out of paying their bill just because the clinic was going to close. The work had been done, so the money was owed. Period.

The bank balances showed enough funds to cover payroll and utilities for the next two weeks, so Joyce sat down and wrote checks for herself and the hygienists. Then she brought up the electronic patient records and did a quick tally. Campos's clinic had just over two hundred patients who needed to be notified that they would have to switch their dental care to a different clinic. She typed out a form letter on the computer explaining the situation, offered her suggestions for other dentists in the nearby area, merged it with the electronic patient files, then hit the Print button.

When the letters were finished, she stacked them in a neat little pile, then adjusted the printer to accept envelopes, did another merge, and hit the Print button again.

All that was the easy part. Because the patient records were also on paper, Joyce knew she'd have to place a note in each file before locking them away in storage. Eventually many of the patients would want their files sent over to their new dentist, so she sat down and typed out another basic form letter to insert into each paper file.

And if Joyce Parker had been just a little more motivated, she would have finished that task as well. But the cleaning had worn her out—not to mention it had made her filthy in the process—so she did what any soon-to-be unemployed person would have done. She told herself she'd get to it tomorrow. She locked up, left, and went home to shower and take a nap.

If she would have stayed and finished, things might have turned out differently for more than one person.

Virgil and Murton found the cemetery in Orange County, in a town called Chambersburg, just south of State Route 150. It wasn't easy to get to, and they had to walk in from the road. The cemetery itself was located within the Hoosier National Forest.

"According to what Sarah found on the Interweb, the cemetery is called Little Africa," Murton said. He was reading as they walked. "It looks like Lindley brought a bunch of freed slaves with him when he settled in the county. They were each deeded 200 acres of land in the heart of the forest, and the area became part of the Underground Railroad for runaway slaves."

"Good to know," Virgil said, trying not to snag his jacket on tree branches. "Are we almost there?"

"Pretty sure we are there, Jonesy. According to this, all that remains today is a cemetery with lost or vandalized headstones." He kicked around in the dirt, and said, "Look, here's one."

Virgil was getting upset. "What a fucking waste of time. How in the hell are we supposed to learn anything out here?"

Murton kept flipping through the notes. "The Thomas Elwood Lindley House in Paoli was owned by Jonathan Lindley's son, and was built in 1869 on land deeded to him in 1812. The house was given to the Orange County Historical Society and—as I said earlier—is listed on the National Register of Historic Places in Indiana."

"Where is it?" Virgil said as he scraped some mud from the side of his shoe with a stick.

"I just told you. It's in Paoli, and open to visitors. I say we give it a look."

"If this doesn't turn into something, I say we burn it down. Let's go."

It took some time, but Virgil and Murton finally located the Lindley house. When they walked up the front steps, Virgil was instantly mad. He pointed at the sign on the door and said, "Look at this. Closed for restoration."

"There's a car alongside the building," Murton said. "Maybe we could get in anyway."

Virgil shook his head. "Yeah, like that's going to happen."

"But you like to stay positive, remember?" Murton said, a little sarcasm in his voice. He knocked on the door, then waited. When no one answered, he tried again, this time using a cop knock.

They waited a few more seconds, then Virgil said, "Let's go, huh? This has been a waste of time from the get." He turned and started to walk away, and Murton followed.

That's when a woman opened the door, stuck her head out, and said, "Sorry gentlemen, but we're closed for restoration. It says so right on the door."

Virgil and Murton turned and walked back up to the house. "Sorry to disturb you, ma'am," Murton said. "We're detectives with the state police. Would you have a few minutes to speak with us?"

The woman looked them over, then said, "May I see some identification, please?"

Virgil and Murton pulled out their badges and let the woman examine them. After she was satisfied that Virgil and Murton were who they said they were, she introduced herself.

"My name is Emma Kennedy. How may I help you, Detectives?"

Murton smiled and said, "My grandmother's name was Emma. You actually sort of look like her."

Kennedy smiled, took the glasses that hung from a decorative chain around her neck, slipped them on, and gave Murton the once-over. "That's because when you get to be my age, we all start to sort of look alike. I think it's the gray hair and glasses." Then, with no segue at all: "You may as well come in. I've been expecting you."

Virgil and Murton both turned and looked at each other. Kennedy saw their expressions, and said, "What's the matter? You look surprised."

THE LINDLEY HOUSE WAS OLD, BUT WELL-MAINTAINED, both inside and out. When they stepped through the door, Virgil looked around and said, "It doesn't seem like the place needs much restoration to me."

"That's because we're almost finished," Kennedy said. Then, with a hint of remorse: "I suppose we should get to it."

"Ma'am?" Virgil said.

"I don't have a lot of money. This is a volunteer position. Do you happen to know how much bail will cost…assuming they grant it to begin with."

"Bail?" Murton said.

"Yes, for all the parking tickets. I assumed that's why you're here."

Virgil laughed in a kind way, and said, "Ma'am, we're not here because of any outstanding parking tickets you may or may not have."

Kennedy put a hand to her chest and said, "Oh, thank heavens. And believe me, I have them. I was sure you guys were going to throw me in the pokey."

"Why not just pay them?" Murton said.

"It's a matter of principle," Kennedy said. "Public streets should have free parking. But I guess you can't fight city hall, as they say."

"You also shouldn't ignore them, either," Murton said. Then he chuckled.

"What's so funny?" Kennedy said.

"You're the second woman we've heard of in almost as many days with the same problem. There's a detective up in Jackson County who told us his mother is a seventy-three year old woman who thinks parking meters are the scourge of the twenty-first century."

Kennedy gave them both a sharp nod. "Well, she's right. Now, how may I help you, Detectives?"

Virgil didn't want to give out too much information, but he knew he had to tell the woman something. "We're investigating the death of Doctor Paul Campos."

"Yes, the whole town has heard," Kennedy said. "What a horrific ordeal. Doctor Paul had been my dentist for decades. That poor man. I can't think of one single person who would want to hurt him. I'll bet it was those darn druggies."

"We, uh, have reason to believe that wasn't the case," Murton said. "Robbery of any kind doesn't seem to be the issue here."

"Then would you mind if I asked you a couple of questions?" Kennedy said.

"Go ahead," Virgil said.

"If robbery wasn't the issue, as you say, what was? And why in the world do you want to talk to me?"

Virgil scratched his cheek with his thumbnail. "You have to understand, Mrs. Kennedy, that it's difficult for us to speak openly about an ongoing investigation. There are certain…mm, pieces of information that haven't been made public."

Kennedy let out a sad little laugh. "In this town? You're kidding, right?"

"No, ma'am, I'm afraid we're not," Murton said.

"Well, here's what I know," Kennedy said, "and if my information is correct, then maybe we can talk about your investigation."

Virgil crossed his arms over his chest and said, "Okay, what have you got?"

Kennedy perched her glasses atop her head. "Well, it seems our dear Doctor Campos was beaten to death with a hammer. Single blow to the top of his skull is what I heard. His teeth were smashed out after the fact, and there was a note left by the killers. Would you like me to recite it for you? I have a very good memory."

Virgil uncrossed his arms. "No, thank you. That won't be necessary. How about we all sit down?"

"That's fine," Kennedy said. "Let me get some tea and cookies first."

"We're fine, ma'am, but thank you," Virgil said.

"I was speaking of myself," Kennedy said.

Murton leaned close to Virgil. "So much for discretion, huh? It sounds like Orange County gossip is alive and well."

"There's nothing wrong with my hearing, either," Kennedy said from the back room.

CHAPTER TWENTY

VIRGIL ASKED KENNEDY A DIRECT QUESTION. "Who informed you of the details surrounding Campos's death."

"Well, I don't think I could point to any single person. Some of the information came from my book club, and the rest I simply heard around town. I assume the information is somewhat accurate?"

Virgil didn't like it, but in the end, he admitted it was. After he said as much, he continued with, "Look, Mrs Kennedy—"

"Please, call me Emma."

"Fine, Emma, then," Virgil said. "The thing is, there's no way for you to unhear what you have already. But there are things we'd like to discuss with you that must remain confidential until this case is solved. We can't have you running around to your book club, or whatever, telling everybody you know what we talked about here today."

Kennedy tucked her chin slightly and said, "I'll try not to take offense at your statement, Detective."

"Please don't," Murton said. "We simply need it on the record that we've advised you that this conversation is to remain between the three of us."

Kennedy seemed to relax a bit. "Not to worry, Dear. I give you my word. I do wish you'd answer my question, though."

Virgil had already lost the thread. "What question, Emma?"

"Why in the world would you want to speak with me about Doctor Paul?"

Virgil had just verbally painted himself into a corner. He knew if he told Kennedy the truth—that it was his father who'd told them to come—Kennedy would probably run screaming from the building. He sidestepped the question slightly and said, "Detective Wheeler, here, is not only my partner, but my brother."

Kennedy gave her hands a single, sharp clap. "Oh that must be wonderful. Brothers working together."

"It's often the highlight of my day," Murton said with a big toothy smile.

Virgil looked at Murton with his eyes half-closed

and said, "Mine too." Then to Kennedy: "In any event, in a roundabout way, we both work for the governor, who recently had a meeting down in Tell City with the National Forest Service."

"I still don't see the connection to me," Kennedy said.

"Actually, until we met, we didn't know who you were," Murton said. "It's Jonathan Lindley we're interested in. We were hoping, as the caretaker of this place, that you might be able to enlighten us regarding Lindley's history."

"Well, I can certainly do that," Kennedy said. She spent the next thirty minutes telling Virgil and Murton about Lindley, his life, where he'd lived, how he founded the county, when he died, and the slaves he helped free. Unfortunately, very little of it was new information. She finished with, "What I still don't understand is what any of this has to do with Doctor Paul."

"That makes three of us," Murton said. Then he pointed to a large map on the wall. "Tell me about that. It's sort of an unusual map."

"Yes, and quite valuable, too," Kennedy said. "That is a map of all the land that Lindley and his family surveyed over the course of their lives. Most of it is now part of the Hoosier National Forest."

Virgil and Murton both walked over and examined the map for a few minutes. Finally Murton looked at his brother and turned his palms up. "I got nothing."

"Neither do I," Virgil said. He turned to Kennedy and practically out of desperation, asked her another question. "Was Doctor Campos involved with the Hoosier National Forest in some way?"

"What do you mean?"

Virgil gave her a shrug. "I'm not sure. We heard he did volunteer work. Did he help pick up litter out there, or something like that? Maybe give tours to Boy Scouts or grade school kids?" The questions were so ridiculous Virgil could feel his face redden even as he asked.

"Paul did do volunteer work, but he never said anything to me about the forest. I'm sure I'd know if he had."

"Why's that?" Virgil said.

"Because we both served on the VOC."

"I'm afraid I don't know what that is."

"It's the committee that makes up the Volunteers of Orange County."

Virgil was thinking about the contents of the notes that had been left at the murder scenes when something occurred to him. "Emma, how long has the restoration of this building been going on?"

Kennedy tipped her head back in thought. "Mmm,

about eight weeks now. We're almost done, as you can see. May I ask why you want to know?"

Murton chuckled. "I'm surprised you have to ask. It's part of the note. Was Doctor Campos involved in the restoration of this building?"

"No, he wasn't. To be honest, I don't think he's ever been here. Even if he was involved, who in their right mind would want to kill someone because a building was being restored?"

"A nut," Virgil said. "That's who."

"You don't think I'm in any sort of danger, do you?"

"Not at all, Emma," Murton said. "I'm sure it's simply a coincidence."

"Well, I should certainly hope so…your nuts notwithstanding."

Virgil was ready to give up. He thanked Kennedy for her time, then asked a question right before they left. "Would you mind if I took a picture of that map on the wall?"

"I'm afraid that's not possible, Detective. This house is on the national registry of historic places. Photography is strictly forbidden."

"I understand," Virgil said. "But it could help us—although I'm not quite sure how—catch Doctor Campos's killers."

"You've both been very kind, but I'm afraid it's simply out of the question. Now, if you'll excuse me, I have some things that need my attention in the back room. I do hope you find whatever it is you're looking for. I'll let you show yourselves out." She gave them an exaggerated wink, then walked out of the room.

"Well, it was worth a shot," Virgil said.

Murton shook his head, pulled out his phone and took a picture of the map.

"What?" Virgil said. "It was a joke. I was going to take the picture."

"Right. C'mon, take a cookie instead, and let's get out of here. There's nothing wrong with Grandma's hearing, remember?"

Once they were back in Virgil's Range Rover, Murton looked over and said, "We've essentially wasted a day."

"I'm aware," Virgil said. "What I don't understand is why Dad would say something that makes no sense whatsoever."

"He didn't."

"Yeah, he sort of did, Murt. He pointed me at

Jonathan Lindley. We came all the way down here and didn't learn a thing."

"So what are we missing?"

"Hell if I know," Virgil said. "Send me that picture, will you?"

"Sure." Murton checked his watch. "What's the plan, Jones-man?" When Virgil didn't answer, Murton said, "Hey, Jonesy, you with me?"

Virgil nodded. "Yeah, sorry. I was just remembering the last case we worked down here."

"Don Whittle?"

"Yep. I wonder how Sam and Danika are doing."

Sam Whittle was a famous author—and quite unfortunately—the brother of a known, but now dead, serial killer.

"Well, if memory serves," Murton said, "they live about two miles from here. Why not stop in and say hello? I heard he's got a new book out."

"Yeah, I'm sure he'd love to take a trip down memory lane with us."

"See, there's that positive attitude again. You better learn to dial it back a little, Jonesy. Otherwise your butt will start glowing."

"Murt…"

"Okay, it was just a thought. Let's head home, huh?

Maybe by the time we get there Becky and her little helpers will have something solid. Can I drive?"

"No."

"Why not?"

"Because I want to make it home in time for dinner. I have plans with Sandy, and I don't want to be late."

"Says the guy who hasn't even started the engine yet."

———

Virgil took a call from Rosencrantz on the way back. He hit the Speaker button on the Rover's steering wheel so Murton could listen in. "Did you get anything useful from Frank Reddick?"

Rosencrantz let out a sigh, and said, "Not one single thing. The guy is definitely not a suspect, and he is completely baffled as to why anyone would want to kill his wife. Did you guys get anything out of Orange County?"

"Yeah, mud on my new shoes," Virgil said.

"I got a picture of a map," Murton added.

"Congratulations," Rosencrantz said. "What's next, Jonesy?"

"Did you get with Becky yet?"

"No, we just got back."

"Where's Ross?"

"In Murton's office with Sarah."

Murton frowned at the Rover's display screen as if Rosencrantz could actually see him. "Rosie?"

"Yeah?"

"Why are they in my office?"

"Based on the intelligence I've been able to gather, I think that's a question you should ask Jonesy."

Murton slowly turned his head and looked at his brother.

Virgil sucked on his cheeks and kept his eyes on the road. "Okay, Rosie. Gotta go. Tell Becky we'll get with her when we get back." He ended the call and refused to look at Murton.

"Virgil?"

"I have no idea what he was talking about," Virgil lied. Then: "Say, I changed my mind. Would you like to drive?"

LUKE QUINN WALKED INSIDE AND FOUND CALEB ASLEEP on the sofa, and for reasons he couldn't readily identify, it angered him. He kicked Caleb in the leg, and said, "Wake up. We need to talk."

Caleb rubbed his leg with both hands. "Christ,

what's the matter with you? Think I need a little more pain in my life?"

"I don't know. But I could sure use a little less whining."

Caleb was growing concerned that his brother was losing his grip on reality. His temper was getting worse by the day, and his drinking was off-the-charts bad.

"We need to start turning up the heat in a big way. Killing these other idiots doesn't seem to be making any difference."

"What the hell are you talking about?" Caleb said.

"Maybe if you spent some time watching the news instead of sleeping all damned day you'd know."

"Know what?"

"The restoration project is moving forward. Apparently someone isn't getting the message."

"Luke…"

"I'll tell you what we're going to do. We're going after the owner of Midway Timber. That'll get their attention."

Caleb didn't want to have yet another argument with his brother, but he didn't know how to avoid one. It was like trying to find a place of peace that was non-existent. "That's about the dumbest idea you've had yet. Don't you realize that they'll connect his murder with my injury, dad's death, and your termination?"

Luke poured himself a full glass of whiskey and drank it down in three large swallows. "No they won't. It's been long enough since all that happened. If we do it right, they won't even think to look at us."

"What do you mean if we do it right?"

"This time we're going to get rid of the body instead of leaving it on display."

"How?"

"Simple. We'll use one of the bastard's own wood chippers."

"Ah, Luke, it's too much, man. We gotta stop."

Luke pointed a wobbly finger at his younger brother and said, "I'm telling you, Caleb, if you want the killing to stop, then their project has to stop. It's the only way I'll ever be able to get these voices out of my head."

"That's not the only way to quiet the voices, and you know it. I don't think I can do it anymore, Luke. I'm not a killer."

"In the eyes of the law you are."

"I'm not talking about the law. I'm talking about myself. I've suffered enough. I don't need this weighing on me any longer. You gotta stop, man. Don't you see that? What happened with Pop…with me…it was an accident."

Luke refilled his whiskey glass and said, "Was it? Is that how you see the whole thing?"

"Yeah, why wouldn't I?"

"Because it wasn't an accident. That tree was spiked. If it hadn't been, Pop would still be alive, and you wouldn't be a cripple. Whoever spiked that tree is the real criminal and that makes them responsible for what happened to you and Pop. Calling it an accident makes it *my* fault. Don't you see that?"

"And killing people over it doesn't make one bit of difference. If anything, it makes everything worse. What do you think is going to happen? Kill enough people and Pop will come back to life…or I won't be hobbling around on this cane anymore? You gotta stop, Luke."

"I'm not stopping until I get the guy I'm really after, and you know who that is."

Caleb had heard enough. "Whatever. It looks like you're gonna do what you're gonna do, but count me out. I'm done. You hear me? As far as I'm concerned, I was never there. You did the killing, not me. And change that fucking note. There is no more 'we.'"

"Where in the hell do you think you're going?"

"Outside to clear my head. You're toxic, Luke. I can't take it anymore."

"So much for going to hell and back with me, huh?"

"In case you haven't noticed, we've already made

the trip. I'm not doing it again. Now get out of my way."

"Or what? You gonna beat me with that little walking stick of yours?"

Caleb shook his head in disgust. He knew there was no talking to his brother when he was like this, so he didn't even try. He sidestepped Luke, and when he did, his brother kicked the cane out from under him. Caleb stumbled, almost caught himself, but then his feet got tangled and he fell. When the back of his head hit the corner of the solid oak coffee table, the sound was exactly like that of a hammer going into the skulls of the people Luke had killed.

CHAPTER TWENTY-ONE

WITH MURTON BEHIND THE WHEEL OF THE RANGE Rover, Virgil played around with the display screen for a few minutes, then put a call through to Becky.

"Hey, Becks. You're on speaker with me and Murt."

"Hi guys. Did you get anything out of Orange County?"

"Not unless you're counting more mileage on the Rover. I hope this thing wasn't leased," Virgil said.

"Are you coming back to the shop?"

"Why do you ask?"

"Because if you are, it'll be a waste of time," Becky said.

"Care to explain that?" Virgil said.

"We're still parsing out the data. Campos had

exactly two hundred and three patients, and Harwood, the car lot guy, has customer records going back nearly ten years."

"How many customers is that?" Murton said.

"Nearly four thousand. Some of them are duplicates, though. You know…someone buys a car, then goes back and trades it in three years later, or whatever. So we've narrowed that down a little from four thousand, but it's still a lot of people."

"What about the Reddick woman and her shop?"

"That's the one bright spot in all of this," Becky said. "She didn't track her customers by name."

"That's hardly a bright spot, Becky," Virgil said.

"Says you. Anyway, it's going to take a couple of days to run everyone through the system. I can tell you this, though: Campos never bought a car from Harwood, and Harwood was not a patient of Campos's dental clinic, so there is no obvious connection between those two. At least not yet."

Virgil had a thought. "Do me a favor, Becks?"

"Sure."

"Take a look at the state's Bureau of Motor Vehicles records, or the Department of Revenue—whichever is easier—and see if you can find any Lindleys. Focus your search on the southern part of the state."

Becky dropped a little exasperation into her voice and said, "Has anyone ever mentioned that you have one of the most common last names in the country?"

"It's been brought to my attention over the years," Virgil said. "Why?"

"Because I'll probably find about two hundred people named Lindley. Then what, and why do you want it?"

"I'll explain later, Becks. But get the search going, will you?"

"Sure, I'll add it to the list." Then before Virgil could respond, Becky added, "Hey, Murt?"

"Yes, my love?"

"If you guys aren't coming back here, will you pick up Ellie Rea from Huma and take her home?"

"You bet. Listen, be careful with the squad car, huh?"

Becky laughed, then hung up.

Virgil looked at his brother. "You let Becky drive your squad car?"

Murton shrugged. "Only if she has to…like today. We rode in together, remember? So unless you want to drive all the way back to the MCU and drop me off, she doesn't have a choice."

Virgil checked the time. "That'll take too long."

Then: "Hey, turn in to that store up ahead. I've got to get some ice cream."

Murton smiled. "Cherry Garcia?"

"That was the request. Listen, when Becky is driving your squad, she doesn't run the lights or siren, does she?"

Murton's smile went away as quickly as it had appeared. "Of course not…you know, unless she's late, or needs to pee, or something like that."

Luke was sitting on the sofa staring at his brother's body, wondering why he didn't feel any sense of remorse. When he thought about it, the only real feeling he could come up with was one of relief. He knew that Caleb would have eventually cracked under the pressure and taken them both down, and that was something Luke didn't want to think about. *Done is done,* he thought. But now he had a problem. Two problems, actually.

One…what to do with the body. It wasn't like he could just drop him in a dumpster somewhere, or bury him in the woods. If he did either of those things, he'd eventually get caught. And the other problem? His sister. They'd never been close, but after their father died, she'd told her secret to Luke in a moment of weakness, and made him swear he'd never tell Caleb what really happened. Luke had agreed, but since then they rarely spoke to each other, although her and Caleb remained in touch. So, what to do next time Sis showed up to see her little brother?

Luke poured himself another drink—just one more for the road—then sat back down on the couch. He looked at his dead brother and said, "You turned out to be a real piece of shit. It wasn't my fault. It wasn't an accident, either."

Luke was so far gone by then, even he didn't know if he was speaking of the death of his father, or his brother.

The whiskey finally smoothed him out, and Luke decided he'd had the answer of what to do with Caleb's body all along. He checked his watch, saw that the day was turning to night, then got to work in a hurry. There were things that needed to be done before morning. He pushed the coffee table out of the way, then rolled Caleb's body up inside the area rug where he'd fallen. With that done, he carried his dead brother out to the garage and tossed him in the bed of the pickup. Then he went back inside, grabbed his father's shotgun and a box of shells, put everything in the truck, then headed north, up toward Brown County.

He had an appointment with the owner of the Midway Timber Company.

Rosencrantz was conflicted. He paced around his house trying to decide if he should make the call, or not. There wouldn't be anything romantic involved, so what was the problem? Besides, he and Lisa Young, the Brown County sheriff did have something in common, as sorrowful as it was. He took out his phone, brought her number up, then stuck the phone back in his pocket. He walked over to the mantle and picked up a framed photograph of Carla, looked at it with a heavy heart, then set it carefully back in place. What was it Virgil had said? If Young didn't make the call, he should?

Rosencrantz took his phone out again, looked at it for a minute, then stuck it back in his pocket and continued to pace. He'd lost his fiancé and unborn child. She'd lost her husband. They were both still grieving. But Virgil had also said something about shared grief, hadn't he? So why was he hesitant? Was it his feelings for Carla, or the fact that Young herself was a beautiful woman who was hurting and in need of some companionship…or both?

But there was something else, as well, and Rosencrantz couldn't quite put his finger on it. Young was vulnerable, of that there was no question. But the depth of her loss seemed greater than it should be. Could someone be stuck in grief for that long? And then he wondered who was he to be the arbiter of others' feelings in their time of need. A calendar wasn't the only way to measure the passage of time. He took his phone out yet again, and finally made the call.

Young's greeting was right to the point. "I'm sure you're not going to believe this, but I've been sitting around trying to decide if I should call you or not."

Rosencrantz chuckled. "I do believe it…only because I've been doing the same thing ever since I got home this evening. How are you?"

"Hungry, and tired of eating alone. I don't know where you live, but if I text you my address, would you be interested in a trip to Nashville? It comes with a no-strings-attached offer of a free home-cooked meal."

"I'll bring the beer," Rosencrantz said. "How does an hour sound?"

"It sounds like the best thing I've heard all day. Hang on." Then, a few seconds later: "I just sent you my address. See you in a while. By the way, I'm vegan. Would edamame beans and tofu be okay? Tom? Are you there?"

"Uh, yeah. We must have a bad connection, or something."

"I'm kidding. I've got a porterhouse in the fridge that'll break your heart."

Too late, Rosencrantz thought.

"What was that?" Young said.

"I said, don't worry, I won't be late. See you soon."

THE OWNER OF MIDWAY TIMBER LIVED ALONE IN southern Brown County in a massive custom-built log cabin tucked back off the road and surrounded by the forest on all four sides. The main drive was gated, but for those who knew the property—as Luke did—there was another way to get to the cabin.

The property where the owner lived was also where he ran his timber company. The company portion of the property was nothing more than a huge lot filled with logging trucks, a series of doublewide trailers converted into office space—much like the kind found on construction sites—and a bunch of equipment stored in large pole barns. The entrance to Midway Timber was wide open, and all Luke had to do was turn into the lot, then follow the hidden trail that led to the back of the cabin on the other side of the property. As a former employee, he'd taken the trail hundreds of times to speak with the boss. It was necessary because the owner liked to start his evening drinking a little before noon. Luke had driven the trail so many times he could do it with his eyes closed.

When he turned into the lot, he drove past the trailers and storage buildings, then killed his headlights, found the switchback in the trees, and headed for the cabin. The radio in the truck was on, the volume turned down low, Mick and the Stones singing something about you can't always get what you want…

When he glanced over at the shotgun resting next to him, it made him wish he'd brought a hammer instead.

…but if you try sometimes, you get what you need…

Luke stopped well short of the cabin, grabbed the shotgun, then made his way toward the back door. He put his hand on the knob, gave it a twist, and wasn't really surprised to find it unlocked. *The bastard probably passed out three hours ago,* Luke thought.

He went through the back hall, then turned through the kitchen and into the great room. The owner of the timber company was asleep on the sofa, a half-empty bottle of twenty-three-year-old Pappy Van Winkle bourbon sitting on the table in front of him. Luke shook his head in disgust. *A four thousand dollar bottle of booze and the guy probably drinks it like water.*

Luke picked up the bottle, took three long swallows, and let the alcohol hit his system like a freight train with bad brakes. Then he poured the rest of it on top of the sleeping man, and said, "Hey, Travis…time to wake up."

Travis coughed, rubbed the bourbon from his eyes, and tried to orient himself. But he was too drunk and couldn't quite make sense of what was happening. And Luke, who was running on a deadly combination of alcohol and adrenaline forgot all about the shotgun. He swung the bottle as hard as he could and smashed it right into Travis's face, knocking him out cold.

Luke dropped the bottle, grabbed the unconscious man by his ankles, and began to drag him outside, a trail of blood following them the entire way.

Still plenty to do.

When Young answered her door, Rosencrantz involuntarily swallowed, then said, "Maybe this wasn't such a good idea."

Young put her hands on her hips and said, "Why the hell not?"

And Rosencrantz thought, *Anger issues?* "You, uh, look nice."

Young grabbed his arm and pulled him inside. "Don't get any ideas. I just wanted some company."

"I brought beer."

"I can see that. How about you offer me one?"

"Got an opener? They're not twist-offs."

"In the kitchen," Young said. "Follow me."

As they were walking to the kitchen, Rosencrantz said, "You're kinda bossy."

"Only when I'm nervous. I haven't had a man in my house since, well, you know." She reached into a drawer and handed Rosencrantz a bottle opener. He cracked two beers and handed one to Young. After a few seconds of awkward silence, Young said, "What?"

"I don't think this really needs to be said out loud, but I'm going to anyway."

"Okay…"

"You lost your husband nearly three years ago. It's only been a few months since I lost Carla and our baby. You're a beautiful woman, but I'm not looking for anything other than friendship."

Young clinked her bottle against Rosencrantz's and said, "Good. We're on the same page, then. The grill is fired up and ready. I hope you know how to do steak, because I never get it right. I can do chicken, but I'll turn a couple of steaks into something you could lace up and run the marathon in."

Rosencrantz felt himself relax. "Yeah, I can do steak." Then he started laughing.

"What's so funny?"

"My boss, Virgil Jones. Do you know him?"

"I've never met him, but I know who he is. Why?"

"That guy couldn't grill a chicken to save his own life. In fact, I'm surprised the American Poultry Association hasn't issued a restraining order against him."

"That bad, huh?"

Rosencrantz took a swig of his beer. "Yeah, I remember this one time, a year or so ago…"

Luke got Travis outside, dumped him in the driveway, then quite unceremoniously put two rounds into his chest with the shotgun. Then he went over to his truck and backed up to the body. He pulled a towing strap from the pickup's bed with some difficulty—the damned thing was wedged underneath Caleb—and once he had it free, he wrapped one end around Travis's ankles, and hooked the other to the trailer hitch on the back bumper. By the time he was finished, he was soaked in sweat.

He jumped in the cab, then dropped the truck in gear and dragged Travis's body along the trail through the woods. When Luke got close to the pole barns, he killed the engine, grabbed the shotgun, and headed for one of the buildings. He examined the door lock with a dull expression, then fired at the handle. It took two shots, but the handle eventually fell away, and Luke pulled the door open and walked inside.

The wood chipper was right there, almost like it had been waiting for him. He fired it up, then turned back to his truck, his jaw hanging open, his tongue stuck against the inside of his cheek, drool dripping off the side of his chin. He wondered who he should put through first, Travis, or Caleb.

Ultimately, he decided to start with Travis. It was a practical decision more than anything. Once he had Travis out of the way, he'd be able to back the truck up closer to the chipper, which would make the whole job easier.

Luke unhooked the tow strap from the bumper and used it to drag Travis closer to the machine. He found a thick heavy branch, tied the strap around the log until he was sure it would hold, then pushed it into the teeth of the chipper.

The machine chewed through the branch like it was nothing more than a toothpick, caught the strap, and began pulling Travis's body closer and closer.

Luke turned away at the last second. He hated to lose that strap. Pop had given it to him that one year for Christmas. *Man, those were the days.*

CHAPTER TWENTY-TWO

DELROY AND HUMA OFFERED TO TAKE THE KIDS OUT TO dinner so Virgil and Sandy could have a little time to themselves. Virgil fired up the grill, tossed a couple of steaks over the coals, then cracked open two bottles of Red Stripe beer. Sandy threw a salad together, and fifteen minutes later they were sitting on the back deck enjoying a quiet meal with each other.

"You look tired," Virgil said. That got him a gentle kick in the leg.

"That's not exactly the kind of thing a woman wants to hear."

"You know what I mean. You look great…I'm simply saying you look like you could use a little rest."

Sandy took a bite of salad, then pointed her fork at Virgil. "You know how it is, Virg. If you don't sleep well for a week, it takes more than one good night to make up for it. I haven't slept well in a month."

"But you had a good day?"

"I had a light day, which is good enough for me," Sandy said. "What about you?"

"I had a wasted day." Virgil explained the trip down to Orange County and why they went, then finished with, "So either we're missing something regarding this Lindley guy, or he's got nothing to do with it at all."

"That seems unlikely," Sandy said.

Virgil wasn't sure if his wife was speaking of him missing something, or the manner in which he had been pointed at Lindley in the first place. They sat in comfortable silence for a few minutes the way couples often do, then Virgil said, "Can we finish what we were talking about this morning?"

"That depends."

"On what?"

"Did you bring Cherry and the band for dessert?"

Virgil smiled. "I did. And I'll get you some as soon as you clean your plate, young lady."

"What's the point of ice cream if you're too full to enjoy it?"

Good point. "Sit tight. I'll be right back."

Virgil returned a few minutes later with a tub of

Cherry Garcia, and two spoons. Sandy looked at the carton, her eyebrows knitted together.

"What's the matter?" Virgil said.

"Nothing. I just thought it'd be bigger."

"And I thought we agreed you'd never say that to me again."

Sandy laughed, then took both spoons. "You won't be needing yours. You can have the rest of my steak, though."

"Deal," Virgil said. "So, this morning…we were talking about your meeting down in Tell City the other day. You mentioned something to the effect of larger issues at play?"

Sandy took a huge bite of ice cream, then pinched her eyes shut. "Brain freeze. Jesus, that hurts." Once the freeze had passed, she looked at Virgil and said, "In a minute, if that's okay. There's something else I wanted to run by you."

Virgil scraped Sandy's steak onto his plate and said, "Sure. Whatcha got?"

"I'd like to throw a party for Jonas's birthday this Sunday. Jonas's friends during the day, and then the adults can have some fun in the evening. What do you think?"

Virgil knew when Sandy wanted to have a party of any kind there was no talking her out of it…not that he wanted to anyway. "Sounds good to me. Are you going to go all out…you know, tent, catering from the bar, the whole nine yards?"

Sandy gave him a wicked little grin and said, "What do you think?"

"I think we should invest in a tent rental company. But yes, that sounds fantastic. Are you sure you're feeling up to it? You've been going non-stop for weeks."

Sandy waved him off. "For one of our kids? Of course." Then: "What's so funny?"

"I was thinking you should invite Mac and have him dress up as a clown."

"Mac will be invited, sans clown outfit."

"It was just a thought," Virgil said. "So…Tell City?"

Sandy nodded. "Okay. Rick's company held—" Then she waved her hands in the air to erase her words. "I misspoke. Let me start over. Rick's company—the one that Mac now runs—*holds* a majority position in a company called Midway Timber. Because Rick held that interest prior to his death, he negotiated the contract with the state, through Mac, to thin the Yellowwood."

"Right," Virgil said. "We covered that already."

"Just making sure you're keeping up. Anyway, as I

mentioned, they also contracted with the NFS to thin the Hoosier National Forest at a future date, if and when the NFS chooses to move forward, which they've decided to do."

Virgil rolled his wrist. "Right, right, and there are larger issues at play."

Sandy tipped her head to the side. "Do you know that there are exactly two people you should never roll your wrist at? One is your wife. The other is the governor. I happen to be both."

Virgil leaned over and kissed his wife. "Sorry. Won't happen again."

Sandy gave him a wink, then said, "The issues are more complex than they might seem on the surface. There are essentially four groups involved. The state, the DNR, the NFS, and a variety of special interest groups we can lump together and label as protesters."

Virgil understood about the protesters, and said so. "I remember when they worked the Yellowwood in Brown County. Things got pretty nasty."

Sandy took another scoop of ice cream, put the spoon in her mouth upside down, then licked it clean. "They sure did. And I'll tell you something, Virg, while I don't agree with some of the things the protesters did —like spiking trees, or sabotaging the timber company's equipment—I can't find fault with what they were trying to accomplish."

"I'm surprised to hear you say that," Virgil said.

"Why?"

"Because the protesters engaged in illegal activity to try to derail the process. The end doesn't justify the means."

"When was the last time you saw the Yellowwood?" Sandy said.

"I haven't been out there since Patty was kidnapped."

"And that was before Mac and the state contracted with the timber company. You should see it now. What was once a beautiful untouched state forest with hiking and walking trails and old-growth trees dating back hundreds of years now has areas carved out that look like they're getting ready to build a shopping mall. That's not an exaggeration. Those trails I just mentioned? They were turned into logging roads covered with slag and gravel that are over twenty feet wide. It will take the forest hundreds of years to recover, and as a point of fact, I don't think it will ever be the same."

"I take it that this is where you and Mac don't exactly see eye-to-eye on the issue."

"That's right," Sandy said. "I'm completely against

the idea of harvesting the Hoosier National Forest. Mac is all for it."

"Why?"

"Think of all the cases you've worked over the years, Virgil. What's the one thing most of them all boil down to?"

Virgil didn't hesitate. "Money, or revenge. Usually both."

"Well, that's two things, but to answer your question of why, this one is about money."

"Said was a money guy, so I can sort of see his involvement, but why would Mac, and by extension, the state, want to get involved in something so controversial?"

"Same answer."

"But that doesn't make sense."

"What do you mean?" Sandy said.

"Well, looking at what happened with the Yellowwood, I assume since it's a state forest, it was the state who hired the timber company."

"It was," Sandy said.

"So the state paid the timber company to come in and cut down a bunch of trees, right?"

"That's right."

"And how much was the contract worth?"

"That's what I meant by larger issues," Sandy said.

"The state paid a little over one hundred thousand dollars to have the trees harvested."

"To what end?" Virgil said.

"I guess that depends on who you're talking to. Mac calls it fiscal responsibility."

"Look, I'm not a financial whiz, but spending over a hundred grand to cut down trees in the state forest sounds like the polar opposite of fiscal responsibility."

"It does, doesn't it?" Sandy said. "But there's more to the story. The timber company harvested trees out of the Yellowwood that were worth millions of dollars, Virgil. Care to guess where all that money went?"

"My guess would be the timber company."

"And you'd be exactly half right. The contract that Mac and Rick Said worked out stipulated that the state would pay to hire the timber company, then any profits gained by the selective harvesting would be split between the timber company and—"

"The state," Virgil said.

Sandy took another bite of ice cream, tipped her spoon at Virgil and said, "Yup."

Virgil thought about that for a few minutes, and Sandy let him. "Ask you a question?"

"Sure," Sandy said.

"You might not like it."

"I'm a big girl. Go ahead."

"How is this different from the way we made our money? We sold two thousand acres of land to the state and Said's company, but kept the mineral rights, and now we continue to generate income from that arrangement."

"The difference is obvious. Our agreement with Rick was put in place to extract natural gas from the shale using new technology. It was a win-win for everybody…us, the state, the Pope's foundation, and Said's company. This is different."

"In what way?" Virgil said.

"In that what we did in Shelby County didn't destroy the land. One of the things the NFS is tasked with is to protect the forest itself…from fire, timber theft, and anything else that threatens its environment.

"Since Mac is now running Said's company, he wants to move forward and do another harvest. Only this time, the profits won't be split between the timber company and the state…they'll be split between the National Forest Service and Mac's company. I'm being boxed out, and it's maddening. Midway Timber and Said, Inc. are going to go in and destroy a large chunk of our state land. Instead of preventing timber theft, they want to cut down the publicly owned forest and keep half the money."

"How large of a chunk are we talking about?"

"The Hoosier National Forest is the largest public land in Indiana. It's eight times larger than all the state forests combined. They want to clear cut over 2,400 acres, and they want to take an additional 700 acres and treat them with pesticides, which, by the way, wouldn't be necessary if they didn't do the harvest. There will be controlled burns of up to 15,000 more acres, and twenty miles of walking trails will end up being converted into logging roads. You know what's so ironic about the whole thing?"

"What's that?" Virgil said.

"There are signs at the entrances to the Hoosier National Forest. They all say the same thing: 'Enjoy but don't destroy our cultural heritage.' Except Mac and the National Forest Service are about to do the one thing the public actually pays them to prevent."

"So what are you going to do?"

"I'm not sure there is anything I can do," Sandy said. "Mac won't budge, and from a business standpoint, I understand. But unless someone can put a stop to it, Midway Timber and the National Forest Service are going to go down to southern Indiana and it'll be like the Yellowwood fiasco all over again, only worse."

Virgil puffed his cheeks. "Wow, so that was your Tell City meeting, huh?"

"Yeah, and it wasn't pleasant, either. I actually

accused them of planning timber theft and hiding behind PR reps and lawyers. Want to know what their response was?"

"I'm guessing it wasn't very polite."

"You're not too far off the mark. Their representative said that some ignorant people might call it timber theft, but they like to refer to it as the Buffalo Springs Restoration Project."

And Virgil thought, *Holy shit.*

CHAPTER TWENTY-THREE

Rosencrantz and Young had just finished their meal when Young's cell phone rang. She excused herself, answered, then listened for a full ninety seconds before responding.

"Tell them I'll be there in thirty minutes. Keep everyone, and I mean every single person out except for the crime scene techs. Got it? Good."

Rosencrantz walked over and said, "What's up?"

"That was our dispatch center. I'm afraid I have to go. We've got what looks like a double homicide. It sounds…pretty bad."

"Tell me."

"I don't have time."

"How about I ride along and you can fill me in? I'll

even drive if you need to work your phone or something."

"Tom, thanks, but maybe you should just go. This is county business."

"If you've got a double homicide it's going to be state business too. I might as well come with you and get the ball rolling."

"It's only state business if I call you in," Young said.

Rosencrantz shook his head. "Not anymore. The state has given the MCU ultimate authority in which cases we work."

"You're pulling rank on me in my own home?"

"No, I'm offering to help. What's with the pushback?"

Young didn't want to debate it. "Fine. Whatever. Let's go." As they were walking out the door, Young looked over her shoulder and said, "You can follow me. Try to keep up."

Luke was furious with himself. He was in his truck, driving back home, beating the steering wheel with his fist over and over and over again. He beat the wheel until his hand came back bloody. The wood chipper had malfunctioned, and Caleb hadn't made it all the way through. Luke tried to get the machine going again, but then he'd heard sirens in the distance and knew he didn't have any choice but to get the hell out. So that's what he did, half his brother's body still hanging from the teeth of the chipper. Luke wasn't even sure which half because Caleb had been rolled up in the carpet went he tried to put him through, and he didn't have time to check because of the sirens. Not that it would have made any difference.

He beat the steering wheel again, then cried out in pain.

Sandy saw the look on her husband's face, and said, "What is it, Virgil?"

"I think you might have just helped solve some murders. I need to call Murt." He stood to go inside and get his phone, but Sandy stopped him. "Virgil, wait. Tell me."

"It's that damned note the killers have been leaving."

"What note? You haven't said anything about a note. Not to me, anyway."

"You can blame the lieutenant governor for that."

"Cora? Why? What did she say?"

"She said that due to the nature of your new position and my job at the MCU, we were supposed to leave you, and her, out of the loop."

"Then she's being overprotective," Sandy said. "I never wanted to be uninformed. I simply wanted a layer of insulation between your operations and the executive office. Tell me about the note."

Virgil laid it out for his wife, then finished with, "We couldn't figure it out. We thought—well, everyone except for Chip—that the BS part of the note meant bullshit. But it doesn't. I think it means the Buffalo Springs restoration project."

"You're saying that the victims are connected to what's happening with the Hoosier National Forest?"

"It's the only thing that makes sense at this point. Anyway, let me get with Murt real quick so we can figure out how to move forward."

"Is there anything you can do about it tonight?"

"Probably not. Becky will have to reconfigure her search parameters."

"You're not going to ask her to start that now, are you?"

Yes, Virgil thought. "Uh, no I guess not. A few hours won't make much difference. I will want her to start early, though. Let me make the call and fill them in. I'll be right back."

Sandy wasn't quite finished. "Wait, Virgil, if what you're saying is true, then you've got someone out there killing people to stop this project from moving forward."

Virgil was getting impatient. "I know. That's why I want to get with Murt and Becky. I want to hit the ground running first thing in the morning."

"You're missing my point," Sandy said. "If your killers are going after people to stop the Buffalo Springs restoration process, Mac could be in real danger."

Virgil nodded. "You're right. Make the call to Mac. Find out where he is, then get at least two troopers on him for the duration. I don't want to take any chances."

WHEN ROSENCRANTZ AND YOUNG PULLED UP TO THE scene at Midway Timber they discovered that half the Brown County cops on duty were already there, as were the crime scene technicians, the fire department, and EMS. Young pulled Rosencrantz aside before they got too close and said, "Listen, I'm still pretty new at this. I thought the sheriff's position was going to be mostly administrative work. That's my way of saying I'm glad you're here."

"Don't sweat it," Rosencrantz said. "I've met your investigator, Ken Mayhall, remember? We can handle the heavy stuff."

They both scribbled their names on the sign-in sheet, ducked under the crime scene tape, then got stopped by one of the technicians.

"Good evening, Sheriff. Sir. You'll have to gear up if you want to get any closer. This one is as bad as I've ever seen." He pointed to his right and said, "Extra suits are in the van. You'll want head coverings, goggles, and masks, as well. Detective Mayhall is over by the body."

Young looked across the lot and into the surrounding trees. "What's with all the flashlights in the woods?"

"I'll let Detective Mayhall explain the particulars if you don't mind. There seem to be quite a few. I need to get back to work. We're going to be out here all night."

Rosencrantz and Young got suited up in Tyvek from head to toe—both of them looking like surgeons about to enter an operating room. They found Mayhall standing outside a tent that had been erected in front of the door that opened into a pole barn. Young looked at him, and said, "Ken, glad you're here. You remember Detective Rosencrantz with the Major Crimes Unit."

"I do," Mayhall said. He looked directly at Rosencrantz when he spoke, a knowing look on his face.

Rosencrantz used as much discretion as possible. "I happened to be in the area and heard about the call. What are we looking at?"

"Probably your worst nightmare. It appears someone fired up an industrial-grade wood chipper and tried to run a couple of guys through."

"Jesus Christ," Rosencrantz said. "Did you say a couple of guys?"

Mayhall nodded. He was sweating heavily and his goggles were half fogged over. "The techs are all but certain there are two victims, and what we've found so far fits with their theory."

"Start at the beginning, Ken," Young said.

"A call came into 911…someone heard some gunshots, so they dispatched one of the deputies out here to take a look around. He found one of the victims rolled up in a carpet, half his body hanging from the teeth of the shredder."

"Which half?" Rosencrantz said.

"He's still intact from the torso up."

"Who's the other victim?"

"We suspect it's the owner of the company. His house is on the property, and we found a blood trail inside his cabin that led from the sofa all the way to the back door. We also discovered a large area of blood spatter consistent with a shotgun blast on the driveway right outside the same door."

"What's all the searching in the woods?" Rosencrantz said.

"There's a path that leads from here up to the house. It's just big enough to get a vehicle through. One of the techs spotted some blood on the ground, and followed the trail. That's what got us to the house, and the two victim theory."

Rosencrantz looked at the tent and said, "How do you know that the guy who is…uh, stuck in the chipper isn't the victim from the house?"

Mayhall pulled his mask down, wiped the sweat from his face, then said, "C'mon, you better take a look."

Rosencrantz and Young followed Mayhall into the tent, then through the door of the pole barn. The carpeting had been cut away from the chipper, and the body of Caleb Quinn hung from the steel teeth of the machine, face up. The sight was so disturbing that Rosencrantz had to look away. When Young saw the body, something inside her clicked off like the power had just gone out. She shook her head and walked out of the tent, her arms extended out from her sides to maintain balance. It was all too much to take. Rosencrantz and Mayhall followed Young outside.

Once they were clear of the body, Mayhall said, "The techs told me—and I quote—that 'there is far too much organic matter to account for only half a body.' So it looks like someone ran the first victim through… the homeowner, a guy by the name of Travis Lindley, then tried to put the other victim through—"

Rosencrantz held up his hand and said, "Wait. Say that again. The homeowner's name."

Mayhall gave him an odd look. "Lindley. Travis Lindley. He's the owner of Midway Timber. Why? What's going on?"

"I'm not sure I know how to answer that," Rosencrantz said. "But I think my boss does. I've got to make a call."

Virgil was on the phone with Murton and Becky, recapping his conversation with Sandy. He finished with, "Becky, I'll want you to start first thing in the morning. Stop any running processes you have going, and get me a connection between the individual victims and anything that is even remotely connected to the National Forest Service, the DNR, any protest groups who opposed the Yellowwood project, or the harvesting of timber from the Hoosier National Forest."

"You got it, Jonesy. Do you want me to go in tonight? I could get the process started and we might have something by the end of the day."

Virgil smiled into the phone. "I appreciate your work ethic, but I'm pretty sure it can wait until tomorrow. Hell, if I hadn't asked Sandy about her Tell City meeting, we wouldn't even be having this conversation."

"Works for me," Becky said.

Virgil said he'd see them both in the morning, then ended the call. He didn't know it at the time, but he'd see them well before the start of the next workday.

CHAPTER TWENTY-FOUR

Delroy and Huma had returned with the boys and Aayla, and everyone was exhausted. Sandy got the boys ready for bed, then Virgil came in and said goodnight. As he was walking down the hall his phone buzzed at him. He pulled it from his pocket, saw that it was Rosencrantz, hit the Answer button and said, "Hey, Rosie. What's up?"

"I'm down in Brown County."

"Say, good for you, man. Decided to take my advice, huh?"

"In a manner of speaking."

Virgil was relieved. He knew Rosencrantz needed someone to talk with, and Lisa Young might just be the person to help his friend move further along with his healing process. Virgil tried to keep any amusement out of his voice but failed. "And how is our lovely Sheriff Young this evening?"

"Right now she's heavily sedated in the back of an EMS unit."

Virgil's relief went away as quickly as it had appeared. "What happened?"

"I think I'm going to need you down here, Jonesy. It's your call, but you might want to get Chip and Mimi headed this way as well."

Virgil had walked himself into the living room, so he sat down on the sofa and said, "Start at the beginning. Tell me everything."

"I'll start at the beginning when you get here. What you need to know right now is this: I've found your connection to Lindley."

It was practically the last thing in the world Virgil expected to hear from his friend. *"What?"*

"You were looking for a guy named Lindley, right?"

"Yeah. Murt and I gave it our best shot, but nothing really stuck to the wall."

"Interesting choice of words," Rosencrantz said. "I just got done looking at the equivalent of a Jackson Pollack organic masterpiece. If that doesn't paint you a picture, this probably will: I'm standing in a timber yard that happens to be one of the worst crime scenes I've ever witnessed. I'll text you the address. We've got a double homicide down here. Two male victims, one unidentified, and all available information strongly suggests that the other is the owner of Midway Timber…a guy by the name of Travis Lindley."

And for the second time in the evening Virgil thought, *Holy shit.*

VIRGIL HURRIED DOWN THE HALL THAT LED TO THE private quarters where Delroy and Huma lived. He knocked on the door, and dialed Murton's number while he waited. Huma opened the door just as Murton answered.

"Hi Jonesy. Are the boys all right?" Huma said.

"Hang on," Virgil said into the phone. Then to Huma: "Thank you. Yes. Can you take Ellie Rea for a while? It might be for the rest of the evening."

"Of course. Is everything okay?"

"Yes and no. Our case is coming together and I need Murton and Becky."

Huma shooed him away. "Go, then. I'll run over and get her right now."

Virgil gave her a quick thank you over his shoulder and got back on the phone with Murton. He dispensed with any pleasantries and said, "Huma is on her way over to get Ellie Rae. Tell Becky to head to the shop and get started. You and me are going down to Brown County."

"What's happening?"

"I'll give you the details in the car, but we've got a double, Rosie is on the scene, and it's connected to us. Pick you up in five."

Murton said he'd be ready. Virgil hurried back down the hall, and almost bowled right over his wife. "What's going on?" Sandy said.

"Things are breaking…or coming together, depending on your perspective."

"Your case?"

"Yep. Huma is going to bring Ellie Rae over here. Becky is headed to the shop, and Murt and I need to get to Brown County. I'll have to fill you in later, but right now I need to know that you've got troopers on Mac. These killers are starting to unravel."

"I've got him covered, Virgil, but please, tell me what's going on."

"It looks like the owner of Midway Timber was just killed. Whoever's doing this seems to be working their way up the food chain. I'm afraid Mac might be next on their list."

Sandy gave her husband a quick kiss, then told him to be careful.

Virgil said he would, then ran out the back door and jumped into the Rover.

Murton had jogged out to the end of Virgil's driveway and was waiting. Two seconds after Virgil stopped, they were on their way. Murton reached down, flipped the flashers on, then turned the Motorola police radio to the proper channel to reach the troopers guarding the intersection by the highway. "Unit one is rolling. We need a clear southbound path at the gate."

The troopers responded and said they'd be ready, and they were. Two minutes later, Virgil saw that the highway had been blocked off as requested. He hit the siren, braked hard, made the turn south, then ran the Range Rover up to ninety and set the cruise control.

"Becky will be at the shop in less than an hour," Murton said. "Wanted you to know she's going to call Mayo and Ortiz in."

"I thought they were getting in her way."

"Naw…she just likes to be dramatic sometimes. So let's hear it."

"I guess Rosencrantz went down to Nashville, um, to hang out with Sheriff Young. It was sort of my idea."

"Didn't think he'd be interested yet."

"He's not. But they met when he and Ross were down there interviewing Mayhall about the Reddick woman. They met by chance, and as it turns out she lost her husband a few years ago."

"So they've got a little something in common," Murton said.

"That's right. I suggested that it might help him feel better if he spoke with someone who's been through it. Apparently he decided to listen. Anyway, the call came in while he was still there, so he went along. What I told you earlier tonight…about Midway Timber and everything else Sandy told me?"

"What of it?"

"That's where the crime scene is…in the Midway Timber yard. The owner is dead. His name was Travis Lindley."

Murton let that sink in for a few seconds, then said, "Holy shit."

Virgil laughed without humor. "My thoughts exactly."

Less than an hour later Virgil and Murton were on the scene. They found Rosencrantz standing next to the back door of an EMS unit. The door was cracked open, and they could see one of the medics taking Young's blood pressure.

Murton looked at Rosencrantz, tipped his head toward Young, and said, "She okay?"

"I think so. She just sort of lost it there for a minute. It was actually kind of weird. She walked away from the body and while I was speaking with Detective Mayhall she went pale, had this catatonic look on her face, then collapsed. The medic said it was caused by sudden onset stress."

"But she's all right…physically?" Virgil said.

"Yeah. She didn't whack her head or anything like that," Rosencrantz said. "She's still new at this. She told me earlier tonight that she thought the job would be mostly administrative. Are you guys going to take a look at the body?"

Virgil puffed his cheeks. "I guess we better."

"You'll have to suit up. There's extra Tyvek in the county van."

Virgil said they would, then asked Rosencrantz a question. "Do you think we need Chip and Mimi down here?"

Rosencrantz shook his head. "I don't think so. Based on what I've seen so far, the Brown County techs are doing everything they can. Looks like they're on top of it."

"Good enough." He looked over Rosencrantz's shoulder. "What's with all the flashlights in the woods?"

Rosencrantz explained the sequence of events and told Virgil and Murton about the trail.

"Okay, we'll take a look up there next." Then to Murt: "Let's suit up."

It took Virgil and Murton nearly ten minutes to get their protective gear on, and less than thirty seconds to look at the body. Both men had seen their fair share of gruesome crime scenes, but by the time they exited the tent, they were both breathing heavily and sweating through their clothes.

"Christ," Murton said. "You know what that reminds me of?"

Virgil ripped off his mask, pulled the goggles down below his chin and said, "What?"

"That time we found what was left of Charlie Esser over in Shelby County after the hogs had gotten to him."

"I think this is worse," Virgil said.

"No argument here. I'm simply making a comparison."

Virgil glanced over at the EMS van. "It's no wonder Young lost it. I might not sleep for a week."

Mayhall walked over and they all introduced themselves. "Detective Rosencrantz told me you guys were headed this way."

"I'm beginning to wish we hadn't," Murton said. "Does anybody know who that is?"

Mayhall shook his head. "No, and to tell you the truth, I don't think we ever will. The way he was rolled up inside that carpet? His arms were pinned against his sides. He went through far enough that his hands were, uh, destroyed."

"What about dental records?" Virgil said.

"That's the only other possibility, but what are you going to do? Go around to every dentist in Brown County and have them compare that guy's teeth against every patient file? You might figure it out in about ten years. Your best bet is to find whoever did this and beat it out of them."

"My thoughts, exactly," Murton said.

Virgil looked at Mayhall and said, "Show us the house?"

"Yeah, but it's easier if you strip out of that gear and we take the road. The trail is still being searched, and I'd like to stay out of the way."

"Let us get on the other side of the tape," Virgil said. "We'll be ready in five minutes."

"That'll work," Mayhall said. "You want to ride with me, or follow?"

"We'll follow," Virgil said. "Just a second." Then he walked over to where Rosencrantz stood. "Mayhall is going to take us up to the house. I want to give it a quick look."

"That's fine. I'm going to wait here, if you don't mind. I've already been up there, and I want to make sure Lisa is doing okay."

"No sweat, Rosie," Virgil said. "We'll be back shortly."

After Virgil and Murton removed their Tyvek suits, they climbed into the Rover and followed Mayhall out of the lot and down the highway that led to the front gate of Lindley's cabin. Mayhall parked next to the gate, then walked over to Virgil's vehicle. "We'll have to walk from here. No one has been able to figure out how to open the gate. It takes a code or something."

"Do you have any deputies up at the house, or is it just crime scene techs?" Virgil said.

"I've got a couple of guys up there. Why?"

"Have one of them go out to Lindley's vehicle. I bet there's a remote for the gate."

"Geez, I didn't even consider that," Mayhall said. He got on the radio, made the call, and less than a minute later the gate started to roll sideways. Once the gate was open, Mayhall wedged a large rock in the roller bar to prevent the gate from closing just in case it was on some sort of timer. He walked back over to the Range Rover and said, "What made you think of that?"

Murton leaned across the seat so Mayhall could see him. "He's getting his own private road. I caught him looking at motorized gate catalogs the other day."

"No you didn't," Virgil said.

"Well, I saw them on your desk."

Mayhall gave them a funny look. "You guys always like this?"

"Like what?" Virgil said.

"Pretty much," Murton said.

CHAPTER TWENTY-FIVE

ONCE THEY WERE AT THE CABIN, EVERYONE PUT SHOE coverings and gloves on, then Mayhall took Virgil and Murton inside and walked them through the sequence the crime scene techs had laid out.

"There's not much to see, really," Mayhall said. He pointed at the small pool of blood on the floor by the sofa. "It looks like Lindley was attacked—with a rather expensive bottle of bourbon, no less—then dragged through the kitchen and out the back door."

Murton squatted down next to a technician who was dusting the bottle for prints. "Pappy Van Winkle, huh?"

The tech nodded. "Yeah. Did you know that this stuff goes for over four grand a bottle?"

"Not for me, it doesn't," Murton said. "I get it wholesale."

"How do you manage that?" the tech said without looking up from his work.

"I own a bar. Are you going to get a good print from that?"

The tech carefully peeled a piece of tape from the bottle, then held it up to the light. "Yep. And based on what I'm seeing, it matches one we pulled from the back door."

"How do you know they aren't the homeowner's prints?" Virgil said.

"Because they match the partials we pulled from two shotgun shells." He stuck the tape to a piece of paper, then put it into an evidence bag.

"Do me a favor?" Virgil said.

"If I can," the tech said. "Who the heck are you guys, anyway?"

"Sorry," Virgil said. "We're with the state's Major Crimes Unit. I'm Detective Virgil Jones." He tipped his head at his brother. "Detective Wheeler."

"What's the favor?"

"Send a copy of that print up to our lab. We can probably get the results back quicker than the county."

"Got a number?"

Virgil gave the tech a number that would go straight to Becky. The tech wrote the number down, then said he'd send it right away.

"Thanks for your help," Virgil said. "We'll let our people know it's on the way." He glanced at Murton and saw he was already on the phone.

Virgil turned to Mayhall. "Show us the outside?"

"Follow me." He walked Virgil and Murton carefully past the trail of blood, then through the back door and out to the drive. He pointed at the blacktop, and said, "Remember when this was the kind of thing that looked bad? After I saw that wood chipper, this is nothing."

Virgil looked at the blood and gore on the driveway and noticed the partial footprint. "Did your guys get a picture of that?"

"They did," Mayhall said. "A good one, too. They tell me it's a Wolverine work boot, size eleven. Maybe eleven and a half."

Virgil looked at his brother. "Murt?"

"I'm on it, Jonesy," Murton said before walking back into the house.

"Where's he going?" Mayhall said.

"To tell the tech to send our people the picture of the boot."

"What can they do with that?"

Virgil shrugged. "Probably nothing…yet. But it's been my experience that it never hurts to have too much evidence." Then: "Tell me about Sheriff Young. I heard she was pretty shaken up."

Mayhall nodded and looked away without answering. Virgil waited a few seconds, then tried again. "Detective? I asked about the sheriff."

"Look, you didn't hear this from me, but I don't think she's got her head in the game."

"If you're talking about what we've seen here tonight, I really couldn't find fault—"

Mayhall held up his hand. "It's not just tonight. She's in over her head. I don't know the whole backstory, but she has some issues."

"Like what?"

"Ah, you know, personal stuff. Lost both of her parents, then her husband gets killed…I think she ran for office with the idea that she was going to push paper, then ended up figuring out there is a darker side of things when it comes to law enforcement."

Virgil knew exactly two things about Sheriff Young. She'd either work through her issues and succeed at the job, or she wouldn't. Either way, it was none of his business. "Well, hopefully she can get up to speed before the county takes action."

Murton walked over, looked at Virgil, and said, "We're all set." Then to Mayhall: "How are you going to get the victim out of that chipper?"

Mayhall scratched at the back of his head. "We're still trying to figure that out. The best idea we have so far is to take the teeth out. If we can do that, the coroner will be able to get the body. As soon as the crime scene people are finished, the fire department is going to give it a try."

"What if that doesn't work?" Virgil said.

"Then the coroner is going to have to…uh, cut him out. I'm hoping the first idea works."

VIRGIL AND MURTON WENT BACK TO THE TIMBER YARD site and found Rosencrantz. "We're going to head back," Virgil said. "Becky's working a print, and there's not much we can do here. How's the sheriff?"

"Pretty messed up. If you don't mind, I'm going to hang here for a little while longer and make sure she gets home safely. See you in the morning?"

Virgil tipped a finger at his friend and coworker. "You bet. At the shop by eight?"

"I'll be there," Rosencrantz said, then he turned and walked away.

Virgil watched him go, then looked at Murton and said, "I think he's doing better."

Murton didn't respond.

After Virgil and Murton had left, Mayhall assured Rosencrantz that he had the scene under control. "Why not get the sheriff out of here? I think she's had about all she can take."

"That's not a bad idea," Rosencrantz said. "She's still a little loopy from the sedative the medic gave her. If I give her a ride in my squad car, can a couple of your guys get her vehicle back to her by morning?"

Mayhall nodded. "Yeah, we can do that."

Rosencrantz thanked the detective, then went in search of Young.

Forty-five minutes later he walked Young through her front door and helped her to the sofa. "Is there anything I can get you before I go?" Rosencrantz said.

"Yeah, a do-over on life," Young said. "Short of that, I'd take another one of those beers."

"Do you think that's a good idea? You've still got some of those meds in you."

"What? You're a doctor now?"

Rosencrantz was having a little trouble figuring the woman out. One minute she was as nice and kind and friendly as anyone he'd ever met, and the next she used a tone of voice that suggested she was about to shoot first and ask questions later. He wrote it off to stress, then calmly said, "No, I'm not a doctor. I just don't want you to end up in the hospital."

"Never mind, then. You're probably right. Maybe you should go, huh? Our night got a little ruined. Mine in particular."

"Sure, whatever you say."

"Listen, Tom, I'm sorry. I haven't been myself lately. I feel like I'm going to crack under all this pressure. Maybe we can try again in a couple of days. Would that be okay?"

"Sure." Rosencrantz moved toward the door, then stopped and examined a framed photo of Young, along with who he assumed were her parents. "This is a great picture. Is that your mom and dad standing there with you?"

Young stood from the sofa, took the picture, and turned it face down on the table. "Yes. I think you should go."

"Your dad looks sort of familiar. I wonder if I ever met him before he passed."

"I doubt it." Young moved to the door and held it open. "Good night, Tom. Drive carefully."

Rosencrantz stuck his tongue in his cheek, then said, "You bet. Take care, huh?" Then he walked out, got in his car and headed for home. He spent the entire drive trying to remember where he'd seen Young's father before. It felt like the memory was right on the tip of his brain.

As soon as Rosencrantz was outside, Young turned around, put her back to the door, then slid down onto her butt and began to cry. It hadn't only been the stress of what she saw tonight that caused her to lose her composure. It'd been the secret she kept buried deep inside her brain ever since her father had died. She had to find a way to get out from under the weight of it all, and when that thought hit her she began to laugh hysterically. "There's some irony for you," she said aloud to no one. "I spiked the tree that killed my own father and destroyed my family."

Young stood up, grabbed her phone, then called her brother. When he didn't answer, she left him a voicemail message. "Luke, it's me. You've got to stop. Caleb was our brother. Please, Luke, I'm begging you. I don't know how many times I have to apologize. I'm coming apart at the seams over here." She was about to end the call, but at the last second she brought the phone back up and screamed into the handset. "Do you hear me, you bastard? I can't take it anymore."

When Virgil and Murton arrived at the MCU facility it was well after midnight. When they walked into the computer lab, both men were surprised to find Mayo and Ortiz working with Becky.

Virgil looked at his two other detectives and said, "I appreciate your dedication, guys, but you didn't have to come in for this."

"Then you'll really love us," Ortiz said.

"Why's that?"

Becky answered for Ortiz. "Because when I tried to call them in I discovered they never left for the day."

Virgil raised his eyebrows...both of them. "No kidding?"

"And it's a good thing, too," Becky said.

"Why's that?"

"Because we found what any reasonable person in

the world would most likely characterize as a clue," Mayo said.

"Believe it or not," Becky said, "Mayo here is actually pretty good at this computer stuff."

"Is that right?" Virgil said.

"I'm more than just a pretty face, you know," Mayo said.

"Okay, so you've got one thing going for you," Virgil said. He laughed at his own joke, but no one else did. "So what's the clue?"

"I figured out what all our victims had in common."

Virgil's eyes got wide. "You're shitting me."

"I shit not upon thee," Mayo said. "Every victim held stock in Rick Said's company when it was publicly traded."

Virgil's excitement drained away a little. "Uh, that's good to know, except there were thousands of people… hell, tens of thousands who held stock in the corporation. That doesn't really get us anywhere."

Mayo gave Virgil a sad little head shake. "Oh ye of little faith…"

"How about you drop the old English routine and tell me the rest of it?"

"When Mac and Nichole took the company private, they bought out all the shares. But before they could do that, the SEC mandated that notices be sent to every shareholder informing them of what was happening, and why. One of the things they sent along with the notice was a small questionnaire that asked—among other things—which company under the umbrella of Said, Inc. interested them the least, and why."

"Yeah, I know," Virgil said. "I got one."

"Did you answer it?"

"It may have slipped my mind."

"Well, Harwood, Reddick, and Campos did, and they all gave the same answer."

"Midway Timber?" Virgil said.

Mayo gave Virgil a single nod. "Yup."

Virgil looked at his brother: "C'mon Murt. There's someone we have to speak with." Then to Mayo: "That's great work, man."

"I helped," Ortiz said.

Virgil ignored him, looked at Becky, and said, "Are you running the print from Brown County?"

"Yes. Nothing yet."

"Okay, stay on it. And give Ortiz a sticker, or something. Murt, let's roll."

Virgil pulled up next to one of the trooper's squad cars, buzzed the window down, and said, "Detectives Jones and Wheeler to see the governor."

The trooper casually glanced at his watch and said, "At this hour? And I think you meant former governor, Sir."

"I know it's late, but it can't be helped. Is he still up?"

"I'm just the keeper of the gate, not the chambermaid."

"Good," Virgil said. "Back your squad out of the way, then open the gate."

The trooper did as requested, and Virgil drove up the driveway of the governor's mansion. Mac was waiting at the door, still dressed in a business suit.

When Virgil and Murton got to the front steps, Mac looked over their shoulders and said, "Nice ride, Jonesy. I see you've let Murton help you with your wardrobe as well."

"It wasn't really my decision," Virgil said. "Sorry to bother you at this hour, Mac. I'm surprised you're still awake."

"I'm not," Mac said. "This private sector stuff takes a little getting used to. Anyway, what's up? I hope you're not here to kick me out of the mansion."

Murton gave him a fake scowl. "No, Sir. Just here to collect the rent check. It's past due."

"It's in the mail," Mac said. "So really…what's going on at this uncivilized hour?"

"We need a little information, and I'm afraid we've got some bad news. Someone murdered Travis Lindley earlier this evening."

Mac let his chin fall to his chest. "Ah, Christ. Okay, come inside. I'll get us something to drink."

CHAPTER TWENTY-SIX

Mac led Virgil and Murton into the library, poured himself a glass of scotch, then turned, held the bottle up, and raised his eyebrows.

"We'd better not, Mac," Virgil said. "We're still working."

Mac took a seat in one of the high-backed leather chairs, then said, "Tell me about Travis."

Virgil and Murton spent a few minutes giving the former governor the details of what had happened to Lindley. When Mac heard the part about the wood chipper, his face turned white.

"The good news is he didn't suffer," Murton said. "The crime scene suggests that he was already dead before he went through the machine."

"And they're sure it's Lindley?"

"All but certain," Virgil said. "The Brown County crime scene techs are going to do a rapid DNA on the organic matter. They'll know for sure in a day or two, but really…there is very little doubt. Lindley is dead."

Mac took a rather large drink of his scotch, then said, "And the other victim?"

"Just as dead, obviously," Murton said. "But no one knows who he is. Not yet anyway. Unless something out of the ordinary pops up, we might never know."

They all sat quietly for a few minutes, then Mac said, "You mentioned there was something else you wanted to discuss?"

"I'd like you to work with Sandy and put a stop to the selective harvesting of the Hoosier National Forest," Virgil said.

"Why?"

Virgil barked out a laugh. *"Why?* I can give you a host of reasons why. We've got five murder victims so far, and it's highly likely that you're at the top of the list when it comes to potential victims. This contract that you and Said put together before he died and while you were still in office seems to be the driving force behind all the killings. It's time to put a stop to it."

Mac leaned forward and rested his forearms on his thighs. "If you want to put a stop to the killings, *Detective*, then do your job and catch who is responsible."

Virgil shook his head and tried to keep his voice even. "No. You do not get to speak to me in that manner anymore. You and I are longtime friends, and now business partners, but you're no longer the governor, or my boss. I don't think I can be more clear than that."

Mac leaned back in his chair, and when he spoke, there was a bite in his tone. "I should hope not." Then, after a moment, and a touch softer: "But you are right. Forgive me. Call it force of habit."

Virgil took the apology with a wave of his hand. "Fair enough."

"Regarding the Buffalo Springs restoration process, I don't think I could stop it if I wanted to, and the truth is I don't. There are tens of millions of dollars up for grabs, and all the NFS wants to do is go in and harvest a few trees. Their position is that it will help the forest not only survive, but thrive."

Virgil tried to keep his expression neutral. "Mac, stop reading from the PR statement and think about this for a minute. It's not the forest that needs our help to survive…it's the forest service itself. They're going to take any profits gained from the harvest and use them to support their own administrative funding requirements, all at the expense of the very thing that the American people are already paying them to protect."

Mac held up a hand, palm out. "Jonesy, there are two sides to every argument. I know you know that. But the hard reality is this: The forest service knows what's best. I promise you…if they thought the project would do more harm than good, they wouldn't even consider it. But they don't believe that. As a point of fact, they have scientific proof that selectively culling certain species of timber from the forest will improve the stability of the natural habitat."

"And help fund their operations," Virgil said.

"Look," Mac said, "you basically have two groups who are on the same side having an argument about how you get to a good and reasonable objective. The NFS sees it one way, and the protesters and their nonprofit tree-hugging organizations see it differently, but they both want the same thing, which is to save the forest."

"Why did you say you couldn't stop it if you wanted to?" Murton said.

"Because the National Forest Service is funded by the American people. It's federal. As the CEO of Said, Inc., I hold the contract on behalf of the state, not the federal government."

"A contract that you helped author while in office," Virgil said. "Why not just back out of the deal?"

"Because it wouldn't change anything except the

balance sheet of the company I run. If I tear up the contract, the NFS will simply hire another timber company. And do you know what that means?"

"What?"

"The company I run, and the state, will be out tens of millions of dollars. I'm not only trying to protect the forest, Jonesy, I'm trying to make sure the state and the company I've been tasked to oversee aren't fiscally damaged. And that's exactly what will happen if I back out of the deal."

Virgil understood Mac's position and said so. "I get it. I really do. And I don't think for one single second that you'd put your own interests above the good of the people or the Hoosier National Forest. But there must be something you can do."

"Let me re-examine the contract. I can probably delay any forward momentum, especially since Lindley has been murdered. In the meantime, if you can figure out who is behind the killings, we might be able to spin the whole mess in a way that brings certain aspects of the situation to light."

Murton held up an index finger. "You're saying that a delay due to Lindley's death would cause your company to re-evaluate your position."

"Yes, it would," Mac said. "I don't think the amount

of money we'd gain is big enough to justify the bad PR that would fall in our lap."

Virgil was confused. "But you just told us that if Said, Inc. pulls out of the deal it will still go forward."

"That's right," Mac said. "It will. The state will lose money, the company I run will lose money, but the project will move forward. Ever try to stop the federal government once they've made up their mind? You can't have it both ways, Jonesy."

Virgil gave up. "Okay. I appreciate anything you can do, Mac. How long of a delay are we talking about?"

Mac let a small grin tug at the corner of his mouth. "That depends. How long will this case be open and active?"

"Probably not much long—"

Murton, nobody's idiot, caught on right away and interrupted his brother. "It could go on for years, Mac. One of the victims out at the timber yard is all but unidentifiable. It'll have to remain open and active until we can figure out who he is."

Mac looked at Virgil and smiled. "There you go."

They talked about it a little more, each of them using as much diplomacy and discretion as possible. Virgil wrapped it up by saying, "Well, if the delay means what I think it does, at least Sandy will be happy."

"She might not be as happy as you think when the next budget session comes into play," Mac said.

Virgil shrugged it off. "Like you said…can't have it both ways." Then: "Listen, I almost forgot. Do you have any plans for this Sunday?"

"Nothing out of the ordinary. Why?"

"Sandy is putting a party together for Jonas's birthday. Tent, music, catering, the whole shebang."

Mac smiled. "That woman knows how to throw a party. I'd be delighted. Would you mind if the Popes came along? The entire crew is going to come up this weekend anyway."

"Absolutely, Mac. That'd be fantastic."

Murton slowly turned his head and looked at his brother. "I guess my invitation got lost in the mail."

"I was going to tell you," Virgil said. "It slipped my mind."

"Until just now?"

The governor glanced at his watch. "I can see where this is headed. How about you two work it out in your car? Now would be ideal."

Mac walked them to the door, then told them good night. As they were walking down the front steps of the mansion, Mac called out to Virgil. "Jonesy, one more thing if you will."

Virgil looked at Murton and said, "I'll be right there." Then he turned and walked back up the steps. "Yes?"

Mac was still holding his drink. He took a long slow sip, and looked at nothing when he spoke. "How is Sandy doing?"

Virgil laughed without humor. "Hell, Mac. I should be asking you that question. You spend more time with her lately than I do...although things do seem to be settling down."

"That's not what I'm talking about," Mac said. He shifted his gaze and held Virgil's eyes. "Have you noticed that she's losing weight?"

Once they were in the car, Murton looked at Virgil and said, "What was that?"

"With Mac?"

"No, the gardener."

Virgil swallowed, then said, "He asked me about Sandy's stress level."

"Those were the words he used?"

"Yeah, pretty much," Virgil said.

Murton loved his brother, so he let him have the lie. They rode home in silence, both men thinking the same thing, but neither of them willing to say it out loud.

CHAPTER TWENTY-SEVEN

The next morning, Joyce Parker was back at the dental clinic, ready to finish what she'd started. The electronic patient files had to be matched up with their paper counterparts, and once she had that finished, she'd be able to insert the form letters into the paper files and box them up for storage.

The first thing she did was pull every record from the filing cabinets, and set them on the counter. With that done, she did a quick count, then couldn't quite remember the number of files stored on the server. She brought the reception computer up, then sat down and ran a quick tally. When she saw the number was two hundred and three, she nodded to herself, the memory of her count from the previous day popping back inside her brain.

But her count of the hard copies didn't match with the computer. Had she miscounted? Parker let out a sigh, then went back and carefully recounted the paper files that sat on the counter. When she was finished, she had the same number as before. Exactly two hundred. Parker was missing three files. But which ones?

Only one way to find out. Joyce Parker didn't want to do it, but there didn't seem to be any other option. She printed off a list of patient names, then started going through the stacks on the counter one by one, matching those against her printout. Since she'd stacked the files on the counter in alphabetical order, she was working through the files starting with Z. It was either that, or rearrange the files, which didn't seem to be worth the extra effort.

When she found a match, she placed a little tick mark on her sheet. She did the Z's—there were only two of those, then moved on to Y—working her way backward through the alphabet. She was only fifteen minutes into the task when she found the discrepancy. The three paper files that were unaccounted for belonged to the Quinn family…Carl, Luke, and Caleb.

Joyce stopped at that point, then thought it was possible that the Quinn files might have been slipped into another patient's records by mistake. She'd seen it happen before…someone was in a hurry and something got stuck in the wrong folder. It took her another forty-five minutes to check, but in the end, she didn't find them. She even went back and checked the drawers to make sure they hadn't somehow slipped out of the rack.

Parker sat down in one of the reception desk chairs and thought about the Quinns. The memories came flooding back so hard and fast it felt like she'd been slapped in the face. The father killed, the youngest son, Caleb, crippled for life. Doctor Campos had fixed Caleb's teeth after the accident. Joyce remembered well because the young man had been permanently disabled. His older brother, Luke, had to help him sit and stand, and Caleb hobbled back and forth from the waiting area to the exam room with the help of the one thing the state detective had asked her about the last time they spoke…someone who used a cane.

Parker dug around in her purse, and found the detective's card. When she called his cell number, it went straight to voicemail. "Detective Mayo, this is Joyce Parker, Doctor Campos's office manager. I have some information that might be relevant to your case. Please call me back."

She set the phone on the counter and stared at the printout she'd been using. Parker had a pen in her hand, and without really realizing what she was doing, she began to circle the name Quinn over and over.

She waited half an hour for the detective to call her back, but he never did, so Joyce picked up the phone and made another call.

Virgil and Murton were sitting in the computer lab with Becky. "You're positive?" Virgil said.

"Absolutely, Jonesy. We ran the print through the state and federal databases. There's no match."

Murton rolled the kinks out of his neck and said, "So whoever killed and mutilated Lindley and that other guy has never been printed. Doesn't help us, but it doesn't really hurt us, either. When we do finally catch the guy, it'll be another nail in his coffin."

"Yeah, but we'd be able to hammer it shut faster if we could figure out who it is," Virgil said. Then to Becky: "What about the Reddick woman?"

"What about her?" Becky said.

"Yesterday you told me that Campos never bought a car from Harwood, and Harwood was never a patient of Campos. You didn't say anything about Reddick."

"Sorry, I meant to," Becky said. "She was neither a patient of Campos nor a customer of Harwood."

"Doesn't really matter at this point, Jones-man,"

Murton said. "We know what the connections between the victims are."

"I know, I know," Virgil said. "But we don't have anything to work with."

Rosencrantz walked into the lab and said, "Anything on the print?"

"Came back dry," Virgil said. "What have you heard out of Brown County?"

"Not much. I spoke with Lisa this morning and she says the crime scene people ended up taking the entire machine back to their lab…body and all. The fire department couldn't get the machine apart at the site. I guess the thing was jammed up pretty bad, so they loaded it on a flatbed and hauled it away. The coroner and his people are surgically removing the remains as we speak."

"Glad I'm not there to see that," Murton said.

"I'm still seeing it," Rosencrantz said.

Virgil looked at Rosencrantz. "Where's Ross?"

"Sick day."

Virgil let his eyes go flat. "Sick, sick day? Or sick day?"

"Yes," Rosencrantz said, averting his eyes when he spoke.

Virgil didn't push it. "What about Mayo and Ortiz? I haven't seen them this morning."

"I told them they could take the morning off," Becky said. "They put in quite a few extra hours over the last couple of days." When she saw the look on Virgil's face, Becky said, "What? I'm simply trying to keep your overtime budget under control."

Virgil didn't really care. "Yeah, okay."

"I'll tell you what we should be looking for," Murton said.

Virgil put his feet up on the edge of the counter and crossed his ankles. "What's that?"

"Someone who had a beef with Travis Lindley. Terminated employees, that kind of thing."

"Seems like a long shot," Virgil said.

"It probably is," Murton said. "But you have to ask yourself…got any better ideas?"

Virgil had to admit he didn't. He looked at Rosencrantz and said, "Get with either Mayhall or Sheriff Young and have them send up Midway Timber's employee records. Just the names for now."

"No problem. I'll ask Lisa. Probably happen quicker if the request goes through her."

"Do that," Virgil said.

Rosencrantz walked out to make the call, and after that, no one had much to say. They were stuck, and everyone knew it. Something else had to happen before they could move forward.

And then it did.

Sarah walked into the computer lab, looked directly at Virgil and said, "There's a woman on the phone who is trying to reach Oscar."

"He won't be in until this afternoon," Virgil said. "Take a message and let her know he'll call back."

"I already tried that. Now she wants to speak with whoever is in charge."

"Tell her I'm not here either," Becky said.

"You guys should take your show on the road," Virgil said. "Anyone ever tell you that?" Then to Sarah: "Did she give her name?"

"Joyce Parker."

Murton tipped a finger at Virgil. "Isn't that the dental clinic woman?"

Virgil dropped his feet from the counter. "Yeah. She probably wants an update. I'll speak with her. What line is she on, Sarah?"

Sarah pointed at the phone, a wry grin on her face. "The one that's blinking." She turned to go back to her desk in the operations area, but Virgil stopped her. "Hey, Sarah?"

"Yes?"

"How's Ross?"

"He's fine. Why?"

Virgil picked up the receiver, pinched it between his ear and shoulder, his finger hovering over the blinking button on the phone. "No reason." He hit the button and said, "Detective Virgil Jones, Major Crimes Unit. How may I help you, Miss Parker?"

"I'm sorry," Parker said. "I tried to reach Detective Mayo, but he isn't answering his phone."

"Detective Mayo won't be in until later this afternoon," Virgil said somewhat impatiently. "If you're calling for an update on the case, I'm afraid we don't have anything we can share with you at the moment. But rest assured that we're doing everything in our power to capture Doctor Campos's killer."

"I'm not calling for an update, Detective. I'm calling to offer one."

"Excuse me?" Virgil said. He punched the Speaker button on the phone so Murton and Becky could hear.

"When Detective Mayo interviewed me, he asked if any of our patients used a cane. I told him we had a few, but they were all elderly. I'm afraid I may have spoken too soon…or perhaps I didn't put as much thought into the question as I should have. A few years ago we had a patient come in who had been hurt very badly in an accident that also killed his father. The patient was a young man by the name of Caleb Quinn. He has a brother named Luke. But Caleb was the one with the cane."

"Would you mind if I put you on hold for just a moment?" Virgil said. "I'll be right back. Don't hang up."

Virgil punched the Hold button without waiting for a reply, then looked at Becky. "Becks?"

"I'm already checking, Jonesy."

Virgil went back to the phone. "When was the last time you or Doctor Campos saw either of the Quinn brothers?"

"Well, not since Doctor Campos fixed Caleb's teeth after the accident. According to their charts they've not been back. I guess that's why I forgot about them."

"What made you remember?"

"I was matching up the patient files and realized that the paper copies of the Quinn family are all missing. I have no idea where they are."

"Okay, please hold."

"Got them," Becky said. "In the electronic patient files we got from the clinic, and the BMV records. Address listed in Orange County, outside of Paoli."

Virgil looked at his brother. "Get Cool headed this way."

As it happened, Cool was making a test flight in the helicopter after finishing up the maintenance on the tail rotor. He took Murton's call from the air and said he could be there in less than two minutes.

Murton told him they'd be waiting. He ended the call, looked at Virgil and said, "Two minutes or less."

Virgil stood. "Okay. If this Parker woman is right, she's about to be our new best friend. Becks, keep the intel coming. I want everything you can find on these two guys. Pipe it right to the sat phones. And tell Rosie to stay on top of the employment records with Midway Timber. If he can't get anyone to cooperate, I want him to go down to Brown County, box them up himself and bring them back."

"You got it," Becky said. "Anything else?"

They all heard the sound of the state helicopter approaching. Virgil and Murton started for the door that would lead them to the roof. Virgil looked over his shoulder and said, "I don't know. You're the boss, remember?"

Once they were gone, Becky said to no one, "You got that right."

CHAPTER TWENTY-EIGHT

THEY WERE A LITTLE OVER HALFWAY TO ORANGE County when Becky called. Virgil grabbed the satellite phone and said, "Talk to me."

"If it's not them, I'll eat my mouse pad. Rosencrantz got in touch with Mayhall who was back out at the Midway Timber yard. He just emailed me the employment records. Caleb Quinn was severely injured in a logging accident while working the Yellowwood with his brother and father. The father was killed, and the older brother, Luke, was fired for cause. I'd bet my trust fund against your new Range Rover that one of them will have prints that match the Lindley scene."

"Great work, Becks. And no bet. What's the name of that Orange County detective again?"

"Buckley. Jason Buckley."

"Hang on a second," Virgil said. He tapped Cool on the shoulder. "That address I gave you?"

"Yeah?"

"What's the closest you can get us without it sounding like an invasion?"

Cool punched a few buttons on the nav unit and fiddled with the display until he saw what he needed. "The Paoli Hospital helipad is about two miles away from the address you gave me. They'll never hear us, and even if they do, it will sound like a hospital medevac."

"That's your landing zone."

"Roger that," Cool said.

"How long?" Virgil said.

"Should be about twenty minutes."

Virgil brought the phone back up. "Becky?"

"Still here."

"Get in touch with Buckley and tell him to meet us at the Paoli Hospital helipad. We'll be there in less than twenty minutes. Don't give him Quinn's address or any names. I don't want the county to screw this one up."

"I'm on it, Jonesy. Listen, you guys be careful."

"We always are. We'll call when we've got them."

After Joyce Parker finished her call with the detective, she looked at the list of patient names she'd been working with. She'd circled the Quinn name so many times she could barely read it. Then the doubts began to creep in. Had she overreacted? The Quinn family had always seemed so nice. Why in the world would they ever want to hurt Paul? It simply didn't make sense.

Then another thought occurred. Didn't the Quinn family have a daughter? Laura, or Lilly, or something like that. She went back to the files but didn't find any more Quinns. Then she remembered. Lisa. As soon as the name came back to her, she remembered that Lisa had married her neighbor's son, Jerry Young.

She went back to the Y files, and Lisa Young was right there, along with her deceased husband. They'd moved up to Brown County, and Jerry had been killed in some sort of accident. And hadn't she heard that Lisa was now the sheriff? Maybe she should call and let her know what was happening…ask about Caleb in case the information she'd given the detective was just a coincidence. Since Young was a law enforcement officer, what was the harm?

Parker got on the internet, found the number for the Brown County Sheriff's Department and made the call.

Two minutes later she was on the phone with the sheriff.

"Sheriff Young? This is Joyce Parker from the dental clinic in Paoli. I'm the office manager for Doctor Campos. Do you remember me?"

Young tried to keep her voice even, but wasn't sure if she succeeded or not. "Yes, vaguely. How may I help you?"

"Well, I'm actually trying to understand why your father and both your brother's files are missing from Doctor Campos's office."

"Missing?"

"Yes, and the police think Caleb might somehow be involved in Doctor Campos's murder. I haven't seen Caleb or Luke since shortly after the accident that killed your father. This must all be some sort of big misunderstanding, but I can't figure it out."

Young squeezed the phone so hard she heard it crack. "I'm sure it's a mistake. In fact, I'm positive. Caleb is dead, Joyce. He's been dead for years now."

"Oh, I'm so sorry to hear that," Parker said. "Your poor family…you've all been through so much."

"I appreciate the call, Joyce, but I'm afraid I have to go. We're a little busy at the moment. It was nice to hear from you." Then Young hung up without waiting for a reply.

Detective Buckley was waiting when Cool landed. Virgil and Murton climbed out, told Buckley where they were going and why, then they all climbed into his squad car and took off toward Quinn's house.

"Are we going to need any backup?" Buckley said.

"Might not be a bad idea to get a few units at the perimeter," Virgil said. "Just make sure they stay back. We don't want to spook these guys. One is supposedly crippled or something, so hopefully there won't be much trouble."

Buckley got on the radio and made the call.

"A crippled guy can still shoot," Murton said.

"Then don't forget to duck," Virgil said.

Nerves.

Young ended the call with the Parker woman, then immediately dialed her brother. "Luke? It's me."

"What do you want?" Luke said.

"Are you drunk?"

"None of your business. Don't call me again."

"Luke, shut up and listen. The cops figured out

what you and Caleb have been doing. They're on the way to pick you up right now."

"Then there's going to be some dead cops." Luke picked up the shotgun and walked to the window. When he looked outside, he didn't see anything.

"Why'd you do it, Luke? Why'd you kill Caleb?"

"I didn't kill him. It was an accident. He tripped and fell. I was only trying to get rid of the body."

"By putting him through a wood chipper? Have you completely lost your mind?"

Yes, Luke thought. *I believe I have.* "I didn't know what else to do."

"Luke, you're the only family I have left. No matter what you've done, I don't want to see you hurt."

"Too late, Sis. And don't worry, I'll keep my mouth shut."

"Luke…"

But Luke was already gone.

Young hung up the phone and realized she was slipping away herself. She wrote a short letter of resignation, printed it out, then removed the badge from her uniform, unstrapped her gun belt, and set everything on the center of her desk. Then she walked out the door and never looked back.

Luke loaded the shotgun and stuck extra shells in his pockets. If they wanted to bring the fight to him, so be it. He looked around the cabin and hoped he would get them all without doing too much damage. Pop always loved the place.

Buckley turned into Quinn's driveway, then stopped. "This place is pretty isolated. If we walk in, they'll never hear us coming."

Virgil looked at his brother. "Murt?"

"It's a good idea. But I'd back the car out to the road and have your other units move up. Keep the drive clear in case we need medics."

Virgil looked at Buckley. "Do it."

Once they were ready, Virgil and Murton and Buckley crept up the long drive, made the bend, and the cabin came into view. Murton looked at Virgil and said, "I'll cut through the trees and take the back."

"Watch your ass," Virgil said.

Murton said he would and disappeared into the trees. Virgil and Buckley continued up the drive, hugging the tree line and doing their best to stay out of sight. When it was obvious that they could no longer remain hidden, both men ran toward the house and flattened themselves on either side of the front door.

Buckley was about to knock and announce their presence, but Virgil stopped him. He lowered his voice and said, "Wait. Give my partner time. He had further to go."

Buckley nodded. They gave Murton another thirty seconds, then Buckley, who was feeling anxious about waiting, touched eyes with Virgil. He held up three fingers, then pointed at himself. The message was clear. Buckley would kick the door on the count of three.

Virgil gave him a nod, and it was the last thing Buckley ever saw because when he moved to kick the door, a shotgun blast blew him right off the front porch. Virgil spun away from the gunfire, got his foot tangled in an old rocking chair, then kicked it free, vaulted over the porch railing and ran around the side of the cabin toward the back.

MURTON HEARD THE BLAST AND KNEW THE WORST thing he could do in the moment would be to try to gain entry from the back. He covered the door for ten seconds, then backed away, turned and ran toward the front of the house to check on his brother and Buckley.

Virgil met Murton at the corner of the house. "Buckley's down. Took it right in the chest. I think he's gone, man. We're going to need those other units up here."

"If they heard the gunfire, they should be on their way."

"And if they didn't, we might lose this guy in the woods," Virgil said.

"I'll run down there," Murton said. "There's a path that leads from the rear of the cabin through the trees. Watch the back. I don't think he'll try the front."

Virgil said he would and moved to take cover behind a tree. He watched Murton move off, and he'd only gotten ten yards from the corner of the house when Luke Quinn stepped out and leveled the shotgun at Murton's back.

But Virgil was ready. He didn't shout out any commands to drop the weapon, or get on the ground. There just wasn't time. He stepped out from behind the tree and began firing so fast he burned through a fifteen round clip in less than six seconds, moving closer and closer to his target the entire time.

Murton spun around at the sound of the first shot, then fell to the ground in case Quinn managed to fire.

He never did. Luke Quinn was dead.

Virgil ejected his empty clip, then slapped another in place and released the slide. He hurried over toward Murton, his gun pointed at the back of the house the entire time. "You okay?"

"I am now," Murton said. "You just saved my life, Virgil."

Both men could hear the sirens screaming up the drive. "I think I owe you a few anyway. Besides, I wouldn't want you to miss the party."

Murton heard shouting from the front of the house, and said, "Holster your weapon, Jones-man. And get your badge out and visible. These guys don't know us."

Murton had no sooner spoken the words when a lone deputy ran around the corner of the house and saw Virgil and Murton standing there with their weapons still in their hands.

Then the deputy did what Virgil hadn't. He began screaming commands that were all but impossible to follow. "Freeze. Down on the ground. Hands in the air. Drop your weapons."

Virgil and Murton both carefully set their guns in the grass, then Virgil said, "State Police. Major Crimes Unit. We're going to show you our badges." Both men slowly pulled their badges out as the deputy approached. "Stop pointing your gun at us. I'm Detective Virgil Jones. This is my partner, Murton Wheeler. You've got a man down out front, Detective Buckley. Get the medics rolling. And watch the house. Our intelligence says there might be two guys here."

When the deputy saw their badges he relaxed a fraction. "Sorry, Detectives. Didn't know who you were."

"Not your fault," Virgil said. "Mind if we grab our guns now?"

"Go ahead. And we won't be needing the medics. Just the coroner. Detective Buckley is dead." Then the radio on the deputy's shoulder mic squawked, and a scrambled voice said, "All clear."

"Looks like the house is empty," the deputy said.

Murton looked at his brother. "Still missing one. He might be out in the woods."

Virgil walked over to look at the man he'd killed. "Hey, Murt, come over here for a second."

Murton and the deputy both walked over. "What have you got?" Murton said.

Virgil was standing in a way that blocked the view of the body. "I want you to take a look at this guy. Just a quick glance, then give me your impression." Virgil stepped aside, and Murton moved forward.

After a few seconds, Murton looked away, closed his eyes momentarily, then said, "He looks a lot like that guy that only made it halfway through the wood chipper."

"That's exactly what I thought."

"Wood chipper?" The deputy said.

"It's a long story," Murton said. "And trust me, you don't want the details. Better get your crime scene people headed this way. We need to print this guy and get DNA samples."

"They're already en route," the deputy said.

They moved around to the front of the cabin and found a cluster of deputies surrounding their dead detective. "Did Buckley have any family?" Virgil asked. "Wife, kids?"

"Nope," one of the deputies said. "He was all alone."

Virgil couldn't decide if that made him feel better or worse.

CHAPTER TWENTY-NINE

It took the next two days to wrap up the minutia of the case. The fingerprints taken from Luke Quinn's body matched those found at Travis Lindley's property, and a rapid DNA test—while not quite as reliable as a standard test—confirmed that the body discovered in the wood chipper was Caleb Quinn. Photographs of the Quinn brothers recovered from their residence backed up the DNA, and a follow-up interview between Mayhall and a longtime senior employee of Midway Timber solidified it.

The sullen man and the fallen boy were both finally gone for good.

DNA testing of the organic matter also showed that the owner of Midway Timber, Travis Lindley, had been the other victim. No one was really all that surprised to hear it.

Mac exercised his rights under the provisions of the contract between his company, the NFS, and the state, and had his lawyers back out of the Buffalo Springs contract.

Once that was done, Sandy and Cora crafted a very carefully worded press release that detailed the murder victims' efforts to stop the Buffalo Springs restoration process. The national press picked the story up and ran with it, and the public at large—always ready for a good fight—took up the cause and started to make some noise. The director of the National Forest Service released a press statement as well, stating in part, that due to the unforeseen and tragic events that had played out as a result of their plan, the harvest of the Hoosier National forest would be put on hold indefinitely while they re-evaluated their position and looked at other options.

It wasn't much, but everyone agreed it was better than nothing.

The Brown County Sheriff's Department wrote Lisa Young's sudden resignation off as job-related stress and kept the whole thing as quiet as possible. Mayhall stepped up and took over in her absence.

In a strategic move, Mac's lawyers helped Frank Reddick file a lawsuit in federal court seeking damages from the National Forest Service. The suit claimed that had the NFS not kept insisting that they were going to move forward with the Buffalo Springs restoration project, his wife—a staunch advocate against the destruction of the forest's natural habitat—wouldn't have been murdered.

No one thought he'd ever see a dime. But it helped keep the pressure up.

John Harwood's ex-wife filed suit against Midway Timber using essentially the same argument Reddick had. She further claimed that she and her ex were in the process of reconciliation. No one believed her story and the case was tossed out before it ever made it to the judge. Not that it mattered. Midway Timber filed for bankruptcy and had to shut down.

The Lindley House received a flood of visitors after all the press, but when it was discovered that Travis Lindley, and the founder of Orange County, Jonathon Lindley, weren't related in any way whatsoever, the traffic died down and went away.

Emma Kennedy, the caretaker of the historical site couldn't have been happier. She later went on to receive the VOC award for volunteer of the year.

Sandy called Virgil at work late in the afternoon on Friday and informed him that the tent company wasn't available for a Sunday erection.

"I am," Virgil said.

"Virgil!"

"Just keeping you up to speed on your options," Virgil said.

"Anyway, I wanted to let you know that they'll be out first thing Saturday morning to set up."

"That's fine," Virgil said. He knew what was

coming next, so he said, "And to answer your follow-up question…that's fine too."

"How do you know what I was going to ask?"

"Because as your husband, I can practically read your mind…especially when it comes to parties."

"Is that right?"

"Yep."

"Okay," Sandy said. "Let's hear it. What was I going to say?"

"You were going to suggest that since the tent will be up a day early, we should invite all our adult friends over on Saturday for pre-party festivities. Dinner, drinks, dancing, like that."

"That's a great idea, Virgil. Will you tell everyone at the shop and let them know they are all welcome?"

"Sure," Virgil said. "But why does it sound like you're trying not to laugh."

"Because you need to polish your crystal ball, or whatever."

"So that's not what you were going to ask me?"

"Nope."

"Well, what was it?"

"I was going to ask if you'd make sure all the dog poop was picked up out of the backyard."

Virgil wasn't sure if his wife was joking about the pre-party idea or not. He did know she was serious about the dog poop, though. He laughed at himself and said, "I can do that."

"And you'll tell everyone at the MCU about the party?"

"That's what I was talking about."

"Very funny, mister."

"Are you okay?" Virgil said. "You sound tired."

"I am. Not to mention I've got a headache that makes me feel like my eyes are bleeding."

"Maybe you should go home and take it easy. It's almost quitting time anyway. I'll be there in an hour or so."

"You know what? I think I'll do just that. See you in a while, boyfriend."

VIRGIL SENT AN EMAIL TO EVERYONE AND INVITED them over for dinner and drinks on Saturday. Then he sent one to Cool and told him to bring Julia if she wasn't working. He also sent one to both Mac and Cora, and made sure Mac knew to invite the Pope crew. He was just finishing up when Rosencrantz stuck his head through the door. "Got a sec?"

"Sure, c'mon in."

Rosencrantz took a chair in front of Virgil's desk and said, "Did you hear about Lisa Young?"

Virgil tipped his head to the side. "No, I've been pretty busy with the paperwork. Is she okay?"

Rosencrantz lifted his shoulders. "Yes and no. She resigned from the sheriff's department."

Virgil drew his mouth into a tight line. "To tell you the truth, Rosie, I'm not surprised. I mean no disrespect when I say this, but based on what I've seen and heard, she wasn't exactly cut out for the job anyway."

Rosencrantz nodded. "Yeah, I was thinking the same thing. Anyway, I talked to her and she sounds like she could use some cheering up. Think it'd be okay if I brought her to the party?"

"Sure, why not? The more the merrier, right?"

Rosencrantz thanked his boss, then said, "If there's nothing else, I think I'm going to take off."

"Yeah, go ahead." Then, "You okay, Tom?"

Rosencrantz stood and walked over to the window of Virgil's office and looked outside. When he spoke, he had his back to Virgil. "I heard Harry was back to work, so I went over to the statehouse today during my lunch break to say hello."

Harry was Chief Justice Harold Freeman, and he'd been injured in the same shooting that had cost Rosencrantz's fiancé, Carla Martin, her life. "How is he?"

"He's fine. Sad about what happened with Carla. He's thinking of retiring."

"Hate to lose him," Virgil said. "He's a good guy."

"He is, isn't he?" Rosencrantz said, his voice monotone and flat.

"What is it, Tom?"

"When I was leaving I ran into Baker and Sandy at the elevator." Rosencrantz turned and faced his boss. "Maybe it's not my place to say, but Sandy doesn't look well."

After Rosencrantz had left his office, Virgil picked up the phone and made a call. "Hey, it's Jonesy. Do me a favor?"

"Name it."

"Hop in the helicopter and fly out to the house, will you?"

"When do you need me?"

"Ninety minutes work?"

"Sure. That's plenty of time. See you then."

Virgil made it home and was waiting on the deck when he heard the familiar beat of the helicopter's rotor blades. He watched his friend fly out over the pond, turn into the wind, then let the aircraft settle gently on the landing pad. Once everything was shut down, Virgil walked closer, opened the door and said, "How are you, Bell?"

Bell hopped out of the chopper, pushed his John Lennon glasses up on his nose, and straightened his mop of gray hair. "I'm fine, Jonesy. How's life in the big leagues?"

"Hectic. Listen, before I forget, we're having a little party Saturday night if you can make it."

Bell made what Virgil could only describe as a Dick Cheney face, and said, "Geez, I wish I could, but I've got plans. Going to an airshow up in Kalamazoo."

"Ah, that's okay. Maybe next time."

"So what's up?" Bell said.

"I've got a patient I want you to look at. She's not going to like it, either."

"Why not?"

"Because I didn't tell her you were coming."

"Sandy, or Huma?"

Virgil's jaw quivered when he spoke. "Sandy." He swallowed, turned away for a second, then said, "I think she's sick, Bell. I mean, like, really sick. She's getting headaches, losing weight, and not sleeping. It's not just me…people are starting to notice."

Bell looked at Virgil over the tops of his glasses and said, "Let me get my bag."

VIRGIL WAS RIGHT. SANDY DIDN'T LIKE IT.

"Virgil Jones, it is not your place to make a doctor's appointment on my behalf."

Virgil stayed calm…as calm as possible, anyway. "You're right. It's not. But since you wouldn't do it, I did. Rosencrantz told me he saw you today at the statehouse."

Sandy had her arms crossed defensively over her chest. "Yes, and what of it? We ran into each other at the elevator, said hello, and that was that."

"He's one of the most observant guys I know, Sandy. And that, as you say, *wasn't* that. When he walked into my office this afternoon he was so concerned he could barely make eye contact with me. Murt has noticed you're losing weight, and so has Mac. Both of them have spoken to me about it. You're the only one who refuses to acknowledge that something might be wrong. It's time to get you checked out. If you don't want to do it for yourself, please, do it for me and the boys."

"May I interject something here?" Bell said.

Sandy turned to Bell. "What?"

"First of all, you do look like you're losing weight. I know it's been a while since we've seen each other, and I hear you are under a tremendous amount of stress lately, but I can tell just by looking at you that an exam is in order."

Sandy loved Bell. He'd helped save her and Wyatt's lives a number of years ago when Sandy was still pregnant, and prior to that, he'd helped Virgil free himself of an opiate addiction. Given all that he'd done for their family, how could she say no?

"Okay, Bell, but what kind of exam are we talking about here?"

"A basic one. I'll draw some blood, do a quick urine dip, listen to your heart, lungs…like that. I'll be out of your hair in no time."

Sandy gave in. "Let's get started then. What do I have to do first?"

Bell reached into his bag and pulled out a sterile plastic cup and handed it to Sandy. "Go into the bathroom and pee in this."

Sandy gave Virgil a look, then took the cup and

disappeared into the master bath. A few minutes later she returned and handed the container to Bell.

"Is your urine always this dark?"

"No, not usually," Sandy said. "Is that bad?"

Bell shook his head. "Not necessarily. It could be simple dehydration, or you might have a urinary tract infection. Maybe both. You said you've been feeling tired?"

"Yes. I seem to ache all over, too. Headaches off and on as well."

"Let's get a quick blood pressure for a baseline," Bell said. He slipped the cuff around Sandy's arm, then pumped the bulb and got the pressure reading.

"Well, you're high on both your systolic and diastolic readings, but that's to be expected given the way you've been feeling."

Bell slipped into a pair of surgical gloves and said, "Excuse me for a moment while I run a quick test." He took the container into the bathroom, and five minutes later he was back. "Any nausea or vomiting?"

"A little of both. You know what it reminds me of?"

"What?" Virgil said.

"When I was pregnant with Wyatt."

Bell chuckled. "Well, we can rule that out, can't we?" Sandy had undergone a full hysterectomy after

Wyatt was born. She'd been shot, and it was the only way to save her from bleeding out.

"I guess so," Sandy said. "What did the pee show?"

"It looks like you've got a UTI. There's a bit of blood in your urine, and that's usually the first sign of trouble. Just a moment please." Bell took out his phone, pressed a series of buttons, then looked at Virgil and said, "What pharmacy do you use?"

Virgil looked at Sandy and said, "What pharmacy do we use?"

Sandy gave Virgil a look that all husbands know well, then answered Bell.

"Thanks." He pressed a few more buttons on his phone, then said, "I just sent a prescription to your pharmacy. It's an antibiotic called Bactrim. I want you to stay on it until it's all gone. You might want to pick up some probiotics as well so you don't upset the good bacteria in your stomach."

"I'll go get that stuff right now," Virgil said. He was already feeling relieved. "I'll be back in half an hour. Will you still be here, Bell?"

"Oh, yes, I'm certain I will be. I'll want to do a quick blood test…I've got strips that can give me some basic information—glucose levels and whatnot—and there's one more thing we need to do."

"Okay," Virgil said. He gave Sandy a kiss, touched eyes with Bell, and said, "Thank you."

Once Virgil was gone, Bell drew the blood, then set it aside. Then he reached into his kit and pulled out a piece of IV tubing and a clear plastic bag that contained a yellowish fluid.

"What the heck is that?" Sandy said.

"This is what we call a banana bag. It's a long-standing treatment used for patients who are in need of rehydration and electrolytes."

"What's in it?" Sandy said.

"It's filled with vitamins and minerals, including magnesium sulfate, folic acid, and thiamine. That's why it's yellow, and why it's called a banana bag. Want to know something funny?"

"Sure."

"Hold still for a minute while I get this needle in." Once Bell had the line in Sandy's arm, he taped it down, then got the IV going.

"You said there was something funny?"

Bell let his head wobble back and forth. "Well, maybe funny isn't the right word, but these things are normally used for chronic alcoholics. You haven't gone to day drinking, have you?"

"Very funny, Bell. And no, I haven't." Sandy looked at the bag, and said, "How long does this take?"

"About forty-five minutes or so. Let me take a look at the blood. By the time that bag is empty, you're going to feel like a new woman."

Bell was right. By the time Virgil returned with the antibiotics, the bag was empty, and Sandy felt like she was ready to run a marathon. "Boy, I haven't felt this good since I was in my twenties," Sandy said.

Bell smiled. "The thing to remember is this: What you're feeling right now is only temporary. Your glucose levels are much higher than they should be, as is your blood pressure. Both of those things can be a result of the infection, so don't fool around and kid yourself that you don't need the antibiotics. If you don't take them, you'll end up in the hospital."

Virgil gave his wife an evil grin. "Don't worry, Bell, she'll take them."

CHAPTER THIRTY

Late the next afternoon Virgil and Sandy's guests started arriving. The tent was up, Robert was manning the grill, Delroy and Virgil were making sure everyone had plenty to drink, and after dinner, as the day turned to night, Huma got the kids settled into bed.

The Pope crew was there, Nichole spending her time with Mac, while Wu and Nicky bent Becky's ear about computer-related issues. Wu's wife, Linda, and Cool's girlfriend, Julia Evans—an ortho doc—spoke with Sandy and Cora about their new positions.

Murton, Ross, Ortiz, Cool, Rosencrantz, and Lisa Young all sat around and talked about the case they'd just closed.

Virgil walked over, looked at Ortiz and said, "Why the heck didn't Mayo show up?"

"I'm not entirely sure. He said there was something bugging him about the Quinn case. He's at the shop trying to figure it out."

"Like what?" Young said. Her tone was just shy of venomous. "I thought you guys had it all put to bed."

Virgil gave her a shrug. "We do. I'm sure it's just a formality."

"Well, I hope so," Young said.

There was something about the woman that Virgil didn't like. She was a little scattered. If he didn't know better—and he wasn't sure he didn't—he thought that there might be a bipolar issue there. The truth was, if it hadn't been for Rosencrantz, Virgil probably would have told her to get lost. Of all the people at the party, she was the only outsider. But he didn't want to upset his friend, or make a scene, so he kept his mouth shut and tried to ignore her.

Someone turned the music up and a few people hit the dance floor. Then pretty soon nearly everyone was out on the helipad, dancing the night away. At one point, Virgil grabbed Murton and pointed at Wu. "You know, for a guy who can fight as well as he does, he sure doesn't float like a butterfly…if you take my meaning."

Murton turned and looked at Wu, who was jerking his arms and legs around like he was having some sort of spasm. Murton laughed and said, "Yeah, but he can sting like a bee."

Rosencrantz and Young sat under the tent. Young said she didn't feel like dancing. Rosencrantz admitted he didn't either.

The night rolled on.

MAYO WAS AT THE MAJOR CRIMES UNIT FACILITY, working away in the computer lab. He knew he was missing a good party, but there was something about the case that just didn't sit well with him. The more he considered it, the sillier the thought seemed, but as a long-time cop, he trusted his gut. The question he couldn't put to rest was why would Luke and Caleb Quinn steal their own dental records after killing Campos. It simply didn't make sense.

Then again, the criminal mind rarely did, but the fact remained, had they not taken their own files, they might have gotten away with it all…at least for a little while longer.

He brought their files up and examined all three. They were mostly filled with medical jargon that Mayo didn't understand, so he focused his attention on the personal questionnaire that every new patient had to fill out. Luke Quinn had listed his father, Carl, as his emergency contact. Caleb had done the same. Carl had listed a phone number, but no name. Mayo thought that odd, so he got into one of Becky's special databases and did a reverse phone lookup, but the number came back as a cell phone. Out of desperation, he called the number and wasn't surprised to find it was no longer in service.

Mayo remembered from the reports that Carl Quinn had died in a logging accident, and his wife had died a few years earlier. He thought the number must have belonged to her. But Mayo was a stickler for details and didn't want to let it go. He picked up the phone and made another call.

"Joyce? It's Oscar…uh, Detective Mayo, with the Major Crimes Unit."

"Of course, Oscar. How are you?"

"Still working, if you can believe that."

"Pretty late for a Saturday, isn't it?" Parker said.

"Yes, and I'm even missing a pretty nice party, to boot."

"Well, at least no one will ever be able to complain about your work ethic. What can I do for you?"

Mayo knew he had to be careful because Parker didn't know that they'd gained access to Campos's patient records. "I'm putting the finishing touches on my report for the boss, and I wanted to ask you a few questions. They probably don't mean anything, but I like to be thorough."

"Sure, go ahead."

"When you discovered the Quinns' files were missing, didn't that strike you as odd?"

"Of course. That's why I tried to call you."

"And it stands to reason that had those files not been missing, you probably wouldn't have remembered about the Quinn brothers. Do I have that right?"

Parker sighed. "Yes, I suppose so. I guess there is always the possibility that I would have eventually remembered, but I guess now we'll never know. Thank God for that, huh?"

"Yeah, that's true enough," Mayo said. "But then let me ask you this: If you were the Quinn brothers, would you have taken the files?"

Parker didn't hesitate. "Yes, I think I would have."

"Why?" Mayo said.

"To cover my tracks. I don't think the Quinn men would have thought that someone would take the time to compare the paper files with the ones on the server. They took their own files to cover the fact that they were patients of Doctor Campos. It makes perfect sense when you think about it. Of course it didn't at the time."

Mayo was confused. "I don't understand what you

mean by that. At what time?"

"When I was trying to figure out why the files were missing. When I called Sheriff Young and told her about the files she didn't seem to understand it either."

"Joyce?"

"Yes?"

"I thought we agreed that any conversations we had regarding the case were to remain confidential."

"Well, we did, but she's the sheriff, so I didn't think that applied to her. Besides, since she's their sister, I thought she might have some idea where the files—"

"Excuse me. Wait. What did you just say?"

"Sheriff Young. The Quinn brothers were her siblings. I thought you knew that. Her entire family has been ripped to shreds. I don't know how that poor woman can stand the pressure of it all."

Mayo swallowed, then said, "Joyce, I'm afraid I have to go. Something just came up. Thanks for your help."

Everyone had worn themselves out dancing, and people were scattered about the backyard in groups of twos and threes chatting amongst themselves. Virgil and Murton were down by the pond, Sandy, Mac and

Cora were standing in the middle of the yard, and Wu was demonstrating some sort of sophisticated chokehold to Ross and Rosencrantz.

Lisa Young sat by herself under the tent.

MAYO RAN FROM THE BUILDING, JUMPED IN HIS SQUAD car and headed for Virgil's house. He knew Young was there with Rosencrantz, and while he wasn't sure she was a threat, he also knew she very well could be. He reached into his breast pocket for his phone to call and warn Virgil, then realized he'd left the MCU facility in such a hurry that he'd forgotten the damned thing.

He hit his lights and siren, then reached down and switched frequencies on his Motorola police radio and made the call to the troopers guarding Virgil's road. He explained the potential threat, and told the troopers to move in and secure the governor.

The troopers jumped in their squad cars, hit their lights and sirens as well and headed for Virgil's house.

YOUNG SAT UNDER THE TENT AND STARED AT MAC. She'd managed to convince herself that as the former leader of the state, he was the man who'd caused her to lose her father and brothers. Something had to be done. Somebody had to take a stand and let the world know that it was politicians and private sector businessmen who always got their way, the people be damned. And here was a guy who fit into both categories. What did she have to lose anyway? Word would eventually get out that she was the sister of Luke and Caleb Quinn, and that she'd known what they were doing. Once they figured that out, they'd know what she'd done as well.

That's when she heard the sirens and saw the blue flashing lights off in the distance as they headed along the road toward the house. Young reached down and pulled a gun from her ankle holster, stood, and started heading toward Mac.

EVERYONE HEARD THE SIRENS AND LOOKED OUT AT THE end of the driveway. Then the sirens died away, but the blue lights were still flashing. Murton looked at Virgil and said, "Something heavy must be happening. Bet they're here to pick up Small."

"Might as well go find out what's going on," Virgil said.

Ross started up toward the drive as well, but Rosencrantz headed for the tent. Later, when asked why, he wouldn't be able to come up with a valid reason for doing so. But that's when he saw Young, her gun coming up, pointed right at Mac.

He pulled his own gun, and like Virgil had done with Luke Quinn, Rosencrantz didn't shout any commands. He simply took aim and fired. It was a clean shot, right through the side of Young's neck.

But he was a half-second too slow. Young got her shot off right before she was hit.

SANDY HEARD THE SIRENS AND SAW THE LIGHTS, JUST like everyone else. She turned to Mac and said, "Looks like my night is over." That's when she saw Young out of the corner of her eye marching toward them, her weapon out and ready. Then three things happened at once: Sandy shoved Mac to the ground…her momentum carrying her forward, and two shots rang out almost simultaneously.

The last thing Sandy saw before she collapsed into a pool of her own blood was Mason. He was standing next to the cross, and for some odd reason, he seemed at peace, his arms opened wide, a beckoning look on his face.

CHAPTER THIRTY-ONE

VIRGIL AND MURTON RAN TOWARD SANDY, AS DID Julia. Virgil slid down in the grass, his thoughts taking him to a place he didn't want to go but was powerless to prevent. Somewhere in the back of Virgil's brain, John Decker was dancing about and laughing hysterically, like he was the sole owner of destiny and ineluctable deeds. Then Murton was there, pulling Virgil back and out of the way so he and Julia could work on Sandy.

Julia rolled Sandy over and said, "No exit wound. She's hit bad. Someone grab the napkins from the tables."

Virgil took his wife's hand in his own, tears streaming down his face. "Hang on, sweetheart. You're going to be okay. C'mon, Sandy, it's time to wake up now."

Murton ripped off his shirt and pressed it tight against the wound. He looked at Evans and said, "Arterial."

"I can see that, Murt. We need more pressure."

Virgil screamed at the top of his lungs. "Somebody call a fucking ambulance."

"We don't have that kind of time," Evans said.

Murton turned to Virgil. "Give me your keys."

Virgil was in shock and didn't know it. He couldn't get the image of Decker out of his head. "What?"

Murton grabbed his brother by the arms. "Virgil. Give me your keys."

"They're in the Rover."

Ross ran up toward the driveway and yelled for the troopers to back out of the way. "Be ready to escort. We're making a hard run to the hospital." He jumped in the Rover, then drove it right down next to Sandy. It didn't escape him that her lips were starting to turn blue. He popped the rear doors, then they got Sandy in the back. "Let's go," Murton said. "We've got to move right now."

Ross went for the driver's seat, but Virgil grabbed him by the collar and yanked him back so hard he fell on his butt. Then Virgil jumped in, hit the gas, and five seconds later they were out the drive and headed down the road, the troopers leading the way.

"You okay to drive, Jonesy?" Evans asked.

"He's fine," Murton said. "I'm starting compressions. You take the breathing. We need more pressure on that wound."

Virgil focused on his driving. It was the one thing he could do to save his wife. By the time they got to the intersection at the highway, the troopers had the traffic blocked off. Virgil took the turn in a perfect slide, working the gas pedal with one foot, the brake with his other, his left hand on the steering wheel, his right on the handle for the parking brake. He made the turn like a pro, released the brakes, then gunned the engine.

The troopers never did catch up.

Not that it mattered.

Mayo didn't make it to the house. He continued to monitor the radio en route, and when he heard the emergency call go out about the governor, he drove straight to the hospital and was there waiting when Sandy was brought in.

The emergency department doctors worked as quickly as possible to get Sandy stable, then rushed her up to the operating room. Rosencrantz showed up thirty minutes later and informed everyone that Young was also in surgery, her condition listed as grave. His shot had hit Young in the neck, and the bullet had clipped her spine.

Virgil got right in his face. "She wouldn't have been there at all if it wasn't for you and your bleeding heart."

"What the hell are you talking about?" Rosencrantz said.

"Ask Mayo. He figured it out."

Rosencrantz turned toward Mayo, who tipped his head and moved down the hall. Rosencrantz followed, and once they were away from Virgil and Murton, Mayo said, "Lisa Young is Luke and Caleb Quinn's sister."

Rosencrantz looked away for a moment as he digested the information. Then he glanced back down the hall at his boss and friend before turning and walking away.

Virgil watched Rosencrantz go and didn't try to stop him.

The surgery took six hours, but in the end, the doctors gave Virgil the bad news. "We did everything we could, but the bullet clipped both her kidneys. The bleeding is under control, and we're pumping her full of fluids and getting more blood into her, but we had to take her spleen and both kidneys. We've got her on a ventilator."

It took Virgil a moment to process the information. "But she's alive?"

"Yes, Sir, she is. The vent is simply a way to take some of the strain off of her system. The spleen isn't an issue, but we'll need to find a kidney donor if she's going to survive. I've already got her on the UNOS list, and sometimes you get lucky, but her best chance of a match is going to come from a blood relative."

When Virgil heard that he had to sit down. Sandy only had one living blood relative.

Their son, Wyatt.

Virgil looked at the doctor and said, "When can I see her?"

"She'll be in recovery for another few hours, and then she'll go straight to intensive care. We're going to keep her in a drug-induced coma for a few days. They'll get her started on dialysis right away, but given the severity of her injuries, unless we can find a donor,

I'm not confident that dialysis alone will do the trick. Even if it does, the survival rate is less than stellar."

"Do you have any good news?"

The doctor nodded. "Yes, sir. If she hadn't been shot, she might not have survived. Has she been feeling ill lately?"

Virgil nodded. "She has a urinary tract infection."

"Among other things," the doctor said. "She also has PKD."

"English, Doc, please."

"Polycystic kidney disease, or PKD, is a genetic disorder that causes cysts to grow in the kidneys, where they can disrupt proper function. Based on what we saw, she was about a month away from end-stage renal failure."

VIRGIL STAYED AT THE HOSPITAL FOR THREE DAYS. When Sandy was strong enough to breathe on her own, the doctors took her off the ventilator, but kept her under sedation. UNOS was doing everything they could to help find a kidney, but Sandy had a rare Rh factor in her blood that made the search much more difficult.

Virgil wasn't a match, and though he was loath to do it, he asked Wyatt and Jonas if they wanted to be tested. Both boys said yes, but neither of them matched either, and Virgil wasn't sure if he was relieved by that or not. How does a parent ask a child to donate an organ?

Every single person that Virgil knew or worked with volunteered to be tested as well...even the Pope crew. Nichole went as far as to have all her people in Jamaica tested, but through it all, no one came close.

Then they almost got lucky.

The neurosurgeon who worked on Lisa Young heard about the governor and tested his patient. She was a perfect match. She was also listed as an organ donor and had no living relatives. Unfortunately, the surgery hadn't gone as expected, and Young was not only paralyzed from the neck down, she was in a coma after suffering a massive stroke on the table. They got her back, but she wasn't expected to ever wake up.

She also wasn't expected to die anytime soon because despite her injuries, her body was strong, her organs—other than her brain—were perfect, and the machines were keeping her alive.

And since there was nothing anyone could do, none of the hospital staff told Virgil. The transplant team decided it would just add fuel to the fire.

But one doctor told a nurse, and the nurse told someone else, and the rumor took hold like someone had just dropped a match on a bale of straw.

JULIA EVANS HEARD THE RUMOR, AND MENTIONED IT TO Cool one night over dinner and drinks. Cool and Sandy had the same blood type, and the same rare Rh factor, so when he had gotten tested, Cool was certain he'd be a match, but he wasn't. "How long do they expect Young to live?"

"It's hard to tell," Julia said. "Other than her injuries and the fact that she's in a coma, from the neck down, she's in perfect health."

THE NEXT DAY COOL WALKED INTO MURTON'S OFFICE at the Major Crimes Unit, sat down, and told Murton what Julia had said. Murton listened but feigned ignorance. "It is what it is, I guess."

"She saved my life, man," Cool said. "That time Bell flew us out of Freedom? She gave me her blood so I could live. I'm sort of wondering if there's anything we can do." Then he caught Murton's eyes and said, "Are you hearing me on this, Murt? I'm wondering if there's anything at all, no matter how…extreme."

"Get those thoughts out of your head, Rich. Do you want to spend the rest of your life in jail?"

"I would if it saved Sandy. Tell me you wouldn't as well."

"Drop it," Murton said. "If something happens to Young, I'll arrest you myself. Is that clear enough for you?"

Cool shook his head and walked out of the room.

Everybody was on edge.

Once Cool was gone, Murton picked up the phone and made a call. "Would you and your partner be willing to meet me at the bar in about an hour? I've got something I want to run by you."

"Sure."

"I'll be in the office upstairs. Come alone."

When Nicky and Wu walked into the office over the bar, Murton put his finger to his lips, then took his phone out of his pocket. He made a show of removing the battery, then setting everything on the desk. Then he tipped his head to the side and raised his eyebrows. Nicky and Wu did the same. Once that was done, Murton said, "There, now—"

Wu rapidly shook his head, held his hand out, and made a shushing noise. Then he walked over to Becky's computer equipment, looked at the entire array for a moment, then flipped a few separate switches. The fans died down, and the lights on the computers went out. "There. Now Wu can talk."

Murton got right to the point. "I'm going to ask you guys to do something, and it has to stay between the three of us. I need your word on that. No one can know. Not Nichole, not Becky, not Jonesy…no one. Can you do that?"

"In case you haven't noticed," Nicky said, "we know how to keep a few secrets. What do you need?"

Murton explained what he wanted, then finished with, "Can it be done?"

"When do you need this to happen?" Nicky said.

"The sooner the better."

"Why do Wu want this?"

When Murton answered, Nicky and Wu looked at each other for a moment, then Nicky checked his watch and said, "Meet us at the Million-Air facility tonight at eleven. Bring your passport."

"Why?" Murton said.

"Eleven o'clock, Murt. Don't be late." Both men put their phones back together, and Wu turned Becky's equipment back on. Then they walked out the door without another word.

Murton drove to the hospital to check in with Virgil. "How is she?"

"Hanging on."

"What can I get you, Virgil?"

When Virgil didn't answer, Murton patted his brother on the shoulder and said, "Things have a way of working out. Keep the faith, Virgil."

EPILOGUE

9 PM - SIX WEEKS AGO:

Becky walked into the bedroom and found Murton sitting on the edge of the bed, lacing up his shoes. She had her phone in her hand, and when she looked at her husband, she said, "Going somewhere?" Her expression was suggestive of someone who already knew the answer to their own question.

"Yeah. Something came up with the case, and I didn't want to bother Virgil with it. He's got enough on his plate right now."

"What kind of something?"

"It's no big deal. I just have a few things to take care of. I might not be home until tomorrow morning."

Murton stood, walked to the dresser, and pulled open the top drawer. He rooted around for a few seconds, growing ever more frustrated when he couldn't find what he needed.

"Looking for this?" Becky said. She held a passport in her hand.

Murton took the passport and tucked it into his pocket. "How'd you know that's what I was looking for?"

Becky brought her phone up, then hit the Speaker button. Murton's voice was as recognizable as if he was speaking the words right then and there.

"I need a power failure in a particular room at the hospital. Specifically on the holding cell floor where criminals are kept while receiving medical care. I'll also need the magnetic door locks jammed for a period of time so no one can enter the room. Can it be done?"

Becky stopped the recording and simply stared at her husband.

"How'd you get that?" Murton said.

"Simple. I've got my own office bugged. You should have checked, Murt."

"I did."

Becky let a small grin tug at the corner of her mouth. "Huh, I'm better than I thought." Then: "Are you sure you want to do this?"

"I've been asking myself that question all day. The answer never changes. Jonesy has saved my life more times than I like to think about. It happened again just the other day. Quinn almost buried a deer slug in my back before Virgil took him out. Everything good that's ever happened in my life is because of Virgil and Small. If those two hadn't ended up together, I'd probably be dead by now. That means I wouldn't have you, and we wouldn't have Ellie Rae. It's no different from what I did after Decker attacked Small when she was pregnant with Wyatt. What's the downside?"

"We could get caught."

"There is no 'we' on this one, Becky. I have to do this alone."

"Yes there is, and no you don't."

"Becky, if this somehow manages to come back on me, I'll be put away for a long time. Maybe for the rest of my life. If you come along, you'll be in the same position. I can't allow that."

"I'm afraid you don't have a choice. I love my family with my whole heart, Murton Wheeler. That not only includes you and Ellie Rae…it also includes Virgil, Sandy, and the boys."

"And if something goes wrong, who is going to take care of Ellie Rae?" Murton said.

"The same loving people we're about to save."

"Becky, I can't let you do it. I'm sorry."

"Didn't you hear what I said a second ago? You don't have a choice."

"What's that supposed to mean?"

"Check the passport," Becky said.

Murton knew without looking that he'd been duped, but he pulled the passport from his pocket anyway. It was Becky's, not his. "Where's mine?"

"What's that you're always telling Jonesy? Don't sweat the small stuff? We'd better get moving. Nicky and Wu seemed pretty adamant about not being late."

"What about Ellie Rae?"

"Huma has her. She's spending the night over there."

Murton checked his watch. "Are you sure about this, Becks?"

"I've never been more sure about anything in my life. I knew from the moment I laid eyes on you that our lives would be filled with the kinds of things most people only see in the movies."

Murton looked at nothing for a few seconds, then said, "Okay, let's go." He handed Becky her passport.

Becky slipped it into the back pocket of her jeans, then turned for the door.

"Hey, Becks?"

"Yeah?"

"Are you going to give me my passport?"

Becky chuckled. "Sure. Once we're on the plane... and in the air."

WHEN THEY ARRIVED AT THE AIRPORT, THE JET WAS ready and waiting. Murton and Becky climbed on board, and when Nicky looked up from his computer, he raised his eyebrows and said, "So much for keeping things quiet."

"It couldn't be helped," Murton said.

"Wu else you tell?"

"As a point of fact, I didn't tell anyone, Wu. Becky has her office bugged."

Wu made a tsk-tsk noise and said, "Paranoia. It come with the territory."

Becky sat down next to Wu, and said, "Show me what you've got?"

Wu shook his head. "It better if we wait until airborne."

Murton looked at Nicky. "Why do we need our passports?"

"Because we're going to be out of the country when

it happens. There's a wonderful little bistro in Toronto right on the water that I haven't been to in years. We'll take care of business, have a late dinner, and be back by…mmm…no later than four." Then: "Buckle up. We take off in two minutes."

The trip from Indy to Toronto took just over an hour. Once they landed and cleared customs, everyone except the flight crew returned to the jet. One of the ground support personnel hooked the aircraft to an auxiliary power unit, and once that was done, Nicky hit the switch to close the plane's door.

Wu got the satellite uplink going, and fifteen minutes later they were all crowded around the laptop looking at Young from a camera mounted in the hospital ceiling.

"How did you get into their system so fast?" Becky said. She was impressed.

"Simple," Nicky said. "We never left. Remember that time we, uh, retrieved Carlos, and Virgil let us all go? We left our entry point intact in case we ever needed back in."

"How is all this going to work?" Murton said.

Wu pointed at the monitor. "Simple. The power

outlets that provide electricity to the ventilators and other equipment are all on separate circuits…as are the door locks. We have access to the central computer that controls the power management system. Once we isolate the circuits, we can manipulate them at will."

"There's only one drawback," Nicky said.

"What's that?" Becky asked.

"We won't be able to watch in real time. Once we jam the magnetic locks and kill the power to the room, we'll have to monitor the hospital's grid and make sure the backup generator's computer system doesn't try to override our commands."

"And you can do that?" Murton said.

"Yes, it will be no problem," Wu said. "The only question is, if we can't see into the room, how long should the power be down?"

"Ten minutes ought to do it," Murton said. "Are you guys sure you're up for this?"

Nicky looked at the screen. "My sister is in love with Mac. I don't think that's a secret. That woman tried to kill him."

Wu picked up the thread. "And who among us is not fond of Miss Sandy?" He pointed at the monitor and said, "That is the woman who has caused all this. Now she will be the one who fixes it."

Then they got to work.

A few of the hospital personnel were in a panic, though most didn't really care. The power had failed in one of the rooms, and the patient, Lisa Young, wasn't getting any oxygen. And for some reason, the magnetic door lock refused to open no matter who entered their code or swiped a keycard.

"We'd better get the fire department up here," one of the nurses said. "They might be able to get the lock open."

A doctor walked by, noticed the commotion, and asked what was happening. When told of the power failure and inability to open the door, the doctor said, "How long has it been?"

"Twelve minutes."

The doctor pushed her lower lip out and shook her head. "It's been too long. She's probably gone by now."

"We've still got to get her out," the nurse said. "She's on the transplant list and a perfect match for the governor."

"I know," the doctor said. "The transplant team is standing by."

"It won't do us any good if we can't get in there."

Then there was a click, the lock let go, and the door swung open a fraction.

The doctor rushed into the room, checked for a heartbeat, then shook her head. "She's gone. Get her to the OR right now," the doctor said. "I'll notify the transplant team…"

NICKY, WU, MURTON, AND BECKY ALL WENT TO THE bistro and had a fine meal, though no one talked much. At one point Wu grabbed his laptop bag, excused himself for a few minutes, then returned without saying a word. When it was time to leave, they asked for separate checks and everyone paid with their individual credit cards. When they arrived back at the airport, the jet they'd flown in on was gone, and a different one was waiting in its place.

"What's with the plane?" Murton said.

Nicky gave him a shrug. "I forgot to mention it at dinner. I guess there was some sort of system failure in the satellite uplink computer. I'm afraid the entire unit has been damaged beyond repair. It will be replaced with a brand new one." Then, "You can't be too careful, Murt."

Murton looked at Wu. "Your laptop bag looks a little light."

"That's what Wu think too."

SIX WEEKS LATER:

Sandy was home and resting comfortably. She and Virgil, along with Murton and Becky had managed a small—albeit late—birthday celebration for Jonas. He said he didn't mind as long as his mom was okay.

Sandy had received both kidneys from Young…the UNOS people unable to locate another matching candidate in such a short amount of time. The doctors told Sandy it'd be a while before she would be able to return to work, so in the meantime, Cora was in charge…and in her element.

Virgil was sitting on the back deck talking with Murton while getting caught up on all the paperwork—both personal and professional—that he'd neglected while Sandy had been in the hospital.

"Hell of a thing, huh?" Murton said.

"That's a bit of an understatement," Virgil said.

"So Small's okay? She's going to be all right?"

Virgil nodded. "There are some meds she has to take now, but other than that, yeah, she's going to make a complete recovery." Then, almost out of nowhere: "You sleeping okay?"

"Sure," Murton said. "Like a rock. Why?"

"Just curious."

"Did you get things patched up with Rosie?" Murton said.

"Yeah. I wasn't thinking clearly that night at the hospital and said something I shouldn't have. I needed someone to blame and he was a target of opportunity. It wasn't my finest moment, but he understood. Everything is fine."

Both men sat in silence while Virgil continued to open envelopes and stack papers into different piles. When he was finished, Virgil looked out across the pond and said, "You made a mistake."

"Is that right?"

"Yeah. You left a trail, Murt."

Murton turned his palms up, curled his fingers, and pretended to examine his nails. "Excuse me?"

Virgil reached into one of the stacks of paperwork and pulled out a billing statement. "You had dinner one night about six weeks ago at a restaurant in Toronto. You used your work credit card instead of your personal one."

"Ah, sorry about that, Jones-man. Don't worry. I'll pay it back."

Virgil waved the statement at him. "According to this, it was the same night that Young died and Sandy got her new kidneys."

"Was it?" Murton said. "The whole thing is sort of a blur."

"It was also the same night that there was some sort of systems failure at the hospital. Something about a power outage and a magnetic door lock."

"Huh," Murton said. "No one mentioned it to me."

"And while all that was happening, you and Becky were out of the country."

"Nicky and Wu wanted to take us to dinner. I honestly didn't know it was going to be in Toronto until we arrived at the airport."

When Virgil didn't respond, Murton stood, arched his back, and said, "You know, for a rich guy, you should get some decent patio furniture. These chairs are harder than hell on my back. I think I'm going to go home and lie down for a while before I start to spasm."

Virgil stood as well. "These things can be traced, Murt."

"We're good, Virgil. I give you my word."

Virgil wrapped his brother in a hug and held on for a long time before letting go. "Thank you."

Murton looked down at the cross by the pond for a few seconds, then turned back to his brother. "What was it you said to me that day we drove to Michigan and picked up my grandmother's ashes?"

"Could you be more specific?" Virgil said. "We talked about a lot of things."

He poked Virgil gently in the chest with his index finger and said, "Family."

Thank you for reading State of Qualms.
Virgil and the gang are waiting for you right now in
State of Remains.

Visit ThomasScottBooks.com for further information regarding the Virgil Jones Mystery Thriller Series, release dates, and more.

Scan me with your Smart phone!

— Also by Thomas Scott —

The Virgil Jones Series In Order

State of Anger - Book 1
State of Betrayal - Book 2
State of Control - Book 3
State of Deception - Book 4
State of Exile - Book 5
State of Freedom - Book 6
State of Genesis - Book 7
State of Humanity - Book 8
State of Impact - Book 9
State of Justice - Book 10
State of Killers - Book 11
State of Life - Book 12
State of Mind - Book 13
State of Need - Book 14
State of One - Book 15
State of Play - Book 16
State of Qualms - Book 17
State of Remains - Book 18
State of Suspense - Book 19

The Jack Bellows Series In Order

Wayward Strangers - Book 1
Brave Strangers - Book 2

**Visit ThomasScottBooks.com for further
information regarding future release dates, and more.**

ABOUT THE AUTHOR

Thomas Scott is the author of the **Virgil Jones** Mystery Thriller series, and the **Jack Bellows** series of novels. He lives in northern Indiana with his lovely wife, Debra, and his trusty sidekicks and writing buddies, Lucy, the cat, and Buster, the dog.

You may contact Thomas anytime via his website ThomasScottBooks.com where he personally answers every single email he receives. Be sure to sign up to be notified of the latest release information.

Also, if you enjoy the Virgil Jones series of books, leaving an honest review on Amazon.com helps others decide if a book is right for them. Just a sentence or two makes all the difference in the world. Plus, rumor has it that it's good for the soul.

For information on future books in the Virgil Jones series, or to connect with the author, please visit:
ThomasScottBooks.com

And remember:
Virgil and the gang are waiting for you right now in State of Remains!

Scan me with your Smart phone!

Made in United States
Orlando, FL
31 August 2024